"I guess it's a little silly to be discussing all this with you," Will said. "I doubt you've ever fallen in or out of love."

The words rubbed Paulie's fur the wrong way. Why was Will blind to the fact that she'd been crazy about him for years?

Never been in love? How could he just assume such a thing?

"That just shows how smart you are!" she said tartly. "You don't know the first thing about me, Will!"

He turned to her, his eyes wide with surprise. "Well, have you?"

Now that she'd started, she wasn't going to back down. "If you must know, I have," she said, tossing her head back defiantly. "Deeply in love."

"Who is the object of all this love you claim to have stored up? Is it somebody I know?"

"I'd say you know him pretty well, Will Brockett," she said. "In fact, sometimes I think it's the person you care most about in the world!"

Dear Reader,

Heroes come in many forms, as this month's books prove—from the roguish knight and the wealthy marquess to the potent gunslinger and the handsome cowboy.

Handsome wrangler Will Brockett will lasso your affection in *A Cowboy's Heart,* a darling new Western by award-winning author Liz Ireland, who writes both historical and contemporary romances for Harlequin. Be prepared to laugh out loud as you watch the guilt-ridden Will try to rescue the fiancée he jilted, with the help of a plucky tomboy who is determined to have him notice *her.* Don't miss the sparks flying!

Fans of roguish knights will adore Ross Lion Sutherland and the lovely female clan leader he sets his sights on in *Taming the Lion,* the riveting new SUTHERLAND SERIES medieval novel by the talented Suzanne Barclay. You *must* meet Nicholas Stanhope, the magnificent Marquess of Englemere in *The Wedding Gamble* by newcomer Julia Justiss. Keep some hankies near as the tension builds between two friends who "marry for convenience" and must deny their love.

Rounding out the month is the irresistible Sheriff Delaney, a mysterious ex-gunslinger who inherits a house—and a lovely young widow—in *The Marriage Knot* by Mary McBride.

Whatever your tastes in reading, you'll be sure to find a romantic journey back to the past between the covers of a Harlequin Historicals® novel.

Sincerely,

Tracy Farrell
Senior Editor

Please address questions and book requests to:
Harlequin Reader Service
U.S.: 3010 Walden Ave., P.O. Box 1325, Buffalo, NY 14269
Canadian: P.O. Box 609, Fort Erie, Ont. L2A 5X3

A COWBOY'S HEART

LIZ IRELAND

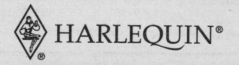

HARLEQUIN®

TORONTO • NEW YORK • LONDON
AMSTERDAM • PARIS • SYDNEY • HAMBURG
STOCKHOLM • ATHENS • TOKYO • MILAN • MADRID
PRAGUE • WARSAW • BUDAPEST • AUCKLAND

ISBN 0-373-29066-7

A COWBOY'S HEART

Look us up on-line at: http://www.romance.net

Printed in U.S.A.

Books by Liz Ireland

Harlequin Historicals

Cecilia and the Stranger #286
Millie and the Fugitive #330
Prim and Improper #410
A Cowboy's Heart #466

Silhouette Romance

Man Trap #963
The Birds and the Bees #988
Mom for a Week #1058

LIZ IRELAND

lives in her native state of Texas, a place she feels gives her a never-ending supply of colorful characters. Aside from writing romance novels and tending to two very demanding cats and a guard dachshund, she enjoys spending time reading history or cozying up with an old movie.

For James and Dana and Will

Chapter One

South Texas, 1883

Trip Peabody would have trouble staying on a horse if somebody glued him onto the saddle. At least, that was Paulie Johnson's assessment of the man's abilities as she watched Trip limp back into Possum Trot leading Feather by the reins. The man just didn't have the gift of balance. Staying permanently upright, whether on horseback or afoot, was a skill he had never been able to perfect.

Paulie, who had been tilting back in her chair on the porch of the Dry Wallow saloon, enjoying the brisk winter morning, brought the front legs of her chair down with a crash and hopped to her feet. "Land's sake, Trip," she called out. "Don't tell me you *walked* Feather all the way to Fort Stockton and back."

Trip let out one of his thin wheezes that passed for a laugh. "Couldn't have made it back this fast if I had, now could I?"

She had sent Trip off four days ago to deposit the Dry Wallow's money in a bank in Fort Stockton, and to see when they might be getting some whiskey. If not soon, she would have to take a wagon and go fetch some herself. Supplies were low—down to tequila, mostly—and she'd already raised the prices high enough that men were starting to grumble. She didn't want a riot on her hands.

But she wasn't much fond of travelling, either. Maybe Trip had good news. "I hope that horse threw you because you had other things on your mind—like where we're gonna put all the whiskey that's comin' our way."

Trip shook his head. "Nope."

Paulie sighed. "Darn that old fool, Oat Murphy!"

Oat, their whiskey trader since Paulie's father had started the saloon at the end of the war, had gone and gotten himself married. And not just married to anybody, but to Mary Ann Redfern, the prettiest, most sought-after girl for sixty miles. This was an especially amazing feat considering that Oat, who was on the sad side of sixty, had no teeth and a curmudgeonly personality; and the last time Paulie had seen him, the man looked like he hadn't said hello to a cake of soap since Christmas.

"It's still the talk all along the road, Paulie," Trip informed her, as if she needed to be told. Oat's marital windfall would be big news around these parts for years. "Heck, people talk about Oat marryin' almost as much as they talk about that durn renegade Night Bird killin' the three men with the railroad payroll. Seems Oat's even given up *drinkin'* whiskey, much less tradin' it. Says he has to be a respectable man now that he has a respectable gal."

"Land's sake!" she exclaimed. "What's he gonna do for money? Mary Ann doesn't eat respectability, I'll bet."

Trip shrugged. "He'll probably try to get himself a herd and start a cattle outfit of some kind."

Paulie shook her head. Men definitely lacked imagination! "We've already got more cows than sense around here. Why doesn't he try growin' turnips or something useful?''

At her peculiar question, Trip staggered slightly and nearly fell off the lowest step of the Dry Wallow's porch. The effort it took to right himself seemed to put him in mind of another puzzling question that had thrown him off balance. "Say, I wonder what Will's gonna think about Mary Ann's gettin' married.''

Will! Paulie had been wondering the same thing herself. Will Brockett had been sweet on Mary Ann Redfern for years, which was no mystery—*every* man within three counties was sweet on pretty Mary Ann. But Will had the edge over all the others because not only was he good-looking, he was also a friend of the family. Shoot, while old Gerald Redfern had been alive, Will had been like a member of the family. He lived at the Redfern place, worked there, and was a favorite of Gerald's. Gerald had been a lawyer back in Louisiana who through some misplaced romanticism had decided late in life to try his hand at ranching out West. Everyone knew that there was no man the Redferns would rather see Mary Ann hitched to than Will.

But Gerald had been gone for three years, dead of pneumonia. A year later his wife had married a man, Mr. Breen, who raised a lot of chickens, and Will had started driving cattle up to Kansas every season. Every winter, he had the dubious distinction of being Possum Trot's sheriff.

But he was, to Paulie's mind, the best-looking thing that ever wore boots, on top of being her favorite person in the whole world. Seven months he had been gone, and every hour of every day of every month had held a twinge of lonesomeness without him there. Paulie was beginning to think the hollow feeling in her chest was bound to be permanent. "Will's been gone so long, he might never be coming back," she said mournfully.

"Oh, I guess we'll see him soon enough," Trip said. "In Fort Stockton I heard that he'd been seen over in San Antonio."

Paulie sucked in a sharp breath. The news almost made her light-headed. "Will, back in Texas?" she asked, unable to keep the excitement out of her voice.

"High time. He's been gone since spring."

And now it was November. That meant Will would probably stick on his badge and winter in Possum Trot again. It wasn't much of a town, so they didn't really need a sheriff, but it was nice to have one occasionally. Especially with that outlaw Night Bird prowling around. Especially when the sheriff was Will Brockett!

Of course, in Paulie's opinion, the man could just sit on the Dry Wallow's porch all day whittling a stick and she'd still call him brilliant. She had been sweet on Will Brockett since she'd first clapped eyes on him. But she'd been a little kid then, and he hadn't paid attention to her. Then, as she grew older, and even after her father died and left her the Dry Wallow saloon, he seemed to view her more as a figure of fun than of romance. He liked to banter with her, but she knew he didn't take her seriously.

"Good old Will." She sighed as her heart fluttered in her chest.

But Trip was once again preoccupied with the topic of the century. "I still can't believe Mary Ann couldn't do no better than Oat Murphy," he said, tugging at one corner of his bushy mustache. He took one of the porch steps and nearly landed flat on his face. "It's got me thinkin' though."

"About what?" Paulie asked, barely able to get her mind

off Will for one minute. He'd been seen already…in San Antonio! She felt like dancing a whoop-de-jig.

"Well…" Trip conjectured slowly, "if Oat can win a girl like Mary Ann, seems like I should at least be able to rate Tessie Hale."

Paulie rolled her eyes in exasperation. "Trip, I bet Tessie Hale's been waiting for you to propose to her since I was in diapers. I swear, you men are so thick it's a wonder anything can stir you up. I'm surprised that poor widow didn't despair and propose to Oat herself years ago."

Trip's eyes widened in panic at the notion. "That would be terrible!"

"Well relax, it can't happen now."

He let out a breath. "That's right. Oat's married to Mary Ann."

It was such a hard idea to swallow! Beautiful, spoiled Mary Ann and Oat Murphy!

"I wonder what made her do it," Paulie said, joining Trip in rumination. Will would surely be disappointed to find his sweetheart married to a toothless old whiskey man.

"People are sayin' that Mary Ann started gettin' restless. She never did like that chicken rancher stepfather of hers none. Called him Mr. Chicken. They're also sayin' that maybe she got scared with Night Bird in the area and all, on account of her blond hair. She thought he'd prize her scalp."

"She would!" Paulie scoffed. "Mary Ann thinks *everybody* loves that yellow hair of hers. Trouble is, nobody seems to hold it in as much esteem as Mary Ann does herself."

Trip laughed. "Still and all, somebody said she was afraid Night Bird was going to come after her."

At the thought of the mysterious Comanche renegade who had been plaguing the area, Paulie let out a sigh of thanks that he had caused her no harm—yet. Twice she had awakened in the night, only to discover the next morning that there were bottles missing from the bar downstairs. Given the Indian's reputation, she would gladly sacrifice a few bottles in exchange for her scalp.

Except now Oat wasn't ever going to bring a shipment. That was troubling. Her stock was running low. Business had declined with Night Bird roaming the area, but it would slam to an absolute standstill if she had nothing to sell.

Yet it was hard to keep her mind on those problems for two minutes. Will was coming home!

And now, without Mary Ann to distract him, maybe he would notice her more, Paulie thought. She looked down at her rough clothes—men's clothes—and began to worry. Will had always made fun of her for dressing like a man, and now she didn't have anything else to wear.

Coincidentally, Trip was giving himself a good once-over, too—no doubt wondering what the widow Hale would think of the worn-out rags he called clothes. Not much, Paulie was sure. She and Trip had fallen a few notches below stylishness sometime in the past decade.

"I wonder if Dwight has any duds my size," Trip said. He was tall and lanky and always looked awkward in the clothes he got from Dwight's Mercantile, the only other business in Possum Trot.

"I know he doesn't have a dress," Paulie said with a little despair.

"What call would I have for one of those things?" Trip asked.

"I meant for me, chowderhead."

Trip's eyes widened. "A dress? Why, you haven't worn one of those since…" He scratched his head. "Since I don't know when!"

"My last one split a seam back in seventy-eight." She

shrugged. She'd never been handy with a needle, and so never replaced the dress. Instead, she wore boots, breeches, and plain cotton shirts, just like all the men who came into the Dry Wallow saloon. Of course, her father wouldn't have approved, but he'd been gone six years now. And the change in her apparel had proved good for business. After a while, people got used to seeing her dressed that way, and became more comfortable doing business with an eccentric woman than a feminine one. She owned the only saloon for thirty miles, and business thrived.

As had her feelings for Will Brockett. She wished she could do something that would make him sit up and take notice of her. "I wish my hair was blond instead of dirt-colored." Mary Ann's hair was the color of corn silk.

Trip assessed her appearance, from her worn-out boots and loose britches up to the crown of her hair, which she wore in a simple long braid down her back. "It ain't so much dirt, maybe, as wood-colored," he said encouragingly.

"Thanks, Trip."

"At least you ain't gone gray," he moped, pushing his hat forward self-consciously. "I guess I look pretty old."

"I hate to break the news to you, Trip, but Tessie's practically white-headed herself now. I doubt she'd hold your age against you."

"Still…" Trip shook his head.

Paulie leaned against the porch rail and let out her breath. "Oh, I guess we're pretty silly to be sitting out here worrying about how we look at this late date. Nothing's gonna turn my stump-colored hair blond any more than you'll ever get your old brown locks back."

Trip eyed her suspiciously. "Who're you tryin' to impress?"

"Nobody," Paulie answered quickly. If Trip ever found

out the extent of her feelings for Will, she'd never hear the end of it. "Can't a person just wish she was blond once in a while?"

A picture entered her mind, of herself, dressed like a real lady in some shiny kind of material—maybe real silk, even. She was at a ball, the kind she'd only read about in some of her father's books, and Will was there, too, handsome as ever. He took her hand, which was mercifully free of unsightly freckles, and lifted it gently to his lips. Then he sent her one of those naughty grins of his. Laughing flirtatiously, with her free hand Paulie tapped him on the shoulder with her fan...

"Paulie?"

At the insistent sound of Trip's voice, Paulie shook her head. "Huh?"

"I said, I think I'll go home. Maybe even clean up a bit."

She felt one of her eyebrows dart up. "You goin' courtin' tonight?"

He stiffened, his expression immediately turning defensive. "Did I *say* anything about courtin'? Can't a body just get clean after a long trip just to...to get clean?"

Paulie shrugged. "You were just talking about Tessie, so naturally..."

"Yeah, well, that road from Fort Stockton was dusty. You might want a bath, too. We're both a sight, Paulie. Rough people for a rough country."

That was the truth. Here she was daydreaming of dazzling Will, when really she was on her way to becoming a female version of poor Trip Peabody. And like Trip, she would probably never work up the courage to admit her feelings to the object of her affection.

Then again, her father had always said that nothing was hopeless until you gave up hope. Paulie liked to think of herself as an optimist. Now that Mary Ann was out of the picture, she just had to think of a way to make Will notice her. And, though it might not have been the most practical dream in the world, she couldn't help hoping that once he did notice her, he would never want to look at another woman again.

"There has to be a way…"

"Way to what?" Trip asked curiously.

"To gussy ourselves up," she said. To his continued quizzical stare she added, "Well, do you want to impress Tessie Hale or don't you?"

"Why sure," he agreed eagerly, nearly slipping off the bar stool. "But what I'm curious to know is, why do *you* want to impress her?"

Paulie rolled her eyes. "Have another drink, Trip."

Will couldn't take his eyes off her. He knew he was staring at Paulie Johnson, but she looked so different, so…strange. All at once, it seemed as if this tiny corner of the world had gone mad.

Possum Trot had always had its eccentricities.

But even given Will's tolerance for strangeness bred of years of living in Possum Trot, he wasn't prepared for the odd sight of Paulie Johnson prancing around in a frilly white dress.

He stood in the door several minutes, perfectly aware that he was gaping at her as she dried glasses behind the bar. Then at last, she looked up and saw him. She sucked in a breath and her green eyes sparked with joy, but all Will could focus on was her hair, which he had somehow managed to miss right up to this moment. Lord, it looked like somebody had taken an eggbeater to it!

In a frenzy of frills and frizzy hair, Paulie practically leapt over the bar in her hurry to get to him. "Will Brockett!'' she cried, launching herself at him in her old exuberant way. ''Will—it's really you!''

''Of course it's me,'' he said. Will allowed himself to be squeezed nearly to death, then held her out at arm's distance. ''The question is, is that really *you?*''

She smiled, and did a lively, if not exactly graceful, pirouette for him. ''Like it?''

He couldn't help staring slack-jawed at her, his amazement utterly unchecked. ''What is it?'' he asked, gaping at the layers and layers of frills covering her.

Offense sparked in her eyes. ''A dress!''

Paulie? In a dress? He wasn't quite comfortable with the idea. And she didn't look particularly comfortable herself. ''What happened to your britches?''

''Oh, for Pete's sake,'' she answered testily. ''I've still got 'em. Can't a girl wear a dress around here every once in a while?''

''Well sure, but…where in tarnation did you get such an outfit?'' It looked like the sort of dress women had worn years and years ago, before the war, when he was a boy. ''I know Dwight doesn't keep his stock up-to-date over at the mercantile, but…''

Paulie frowned and planted her fists on her slim hips—although they didn't seem so slim given her ridiculously flared skirts. ''It's not from Dwight's. It was my mother's.''

''Are you actually wearing a hoop skirt?'' he asked in amazement, using his toe to investigate exactly what was beneath those voluminous skirts.

With a scowl, Paulie slapped his leg away. ''Of course! I'd look pretty silly without it,'' she said.

She looked pretty silly *with* it, but Will didn't dare voice the rejoinder on the tip of his tongue. Paulie, engulfed in flounces, ribbons, bows and lace, already appeared defensive, her pert chin tilting belligerently. From past experience, he knew that once in a fighting mood, Paulie could be a tough one to wrangle with. And in her current state, he didn't think that would be pleasant at all. Like wrestling a cream puff with claws.

Unfortunately, he couldn't help asking, "What did you do to your hair?"

Immediately, he knew he'd made a mistake. She scowled. "I *curled* it, you cowpunching clod!"

"I see." But while other women sported neat sausagelike ringlets, Paulie's curls were completely untamed, crimping and sticking out at the oddest places. "Sort of looks like you wound your head around a cactus."

She drew a hand over her unruly hair and looked at him defiantly. "Well, it's better than it was!" she said. "I've been practicing. I think I'm finally getting the hang of it, actually."

She stared at him for a few more moments, and the irate expression in her eyes slowly faded, replaced by one of her old huge smiles. She reached out and poked his arm. "Will, it's good to see you! Come have a drink."

He crossed the room, feeling strangely disoriented as he walked behind Paulie. Her skirt swayed like a dainty dress, but the square set of her shoulders and the clomping sound he heard every time she took a step made him shake his head. "What are you using for shoes, Paulie?"

She turned, her face a mask of long-suffering frustration. "Wouldn't you know it—my mother's feet must have been five sizes littler than my old dogs. So I'm havin' to wear my work boots!" She lifted her layers of skirt and the hoops and revealed her old scuffed boots.

Will tried to control his mirth. "That's your mother's dress?"

She stuck out her chin. "Yes."

Paulie's mother had died shortly after the family had

moved to Texas. "Why would you have saved that all these years?"

"Well…" She hesitated a moment, a faint blush tinting her cheeks. "Oh, well…it was her wedding dress, so I felt obliged to."

Will scratched his head in wonder. Paulie, wearing dresses, and blushing? Things in Possum Trot sure had changed!

He eased himself up on a seat at the bar, and for the first time noticed they had company. Trip Peabody was face down at the bar. He was also wearing the most ill-fitting suit Will had ever laid eyes on, with cuffs practically skimming his elbows.

"Trip?" he asked, shaking him. "Trip?" When Trip failed to respond, Will turned back to Paulie. "What happened to him?"

"He's thinking about courting Tessie Hale," she said matter-of-factly.

Here was another puzzler. Old Trip had always been half gone for Tessie, but he'd never found it necessary to dress up just to think about it.

"What would you like, Will," Paulie asked, "tequila, or tequila?"

Will frowned. "Don't you have any whiskey?"

Paulie looked uncomfortable. "Nope, just tequila."

Will frowned. "Say…what's happened around here?"

The expression on Paulie's face turned from uncomfortable to downright miserable. She opened her mouth to say something, but still she didn't speak.

"What is it?" Will asked with growing impatience.

"Our whiskey trader sort of…" Her eyes said she would rather talk about anything else. "Well, you remember Oat Murphy, don't you?"

Of course! Will felt his shoulders fall a few inches.

Somehow, seeing Paulie in that strange getup had made him forget his troubles for a few moments. But Oat Murphy was right at the center of them. Now Will felt about as low as Trip.

How could Mary Ann have married that old man? It seemed impossible. He wished it wasn't true. But it was, apparently, and now there was nothing he could do about it.

Gerald Redfern would probably haunt him for the rest of his days for this, Will feared. The older man's last breath had been spent asking Will to take care of his wife and daughter. For Will, making the deathbed promise had been easy. He owed Gerald so much—for taking him in when he was a raw youth with no home, giving him a job, treating him like family. There wasn't a time from the moment he met the Redferns when he *hadn't* thought of taking care of Mary Ann. Even after Gerald died, and Mary Ann's mother had married Mr. Breen, everyone had always assumed he and Mary Ann would marry. Including himself.

Until he'd gone off to Kansas this year. As much as he liked Mary Ann, and was positive that she was the woman he would marry, he'd always known she was a little…well, immature. She tended to be flighty, pouty, and overly whimsical in her ideas. None of these were good characteristics for a ranch wife, and Will wanted to start his own ranch. He had been saving for it for years. He was just waiting till he was good and ready to settle down; actually, he was waiting for that day when he fell in love with Mary Ann and couldn't stop himself from proposing to her. And yet love, which every man seemed to find at least once in his life—and some cowboys he knew found on a weekly basis—eluded him.

At first Will had thought that Mary Ann would grow out of her childish side. *Then* they would fall in love. But finally, two months ago, while lying on the hard ground, his bones aching from the discomfort of the trail, he realized he wasn't getting any younger. And, unfortunately, Mary Ann didn't appear to be getting any older. And neither of them seemed any closer to being in love with the other. She was still as much a flirt as ever, still putting off the idea of settling down in Possum Trot. A decision had to be made, and the very next day he wrote Mary Ann a letter, telling her they would both be better off if they stopped letting her mother entertain the notion that they would be married one day. He remembered now writing that he would always feel as a brother to her....

Now he could have kicked himself. Some brother! Poor Mary Ann had been alone all autumn, and apparently out of desperation she had turned to the first man who came along. Oat Murphy—a whiskey-stained old geezer. What business did that broken-down wreck have asking a girl half his age to marry him?

A sharp, sickening pang of regret shot through him.

Paulie shoved a jigger of tequila across the bar at him. "Have some Mexican milk. You don't look so good." He drank it, and she stared at him evenly. "So...I guess you heard."

"About Mary Ann?" he asked, stiffly, still not comfortable discussing the topic even after endless practice. "I heard."

Paulie leaned her elbows on the bar. "I sure am sorry."

"Don't be," he said. "If it's Oat she wanted, then I'm glad she got what she was pining for."

Paulie tossed her head back. "I don't think she knew what she wanted. Couple of months ago everybody said she was sweet on some gambler who came through here, a man named Tyler. Your Mary Ann never has been exactly discriminating, if you ask me."

"I didn't ask you."

Paulie ducked her head and refilled his glass. "Well, anyways, I'm sure sorry. I know you set a store by her."

He looked into Paulie's eyes, wondering what she would think if he told her the truth. That he was being torn in two directions—relief that he had escaped marrying someone so flighty as Mary Ann, and regret that she had run off with someone so inappropriate. If only she had married Dwight the storekeeper, or...well, just *anybody* besides Oat. Then he could have rested easy at night, knowing Gerald Redfern wasn't looking down from Heaven, scowling at him for breaking his promise to look after his daughter.

That's why he'd come directly here, to the Dry Wallow. Paulie and Trip were always good listeners, and both were adept at putting a man's head straight, too, most of the time. But now this place was topsy-turvy. Paulie was flouncing around in her late Ma's wedding dress, and dependable old Trip Peabody was passed out at the bar.

He gave Trip a slap on the shoulder. "Hey, Trip, aren't you even going to say hello?"

Trip raised one bleary eyelid. "That you, Tessie?"

Will laughed. "Not even close."

Woozily, the man lifted his head of gray hair off the bar. "Why, it's Will! Son of a gun!"

The two men shook hands, and Will couldn't help noticing again the freshly store-bought state of Trip's clothes. "Those are some stiff new duds you've got on, Trip. I don't see how you were even able to pass out in them."

"I was just restin'," Trip said.

Paulie laughed. "He's been 'resting' for two solid days now, trying to screw up the courage to propose to Tessie."

The awkward silence in the bar stretched almost past bearing. Trip cleared his throat. "So I guess you heard about Mary Ann Redfern."

"You mean Mary Ann Murphy," Will said shortly.

Trip nodded. "I guess everybody's heard."

Paulie shifted impatiently. "Everybody's heard *too* much about those newlyweds, if you want my opinion. The way people talk, you'd think Mary Ann was the only unmarried girl in this county."

Trip's eyebrows knitted together, and even Will was intrigued away from brooding by this statement. There *weren't* many unattached females in the area, and that was a fact. Now that Mary Ann was out of his life for good, he supposed he would have to give more consideration to these matters.

"There's the Brakemen twins out north, I suppose," Trip said.

Will smiled. "What about Tessie Hale?"

Trip shivered nervously.

"But most people consider her accounted for," Will assured him.

Paulie cleared her throat, patted down her voluminous skirts, and smiled. "Aren't you two forgetting someone?"

"Tunia Sweeney!" Trip exclaimed. "Nobody's married her yet."

Will wrinkled his nose, dismissing the idea. A woman people called Tunia the Tuna wasn't exactly his dream gal.

"You can't think of anybody else?" Paulie asked, glaring at them as if they were dumb clucks.

Will shook his head. "Still, even counting Tunia, that leaves pretty slim pickings around here."

A bottle shattered on the floor, sending glass shards shooting off in all directions.

"Oh, darn!" Paulie yelled. "Look what you made me go and do!"

The two men looked at each other and blinked. "Us?"

"What did *we* do?" Trip asked.

"Never mind!" Paulie said, bending down to wipe the clear liquid off the floor before sweeping up.

"Well, what are you so lathered up about?" Will asked her.

"I'm just tired of hearing about weddings and courting and such. I swear that's all you men talk about these days. Don't you have anything else to keep yourselves occupied?"

"I guess I should start thinking about what I'm going to do now," Will said.

Trip glanced at him anxiously. "We could sure use a sheriff again with Night Bird roamin' around."

Will frowned. He'd had his heart set on starting a ranch. "Night Bird," he said, repeating the name that he'd heard spoken with fear so often since returning to South Texas. "Is he harassing folks around here?"

"He's been here several times," Paulie informed him. Mention of the renegade seemed to have shaken her pettish mood a little. "I haven't seen him, but he's taken several bottles of my whiskey."

"How do you know?" Will asked.

"'Cause they say when he comes you can't even hear him," Paulie answered. "Those three railroad men who got their throats slit probably never knew what hit them."

Trip shivered. "The first one maybe. But I bet the second and third knew right enough what was happening."

Will frowned. "When it comes to renegades, people are likely to swallow any tall tale." Granted, some gruesome stories were true, but usually people believed what they wanted to believe. "Folks will blame Night Bird if cattle prices fall," he said.

Paulie lifted her chin. "He was here. I know it."

"Maybe," Will allowed.

"Anyways, we sure could use a lawman hereabouts," Trip put in again. "I know I'd sleep better."

"I'll think about it," Will said. If he was going to start up that horse ranch, with or without a wife, it would take him a while to get his hands on a place and accumulate stock. He might as well winter in Possum Trot as anywhere else.

"You sound like you aren't even sure you're going to stay," Paulie said, looking at him anxiously. "You know you're welcome to bed down here, Will. There's a room in the back, next to Trip's."

He looked into Paulie's shiny green eyes and felt gratitude welling in him. "I'm obliged, Sprout," he said, using his old nickname for her.

She blushed again and pushed back a lock of frizzy hair that had fallen across one eye. "There's no obligation, Will. You know that."

For a moment, he stared at her, rapt by those eyes of hers. He could almost swear there was something different-looking about Paulie—besides the obvious change in her getup. Yet in spite of the shambles her hair was in, it was the same light brown color. Her eyes were the same lively pools. She was still skinny, and still had freckles galore, too. Yet, when taken all together, she seemed...different. More frail, more vulnerable almost. He couldn't explain it.

And then it struck him.

"Say, have you been feeling poorly?"

Paulie blinked at him, seeming to snap out of the same daze he'd been in for the past few minutes. "What?"

He shrugged. "You look different somehow," he remarked. "I thought maybe you had been sick."

"Sick!" she cried, sounding offended.

He stared at her quizzically. "What the heck's gotten

into you, Paulie? You didn't used to be this prickly unless I commented on that freckle crop of yours.''

"I don't have *that* many freckles," she shot back heatedly. "Never did."

"Ha!" He laughed. "Knit them together and you'd have skin as brown as an overripe berry."

Her face turned a fiery red. "Why you—"

Before she could explode, and before he had a chance to elaborate on his remark, bootsteps were heard coming up the Dry Wallow's porch. Paulie was the first to look up to see who their visitor was.

From the look of horror on her face, Will was half expecting Night Bird himself. But when he turned, he found himself staring at someone even more surprising. Oat Murphy.

Oat's expression was even more hangdog than usual. Will felt a pang of anger rise sharply in his breast. What did that old man have to be sad about?

Paulie was a bit more generous. "Land's sake, Oat. What's the matter with you? You look like you just lost your best friend!"

Slowly, the grizzled ex-whiskey trader looked from one to the other of them. His droopy eyes were bloodshot and edgy, and his shoulders slumped even more than usual. Even his gray beard seemed to droop.

"Ain't my best friend I lost," he said in his gruff rasp of a voice. "It's my wife."

Chapter Two

"**Y**ou *lost* Mary Ann?"

Paulie finally found her voice and spoke to Oat, who was clearly embarrassed to have to make such a confession. He shuffled to the bar, where she handed him a glass of tequila. He slugged it down, apparently without a thought to his recent vow to abstain from drinking.

"Sure as shootin'," Oat grumbled in his terse brand of speech. "Can't find her. I tell you, I looked everywhere."

Trip appeared so astounded Paulie was afraid he was going to slip clear off his bar stool. And Will was simply incredulous.

"What do you mean, you *lost* her?" he asked Oat, looking as if he wanted to throttle the man. Paulie could understand his frustration. Will probably looked on Oat as having won what he had failed to obtain himself. To misplace Mary Ann was careless in the extreme.

But Oat was evidently tired of having to justify his loss. "I mean, she ain't at home," he said, frustrated. "Ain't anywheres that I can tell." He glanced up at Paulie, and almost as an afterthought, asked, "Ain't here, is she?"

"I haven't seen her. Have you, Trip?"

Trip blinked. "Sure haven't. Not since long before she married you, Oat."

"That's it, then." Oat shrugged. "Just plum lost her."

Will looked as if he might explode any second. "Wait a cotton pickin' minute, Oat. You can't simply *lose* a woman. Are you sure she didn't go somewhere?"

Oat shook his head. "Not that she told me."

"Maybe she went back to Breen's place to be with her ma for a spell," Trip suggested.

"First place I looked," Oat said.

"Could she maybe have had an accident?" Paulie asked.

The old fellow rubbed his tobacco-stained beard and considered this possibility. Finally, he admitted slowly, "Ain't likely. See, I just woke up one morning and found her missin'. What kind of accident can a woman have in the middle of the night in her own house that would cause her to disappear? The only trip she was liable to take in the night was a short one to the outhouse, but I checked that first thing. Wasn't there, or anywhere abouts the house."

Paulie crossed her arms, dismayed. "We didn't think it likely that she's been locked up in the outhouse all this time, Oat. When did you lose her?"

"Two days ago."

"Two days!" Will cried. "Poor Mary Ann's been gone two days?"

Oat looked defensive. "Well, the first day I waited for her to come back. That night, I started to look around. Next day I started *askin'* around. And today I decided I should come to town and ask here. But as of now, I'm concludin' she's lost."

The three men sitting at the bar bore three different expressions of dumbfoundedness.

"She must have run away," Paulie explained. "She always did want to go to the city."

Will shot her a sharp glance. "Then why would she have married Oat and settled down in the country just weeks ago?"

Trip nodded. "He's got a point there, Paulie."

Paulie sighed. "This is pure foolishness!" Men were so dense sometimes—especially this crew. She was still steaming from being left out of the tally of marriageable females in the county even as she was parading around in front of them all decked out in a frilly white dress. Now having to explain the obvious to these men irked her in the extreme. "Mary Ann didn't just *disappear*. That can't happen. A body either has to be lost, or snatched, or to run away. I doubt Mary Ann would get lost. She's lived in these parts for years."

Oat nodded. "That's a fact. She was a smart one, too."

Paulie could have debated him on that point, but felt it would be bad form. The man was grieving, in his own way; he was apt to think of Mary Ann as better than she actually was.

"Did you two ever fight?" Paulie asked him.

"Fight!" Oat let out a bitter laugh. "All we did was fight."

This news perked up everyone's ears.

"What about?"

"Didn't want me to give up my whiskey route." Oat lifted his shoulders. "But I said, what's the point of gettin' hitched, if'n you're gonna be gone all the time? I was figurin' on raisin' some stock and settin' around the house some. Peaceful like. Gettin' old, you know."

That was an undeniable fact, but the strange truth was that the man actually looked older after his few weeks with Mary Ann than he had when he was travelling incessantly around South Texas with a wagonful of liquor.

"Was Mary Ann worried about money?"

Oat nodded. "Yep. So worried about money that she wanted to go with me on my route to make sure I handled things right."

Paulie and Trip, remembering Mary Ann's weakness for one passerby, the gambler, exchanged glances. "She mention anyplace in particular on your route?"

Oat downed another glass of tequila and shook his head. "Nope."

But everybody knew Oat's route took him as far as San Antonio. And San Antonio was the place that the gambler had been heading. "Say, Trip…" Paulie said, trying to sound casual, "what was the name of that snappy gambler man who came through here last August?"

Despite her attempt to strike a nonchalant chord, Will's sharp gaze honed in on her immediately.

"Tyler," Trip said. "Name was Oren Tyler."

Will scowled. "I don't like what you two are thinking."

"Everybody knew she was crazy about him," Paulie explained. "A real good-lookin' dude. I heard tell he stopped one night over at Mary Ann's stepfather's farm."

Even Oat remembered him. He nodded enthusiastically. "I remember Mr. Tyler all right." He looked almost relieved to be solving the mystery of his missing wife, even if the solution pointed to another man. Paulie's guess was that Oat had been just as ready as Mary Ann to wiggle out of the hasty marriage.

"Sure," Trip said, "and after he left, Mary Ann came around here once, askin' if Tyler was still here."

"But he'd gone by then," Paulie remembered.

Will raised a skeptical brow. "And that was August?"

They all nodded.

Will considered for a moment. "Did Mary Ann ever mention this Tyler fellow to you, Oat?"

"Nope."

Will spent another minute ruminating, and for some reason, the other three watched him as if awaiting his verdict on the issue of Oat's missing wife. Of course, Paulie actually looked at him because she hadn't been able to take her eyes off of him since he walked through the door. Lord, he was even handsomer than she remembered! His dark hair was grown almost to his shoulders and his face was bronzed from his months on the trail, making his dark brown eyes appear as if they had some kind of fire in them.

Staring at him almost made her forget how mad she was with him.

Then, finally, he shook his head. "Can't be," he announced.

"Why not?" Paulie asked. "Makes perfect sense to me. Mary Ann started sweet-talkin' Oat so she could go to San Antonio and hitch up with Tyler."

Will's sharp glance melted her insides like butter, even if his gaze was brimming over with condescension. "Think about it. We're not sure that Mary Ann was in love with this man. In fact, we have good reason to doubt it."

"Why?" Oat asked.

Will shot the old codger an even stare. "She married you, didn't she?"

Oat looked abashed at having to be reminded. "Oh, right. Well sure, but…"

"But even putting that fact aside," Will continued, "why would she have *married* Oat if she simply wanted to get to San Antonio? Why didn't she just cadge a ride?"

Paulie had to admit, that would have been an easier alternative.

"And how did she leave?" Will went on, his voice gaining intensity. "Oat didn't mention his wagon was missing, or any horses."

"Nope," Oat admitted. "Didn't take anything that I could tell."

"There. Now what kind of woman sets out to meet a man on foot with just the clothes on her back?" Will asked.

"It's like I said," Oat concluded. "I just plum lost her." And there was more than a hint of relief in his voice when he said it.

Against Will's explanation, and Trip's defection, and Oat's resignation, Paulie lost much of her gusto for the whole argument. "Well, maybe she'll come back," she offered.

"Yeah," Trip agreed. "That could happen."

"Maybe," Oat said, not sounding particularly brightened by that prospect, either. "Anyways, guess I'll be takin' up my whiskey route again."

Paulie nearly collapsed with relief at this news. Thank goodness! Maybe things would be returning to normal soon. Will was back, and perhaps with a sheriff, Possum Trot folks would feel a little safer. At least she would rest easier knowing an officially designated gun stood between her and Night Bird. Everyone else in the area probably would, too. And with Oat making deliveries again, business might pick up.

"Of course, now I got to start worryin' about that old Injun again," Oat grumbled.

"Night Bird?" Will asked.

"Yessir," Oat said, practically shivering at the mention of the name.

Will frowned, causing three deep creases of worry to appear in his forehead. "That's it!" he said, then muttered, "Damn."

The three of them stared at him, but Will just looked straight ahead, brooding.

"What's it?" Paulie asked.

"Night Bird," he said, his lips forming a grim line.

Paulie sucked in her breath. Was he thinking that Night Bird had taken Mary Ann? "Night Bird!" she repeated, the terrible thought attempting to catch hold of her mind like the fleeting memory of a nightmare. Trip stood and then nearly collapsed on wobbly legs, and Oat straightened in his chair, looking truly disturbed for the first time during the whole discussion.

"Of course!" Trip said.

But Paulie, after the first shock, wasn't so certain. She tilted her head, mulling the idea over. "I've never heard of Night Bird kidnapping women."

Will sent her a dead serious look. He didn't even have to say it. When it came to a renegade Comanche, a consistent code of behavior couldn't be expected. "You said yourself that when Night Bird stole your liquor those times, you didn't even hear him."

"Sure, but that was whiskey," Paulie explained. "Wouldn't Mary Ann put up more of a fuss?"

Trip shook his head slowly, in an awed trance of dread at the very idea of Night Bird. "They say those three men he killed didn't even know what hit them."

Paulie frowned. It wasn't that she didn't think Night Bird was capable of abduction—it just seemed so unlikely. Texas Rangers had taken care of most of the Indian trouble in these parts. For an Indian to just walk into a man's house and steal his wife, or ambush her on her way to the outhouse, didn't seem worth the trouble that he would bring upon himself by such a heinous act. "Wouldn't there be at least a sign of a struggle? Mightn't we have heard that someone had seen them somewhere?"

"Maybe not," Will said.

"And what would Night Bird want with Mary Ann anyway?"

Trip and Will exchanged stony glances, and Oat just looked depressed.

Paulie shook her head. "I meant, why would he want her specifically? Killing three men is one thing, but he's bound to know that kidnapping a woman is going to cause big trouble for him."

"You bet it is." Will's voice was thick with determination.

A creeping dread began to snake through Paulie's body. The two other men turned to him with questioning glances.

"I'm going after her," Will announced.

"After Night Bird?" Trip asked.

"After Mary Ann," Will clarified.

Oat was startled. "*You're* going?"

"I've known Mary Ann a long time, Oat," Will explained. "I promised her father I'd look after her."

"Well, sure," the old fellow rasped, "but after all, I'm her husband."

"Of course, you can come along if you want to," Will allowed.

At that suggestion, Oat looked even more startled than before. "What I meant was, *I* should be the one to go get help." Even given his marital tic, the old man didn't look at all eager to chase after a renegade Comanche to find Mary Ann. And who could blame him?

"There's no need for you to go anywhere, if you don't want to," Will said sharply. "I'll find her."

The room was thick with tension. Paulie felt she was going to pop if she didn't say something. "Why should either of you go after Night Bird? Oat's got the right idea. Go fetch the army—or the Rangers. It's their job!"

"That's true," Trip said.

"Should I ride all the way to Fort Stockton?" Will asked

them. "Why waste precious days while Night Bird might be dragging Mary Ann into Mexico or God only knows where?"

Because you'll be killed! Paulie couldn't voice the fear in her heart. It wasn't necessary anyway; Will obviously knew the risks involved. So did Oat, who, wisely, was still hesitating. He took his third swig of tequila, bracing himself.

A kind of hysteria began to build in Paulie. Here she'd been thinking that her problems were almost over—thanking her lucky stars that Will was back. She'd thought Will would be around for a while, had even fancied the idea that he might develop a yen for her, even if he did think she looked like a crazy lady in her dress. But instead, no sooner had he arrived than he was going to ride off and get himself scalped or worse.

"You sat there a while ago telling us that people attribute all manner of things to renegades, just to suit their own purposes," she argued.

"You think I *want* to believe that Mary Ann's been kidnapped?" Will asked.

His look of accusation was more than Paulie could bear. Of course he didn't. No one would, but for Will it was even worse. He might convince Oat that he was running after Mary Ann just because of some promise he'd made to Gerald Redfern, but Paulie knew better. He was in love with Mary Ann. More than Paulie had even suspected, apparently—enough to risk his life for her. But she couldn't bear the thought of his going. "Bad enough that we have to worry about Night Bird coming after us," she said, "without us going after *him.*"

"Maybe if I go after him, we won't have to worry anymore."

"*You* won't have to worry if you get your throat slit like

those three other men," Paulie said, too upset to mince words, "but where does that leave the rest of us?"

The thought of something happening to Will nearly drove her to distraction, but she faced him, holding back tears.

Will stared evenly at her, his expression softening. "I'm not going to get killed."

He appeared so determined, so sure of himself and of what he had to do, in that instant even Paulie couldn't imagine Night Bird getting the best of Will Brockett. But Will was a cowboy, not an Indian fighter! Sure he was good with a gun, but so were plenty of army men who had lost their lives to the Indians.

"Can't let Will ride off alone," Oat said out of the blue. Clearly, he'd been off in his own daze struggling with this moral dilemma. "Me being her husband and all."

Will stood. "Come or don't," he told Oat. "I'm leaving in an hour." And with that, he turned and strode out of the saloon, headed for Dwight's mercantile.

"Guess he's going to get provisions," Trip said.

Paulie felt like running after him, but what purpose would that serve? She wasn't going to change his mind. Once Will Brockett got it into his head to do something, that something always got done. She caught sight of herself in the mirror behind the bar. Her face was worried and pinched. And suddenly, she looked unbearably silly with her wild hair and her mother's white dress. She didn't want Will to ride off remembering her like this.

She didn't want him riding off, period. "Watch the bar for me, Trip." She went back to the narrow stairwell that led to her room above the saloon. Her mind was racing, trying to think of some way to get Will to stay. As she was halfway up the stairs, she heard the sound of Oat gulping down his fourth glass of tequila.

"Gol-darn it!" he hollered decisively, bolstered by spirits. "I'm a goin' with him!"

Poor old man, Paulie thought. Poor Will, too. Oat wasn't going to be much of a help. She'd feel a lot better knowing Will had somebody along who would really watch out for him.

Paulie froze for a split second as an idea began to hatch. *Why not?* Why shouldn't she follow along with Will? She would be as much use to Will as Oat would!

As decided as Oat was himself—only more so, because she was sober—Paulie ran the rest of the way up to her room, a blur of white frills and lace, smashing her hoop skirt close to her body as she took the stairs two at a time. Maybe it was a good thing that she looked silly in dresses, she thought, her mood picking up. They sure were a nuisance!

When Will finally emerged from Dwight's mercantile, he was nearly flattened by Paulie on her way in. He almost didn't recognize her, though she had changed back into the shirt and breeches that should have been most familiar to him. For some reason, he couldn't get the thought of her in that white dress out of his mind.

"I'm going with you," she told him in passing.

By the time the words registered, Paulie had slapped the door shut behind her and disappeared inside. Will stood on the porch of Dwight's building for a moment, sure he'd heard wrong. Or seen wrong. That *was* Paulie he'd just bumped into, wasn't it? He pivoted and went back inside to check.

Sure enough, there was Paulie, her crazy hair braided and smashed under one of her pa's old hats, moving along the shelves of Dwight's, scooping up matches, pointing to dried beef and fruit and quickly calculating the amounts of corn meal and coffee she could take along with her.

Will strode toward her. "Never mind, Dwight," he told the store's short, balding proprietor. "You can just put all that stuff away, Paulie. Unless you're buying it for Oat."

His words barely fazed her. "I'll be more of a help to you than Oat will," she said matter-of-factly. Then she turned back to the store owner. "I guess a pound of coffee will do, Dwight."

Will rolled his eyes. "You don't know what you're talking about, Paulie. For heaven's sake. I can't be hauling a girl along with me."

"Why not? You can haul an old boozy whiskey trader."

"That's different."

"Why?"

"He's a man, that's why." He'd be damned if he was going to spend precious minutes explaining the facts of life to Paulie. "Now be reasonable, Sprout."

She put her hands full on her hips and glared up at him. "You can't go out alone, and if you go with just Oat, you'll be as good as alone. Now I've told you my opinion on the matter. You should call out the proper authorities. But since you won't take my very sound advice, you'll just have to put up with my company."

Will looked away from her, annoyed. Dwight still had his hand in a large sack of coffee, not certain whether he should start scooping it out or not.

"You'll slow us down."

Paulie hooted at that idea. "I can ride better than Oat, and I can shoot better, too. And see better."

"Leave Oat out of this. As far as I'm concerned, adding you to the crew will be travelling with two handicaps instead of one, only you're a different kind."

"What kind?"

"The female kind," he said.

She screwed her lips up wryly. "*That's* a fact I suppose you're just apt to notice when it suits you!"

"You're not going," he repeated, more forcefully.

"You can't stop me," she said. "If you don't allow me in your party, then I'll follow you. And that would be even more dangerous, wouldn't it?"

He took off his hat and slapped it against his thigh. "Darn it, you know chasing an Indian is no job for a girl."

"It's no job for a cowboy, either, but that isn't stopping you."

He sighed, then appealed to Dwight for assistance. "Will you please tell this stubborn girl that she can't just pick up and chase after Night Bird?"

Dwight had been standing in blank confusion, but now that he understood exactly what they were up to, the wrinkles disappeared from his endless forehead and his mouth dropped open in awe. "Night Bird!" Dwight exclaimed, in the same fearful tone that everybody used when referring to the infamous criminal. "Well, I'm glad somebody's chasin' him—as long as they chase him away from these parts. I haven't slept a wink for weeks."

Thanks, Dwight, Will thought with disgust.

Paulie beamed at him triumphantly. "See?" she asked, taking her purchases up to Dwight to tally up. "Even Dwight wants me to go."

"What I *don't* see is why you feel so all-fired determined to tag along with me and Oat. Don't you think we can find Night Bird ourselves?"

"It's the part *after* you find him that's worrying me— and it would be worrying you, too, if you had the sense God gave a garden slug."

"She's right, Will," Dwight put in. "Night Bird is one mean hombre to mess with."

Paulie paid for her purchases, and they left the store. She was headed straight back across the way to the saloon, but Will stopped her with a hand to her shoulder.

She flinched under his grasp, and two splotches of color appeared on her cheeks. Funny, he couldn't remember the old Paulie blushing before—except occasionally when he'd teased her. Now she was turning pink all the time.

He chalked it up to nerves.

"Look at you," he said. "You're already skittish. Have you considered how you'll feel when we're that much closer to finding Night Bird?"

"You don't have to worry about me," she said. "I can take care of myself." She ducked her head, and lowered her voice as she assured him, "I'll take care of you, too, if you'll let me."

Something in her tone, in her gaze, made him assure her, "Nothing's going to happen to me." He squeezed his hand more firmly on her shoulder. "Honestly, Paulie. There's got to be some reason why you're willing to risk life and limb by going on this expedition."

She looked up at him for a long moment, studying his face. He could see his own concerned reflection in her green eyes. And then she glanced away. "You might find this hard to believe, but while you were away, Mary Ann and I got to be friends."

He *did* find that hard to swallow. Not that Paulie wouldn't befriend Mary Ann—Paulie would talk to anything that talked back. But what would delicate, feminine Mary Ann have in common with a rough ragamuffin like Paulie Johnson?

She licked her lips, then looked up at him again. "Pretty good friends," she continued. "So you see, I've got my own reasons for wanting to go. I'm just going to look after somebody I care about, too."

He nodded curtly, touched by her words. Somehow, her claim of friendship changed things. He had a respect for friendship, for people looking after one another. Maybe it went back to the way Mary Ann's dad had always looked after him. "I admire you, Paulie," he said. "Not many people feel the bond of friendship so strong, especially for someone as different from themselves as Mary Ann is to you."

She shrugged modestly. "It's nothing I wouldn't do for any number of people."

A thought suddenly occurred to Will. "What you were saying before, about Mary Ann going to San Antonio...she didn't confide any such scheme to you, did she?"

"No," she replied, "it was just a hunch."

They crossed to the old lean-to Paulie used as a stable and she began readying her saddlebags with the things she'd bought at the store. Will did likewise. As they stood side by side, Paulie finally piped up, "Are you sure you aren't going after Night Bird just to prove something, Will?"

"Prove something? Like what?"

"Well, maybe that you were the man who truly deserved Mary Ann."

He felt a muscle in his tense jaw twitch. For a moment, he considered confiding in her, telling her how guilty he felt for sending that letter, for not just waiting till he got home to explain to Mary Ann why he just couldn't see them getting married. Maybe then she wouldn't have gone off and married Oat, and then been kidnapped by that madman.

But he couldn't think about that now. He just had to concentrate on his responsibility toward her. "I'm not try-ing to prove anything. I just want to find her. It's not right for people to sit around and do nothing when a renegade is snapping innocent young women out of their beds."

They saddled up Paulie's horse in silence and then led their mounts out to the front of the saloon. "I'd better go in and get Oat," Will said.

But Trip was already pushing the older man out the door. "Don't forget this," he joked as he presented Oat to them. He looked over at the sight of Paulie's own saddled horse. "Oh, no," he breathed. "Are you goin' too, Paulie?"

She nodded.

Trip looked from Paulie to Oat. "Then it looks like I'm settin' out again."

"No, you can't," Paulie insisted. "Who'll mind the bar?"

"Heck, Paulie, I'm your best customer," Trip argued. "Besides, you don't have anything to sell."

Will let out an impatient sigh. "This is beginning to look like a posse."

Well, he thought, trying to keep his spirits up by turning to more practical matters, if he was going to search for Mary Ann and Night Bird, posses weren't actually such a bad idea. After all, there was safety in numbers—even when that number included a cranky geezer, a switch of a girl, and a man who couldn't stay upright.

Chapter Three

Paulie whistled four notes of "Oh! Susanna," keeping her eye on Will's ramrod-straight back. For the past four hours he'd been riding ahead of them, and was wound tighter than a pocket watch. Though so far their journey had been completely uneventful, Will was ever-alert, tense. She was just waiting for some part of him to snap.

"'I Gave My Gal a Penny Candy!'" Trip guessed.

Paulie sent him a sidelong glance. "Honestly, Trip, you've got a tin ear."

He looked offended. "It's you that's got a tin whistle."

She whistled again, this time five notes. Their old game cut down on the endless monotony of the day-long ride, but every once in a while she thought she caught Will glancing back at them, annoyed.

He looked close to madness already, in Paulie's opinion. "Land's sake, Will, don't get your dander up. It's just a song."

"Well, it's a damned irritating one."

They stopped long enough for Oat to catch up with them. For the past few miles he had been trailing farther and farther behind. Paulie had begun to wonder whether the old man might be hoping that they would leave him so far in their dust that they would forget about him entirely and he could then go back to his safe house and warm his old toes by a fire.

Right now, he just looked startled to find the three of them huddled together. "Night Bird?" he asked anxiously, trying to guess the reason for the holdup.

"No," Trip answered. "Just 'Oh! Susanna.'"

Will's exasperation was bumped up another notch. "We need to be concentrating on the landscape—not some damned song. Now let's get going." He whirled and spurred his horse into a canter.

Paulie exchanged glances with Trip and blew out a breath impatiently as Will rode ahead of them once again.

"I wonder what's eatin' him," Trip said.

As if anyone had to guess! Paulie felt angry just thinking about how torn up inside Will must be over Mary Ann's disappearance. Frankly in her opinion, Mary Ann just wasn't worth all this fuss. She still had her doubts about Mary Ann's being spirited off by Night Bird. It didn't make sense. For one thing, they said Mary Ann had always been scared of being abducted by Night Bird, and in Paulie's experience, the thing you're afraid of happening hardly ever does. It's the things you didn't expect that sneaked up and changed your life for good.

She kicked her horse into a gallop. In no time at all, she raced up alongside Will and skidded her little bay gelding, Partner, to a quick stop.

Will didn't appear glad for the company. "Don't you ever stay quiet?" he asked.

Paulie tried not to take the remark to heart. In better days, Will had always seemed to enjoy jawing with her. "Don't you ever plan on acting civil again?" she shot back. "I swear, you roam around for months at a time, clear off to

Kansas, then you ride back in and start barking orders at us like you're paying us money to take them.''

Her tart response brought a sheepish shrug.

"Maybe I do stay away too long," he said. "I know I did this time. But I'm back now, and I've decided to settle down.''

Paulie didn't know if she felt like dancing or weeping. It all depended on *where* Will planned on setting himself up. "You thinking of staying in Possum Trot?"

"Probably not."

"Well then, where?"

"That depends on Mary Ann."

For a moment, all she could do was stare at him. What was he talking about? He didn't look at her as if he'd said anything odd; he wasn't looking at her at all, in fact. Just staring straight ahead, his expression faraway yet strangely determined.

"Mary Ann!" Paulie cried. "Have you gone crazy, Will?''

His face remained stony. "Nope."

"She's married, Will!''

"Oat doesn't love Mary Ann."

"Oat, Mary Ann's *husband*, is riding just in back of us, in case you've forgotten.''

"He didn't want to come," Will insisted.

"But he did.''

"He had to talk himself into it."

Paulie rolled her eyes. "So would anybody with any sense, Will! It's because we're going after a killer.''

"A killer who has Mary Ann. His wife." He turned his dark eyes on Paulie, his expression softening. "*You* were more resolute than that old toothless husband of hers, Paulie.''

"That's because—" She was about to say, *because I was*

so worried about you. But she couldn't. She'd already lied and told him that she was only coming along because she and Mary Ann were friends. And he'd believed her! Which just proved that something in the man's mind had shook loose.

"Because you care about Mary Ann," he finished for her. "You see? That proves my point. Oat doesn't care about his wife even as much as her friends do."

"Oh, Will, you can't be sure of that." Although *she* felt fairly certain that Oat wasn't a head-over-heels newlywed, she hated to see Will eating his heart out over a woman who didn't deserve him. And even more to the point, who wasn't even available.

And, she admitted to herself shamefully, who wasn't herself.

"You heard him talking, Paulie. He said he just lost her—the way a man would talk of misplacing his fountain pen. And it was almost as if he was *hoping* that she was lost."

Paulie had sensed the same thing. But she hated to think it. Because if Oat gave up on Mary Ann... Oh, it was selfish of her to want Will for herself—not to mention hopeless—but she couldn't help it. As long as Oat was married to Mary Ann, Paulie at least stood a tiny chance of making Will appreciate her. "He's *married* to her, Will."

"Marriages don't always last," he said tersely.

Paulie couldn't believe her ears. "Will, you're talking crazy!" She'd thought all along that he looked half-crazy, but even so she'd had no idea that thoughts like these had been running through his head. And as he spoke, it didn't even seem as if he *wanted* to wed Mary Ann; instead, it was almost as if it were something he *had* to do.

He shot her a look that had a hint of desperation in it. "You can't imagine what I feel, Paulie."

If only he knew! Maybe she would never work up the nerve to tell him about her own experience with unrequited love, but she could keep him from hatching these unrealistic plans.

"You know what your trouble is?" she asked him.

"No, but I'm sure you'd love to tell me."

She ignored the barb. "You've got an overworked sense of responsibility. When you're sheriff, you feel responsible for the whole town. I bet when you're out on the trail, you feel like you personally have to account for the fate of every one of those beeves. But I'm telling you, Will, Mary Ann is not your problem."

He shook his head. "You don't understand. When Gerald was dying I told him I'd look after his daughter."

"Things are different now. Gerald couldn't know that Mary Ann would one day up and marry Oat and you don't know that the two of you would be any better off together than Oat and her are," Paulie pointed out.

"What do you think I should do—leave her with a toothless old man who obviously makes her unhappy?"

"How do you know they're unhappy?"

"Oat himself said they fought all the time," he insisted, his jaw set stubbornly.

"So do all married people. I think if you respected Mary Ann at all, you'd trust her to make her own decisions."

Will shot her a keen glance. "You're Mary Ann's friend. Has she ever spoken to you about me?"

Paulie hesitated. "No, she hasn't."

"Not even before she ran off with Oat?"

Paulie couldn't help feeling a sharp stab of guilt. "She doesn't tell me everything, Will," she admitted, though even that was a pale reflection of the truth. Mary Ann could be thinking about Will twenty-four hours a day, and she wouldn't know about it.

He let out a ragged sigh, then looked at her, his brown eyes full of kindness. "I guess it's good you came along after all. You always did know how to put me in my place, Sprout."

She revelled in the pet name almost as much as she resented it. Why couldn't Will think of her like he did Mary Ann, not just as a kid?

He shook his head. "I suppose I'm still a little confused over why Mary Ann would marry Oat to begin with."

Paulie remained silent. The whole world was confused on that point.

He shot her a patient glance. "I guess it's a little silly to be discussing all this with you," he said. "I doubt you've ever fallen in or out of love."

The words rubbed Paulie's fur the wrong way. Why was Will blind to the fact that she'd been crazy about him for years?

Probably because he was so stuck on Mary Ann he couldn't see anything else!

Or maybe because he just didn't have the slightest interest in her. That was an annoying—though highly likely—possibility. Paulie knew she could never even be a substitute for Mary Ann. She didn't know the first thing about batting her eyelashes at a man, or flirting. Heck, the only time she'd ever worn a real grown-up long dress in front of Will, he'd said she looked like she'd been sick.

Sick! At the mere thought, she felt her dander rising all over again. *Never been in love?* How could he just assume such a thing?

"That just shows how smart you are!" she said tartly. "You don't know the first thing about me, Will!"

He turned to her, his eyes wide with surprise. "Well, have you?"

Now that she'd started, she wasn't going to back down.

"If you must know, I have," she said, tossing her head back defiantly. "Deeply in love."

"Who?" he asked.

She blinked. "Who what?"

"Who is the object of all this love you claim to have stored up?"

This wasn't something she was prepared to confess. Especially not to Will. Especially not when he asked her using that sarcastic tone. "None of your business."

He looked at her skeptically. "Is it somebody I know?"

Clearly he didn't believe her—a fact that made Paulie spitting mad. Men had so little imagination! Just because she owned a bar and wore men's clothes, was it impossible to comprehend that she had feelings just like every other woman in the world?

"I'd say you know him pretty well, Will Brockett," she said. "In fact, sometimes I think it's the person you care most about in the world!"

She tapped her horse's flanks and wheeled around. Will attempted to stop her. "Paulie, wait—"

She kept going, though, hesitating only long enough to holler one parting shot over her shoulder. "And for your information, I'll whistle whenever I want to!"

Will sat apart, with one eye on the others and the other watching for signs of trouble. Trip and Paulie were splayed out near the glowing warmth of the fire, rattling on as usual. Oat was close to them, sitting up but half-asleep. Occasionally the old fellow would jolt awake again, especially when Trip or Paulie happened to mention something about Night Bird.

"I wonder if we'll ever find him," Paulie said.

Trip shook his head. He was always more sure of himself when he was on the ground, where there was nowhere to fall to. "I imagine if'n we do, it'll be down in Mexico. They say that's where he lives, 'cause the law won't follow him there."

"What about the Mexican law?" Paulie asked. "Mexicans can't like having a renegade Comanche running loose any more than we do."

Trip scratched his head. "They say Night Bird is part Mexican himself—the son of a captive woman from a border town."

Oat's eyes snapped opened and he bolted upright, his hand reaching down for his gun. "Night Bird?"

Trip chuckled. "We were just talkin', Oat."

"We've haven't seen or heard anything," Paulie assured him.

Oat shook his head with such force that the bulbous end of his nose quivered. "When Night Bird comes, you won't hear him."

The three exchanged anxious glances.

Will decided to put his two cents in. "If that were the case, then we might all just as well go to sleep." They looked back at him quizzically. "No man is invisible. If Night Bird comes, one of us will see him."

"Those three railroad men didn't see him—they were all three armed and none of them looked like they had even had time to reach for their guns," Trip said.

The story of the three men who had been ambushed by Night Bird had been through so many versions that it was hard to know exactly what had happened. Most people seemed to want to believe that Night Bird silently appeared and disposed of his victims as easily as an owl swoops down on a mouse.

"I wonder what would turn a man so mad that he'd take up thievin' and murderin' that way," Trip said.

"Having your land stolen out from under you would

make you a little bitter, too,'' Will told him. He bore little sympathy for Night Bird, but he thought he could understand what could turn a man so wrong.

''What land did that Indian ever own here?'' Trip asked.

Will nodded toward the horizon. ''We fought a war to win this land from the Mexicans, but we just took it from the Indians and expected them to be happy about being nudged up to less desirable parts.''

''We wouldn't have nudged anybody if they'd just left us be,'' Trip argued.

''But we were the trespassers, and then we expected them to abide by our laws—not their own.''

Trip looked disgruntled, but said nothing more.

''I guess Will's right,'' Paulie said, turning back to the fire. ''Maybe we're lucky there's only one Night Bird, not thousands.''

''Thousands!'' Oat cried, startled by the very idea.

Will kept his eyes on Paulie. He was surprised that she would take his side after their scene earlier in the day. She had seemed so annoyed. In fact, since he'd come back, she'd been more moody than he could remember her ever being. Especially with him.

Of course, he'd been moody, too, but he knew the reason for his own odd behavior. He was perplexed and torn up over all that had happened with Mary Ann. But could what Paulie said be true? Was she really in love? And with whom?

He'd been pondering those questions all afternoon. He had to hand it to her; her little revelation had completely distracted his mind from brooding about Mary Ann.

Paulie's being in love seemed so unlikely! Yet why not? She had to be over twenty now. *But who?* Who could she have fallen for?

For a while he thought perhaps Paulie might have developed a yen for Dwight Jones. That would have made sense. Though he'd been a widower for half a decade, Dwight was still fairly young, and his mercantile probably made a decent profit. He and Paulie were practically the only people in Possum Trot proper, too. Dwight was the shy, anxious type, though Lord knows, in that empty town and with his booming voice, the man could sit and sing love songs all day to Paulie across the street in the saloon without even having to leave his store.

But the more he thought about it, the less likely a love relationship developing between Paulie and Dwight seemed. Dwight was completely devoted to his wife's memory. The woman had run his store and his life; Dwight still only stocked what his dear Pearl had approved during her tragically short lifetime. And he never stepped foot in Paulie's place, because Pearl had been a devout temperance lady. That was the clincher. Given Dwight's devotion to Pearl's memory, he would never take up with a woman who not only sold liquor, but was not above taking a gulp or two of the stuff herself on occasion.

So that took care of Dwight.

For a brief moment, Will had even considered the possibility that Oat was the object of Paulie's affection. She saw him often or had when he'd been her whiskey man. From that angle, he could see a certain logic to her becoming dependent on Oat. And perhaps that's why she had developed a closeness to Mary Ann, because she wanted to see more of Oat...

But just one look at the old fellow, slumped against a tree, with his mouth hanging open and snoring loudly, made Will dismiss this notion. One woman falling for Oat's questionable charms was amazing in itself; *two* would be entirely incomprehensible.

Trouble was, there were so few people Paulie saw on a

regular basis, every possibility he winnowed out left the field exponentially smaller. He'd never heard her mention any of the other men who lived around the area. Furthermore, when he'd arrived at her saloon that morning, it seemed she had been expecting someone.

For a brief, crazy instant, he wondered if it could even be himself. But what were the chances that she'd known he would be coming home in time to gussy herself up for him? After all, she said she had been practicing doing her hair. And she hadn't exactly welcomed him with open arms; not after the first moment, at least. She'd seemed almost angry with him at times. Not at all flirtatious, like all the other women who had even the slightest interest in him had behaved. Besides, he and Paulie were just old friends. Very good, old friends. That was how he was most comfortable thinking of her.

So who was it?

He glanced again at her, cracking wise with Trip by the fire, and the obvious hit him with the force of an avalanche. *Trip Peabody!*

Of course. It made perfect sense! Trip had been one of her father's cronies, and since her father's illness had lived in the room behind the saloon. Paulie was financially independent, but she had probably turned to Trip for advice innumerable times. Trip wasn't even too bad-looking...

But he was about twenty years older, and practically everybody south of the Red River knew Trip was in love with Tessie Hale.

Wasn't he?

Will frowned, thinking about that very morning, finding both Paulie and Trip dressed up in stiff, unfamiliar clothes. A stiff dark suit...a wedding dress. Trip had been drunk. That was odd in itself. Then there was the eternal question of why Trip hadn't ever actually asked Tessie to marry him.

Maybe Trip's affections were more divided than he let on.

Will felt a twinge of sadness for them all if this was the case. But especially for Paulie. She deserved better than to be stuck in some unhappy love triangle, running around in her mother's old dresses trying desperately to be something she wasn't. He wondered whether Trip might even have taken advantage of her youth and innocence...

A flash of anger so sharp welled in him that he sucked in his breath. He pushed himself to standing and walked away from the group.

Paulie was in love with Trip. For some unfathomable reason, he didn't want it to be true, but the idea made too much sense to ignore. The two of them enjoyed talking, laughing, and playing games—like they'd been doing this afternoon. They were always together, and they shared some of the same rough ways in dress and manner. Will had to concede that there was no better man on earth than Trip Peabody, and yet...

Paulie deserved better.

Damn. Maybe he was just unhappy with *all* the men women picked to pin their affections on these days. He had no call to care one way or the other who Paulie chose to fall in love with. He'd never even given the possibility a thought before now that she might even be of an age to fall in love. She'd always seemed like a tomboy to him. A figure of fun, good for a laugh or someone to talk to.

But the fact was, he *did* care who she fell in love with. Couldn't imagine himself not caring.

"What are you doing out here?"

At the sound of a voice, Will nearly jumped out of his skin. He pivoted, tense, only to come face-to-face with Paulie herself, who stood blinking up at him.

"Did you hear something, Will?"

He swallowed, noticing for the first time how fetching her green eyes really were. He could well understand how Trip might fall for Paulie. "No, why?"

She lifted her narrow shoulders in a shrug. "I saw you over here, pacing, then I came over, only to find you nervous as a cat. Is something wrong?"

Nothing except that he felt a fierce new protectiveness for the young woman standing in front of him. "Actually, I was thinking about you."

Her eyes grew as round as saucers. "Me?"

He nodded, trying to look at her closely in the darkness. Would she try to hide the truth about Trip from him? Or, more important, would she let him know if Trip was pressing his attentions on her unwanted? A young woman in her situation might feel indebted to the older man, might even allow herself to be coerced into something she wasn't ready for. He hated even suspecting such a thing of Trip, but he felt he owed it to Paulie to find out the truth.

"At least you weren't wasting your time," she joked approvingly. "What, exactly, were you thinking about me?"

"Well…" He wasn't sure how to start. "I guess I owe you an apology for what I said this afternoon, for assuming that you've never been in love."

She looked down at her feet and dug her toe into the dirt. "Oh, that."

"I guess I forget sometimes that you're all grown up."

Her head snapped up, and though it was dark he could have sworn that two bright red stains appeared in her cheeks. "Oh, shoot!" she cried, shaking her head. "About what I said this afternoon, Will—about being in love. I didn't mean it, really." She stopped, flustered. "Well, no, I *did* mean it, but, I mean…"

He kept his gaze locked with hers as her words sputtered

out like a dying fire. His heart went out to her, trying so hard to cover up now that the cat was out of the bag. "I know you have a secret, Sprout."

Her cheeks grew redder. "You do?"

He nodded. "You don't have to keep it from me anymore. In fact, you can tell me all about it, if it would help."

She hesitated, looking extremely doubtful. "Will, I'm not sure you're ready to hear what I have to say."

"Why not?" he asked. "It's only fair. I told you all my woes with Mary Ann and you helped me, you really did. I'd like to do you the same favor, if you'd care to tell me."

She shook her head. "I'm not certain where I could even begin…"

He tried to help her out by giving her a starting point. "Are you sure it's love and not something else?" he asked, trying to keep his tone big-brotherly.

She blinked. "What else could it be?"

He bit his lip. Despite her rough exterior, she was so innocent, so sheltered in her own way. He hated to think of some man taking advantage of that innocence. "This man you said you cared about… Maybe you feel an obligation, because this person is an old friend."

Her lips parted and she gasped in a breath, indicating his words had hit close to the truth. "I don't think it's an obligation, Will."

That, at least, was a good sign. "Then, you feel as if you would go to him of your own free will, without any thought of what you might owe him, or how long you've known him?"

"Of course…I mean, I don't know." Paulie looked confused. "What do you mean by 'go to him?'"

Will wasn't quite sure how to explain. "Well, have you kissed this man?"

"Oh, sure!" she said, then her brows knit together.

"Well, you know, he gives me a peck on the cheek every once in a while. That what you mean?"

"No."

She blinked. "Well…how many kinds of kisses are there?"

He smiled. "A couple."

"Oh." She thought about this for a moment. "Well, what kind in particular are you trying to find out about?"

Will hesitated. She looked so anxious, so sweet. The poor thing had grown up without a mother, and since she was fifteen, had been deprived of a father as well. The least he could do was show her what kind of kisses to watch out for.

Of course, it didn't escape his notice that Paulie had very kissable lips, now that he put his mind to studying them. Or that she looked willowy and almost fragile beneath her bulky clothes. Why, he could probably encircle her waist just with his two hands.

He stepped forward slowly and tilted her chin upwards with his knuckle. Her eyes were two liquid green pools as they looked up at him. "Do you really want to know?"

She nodded her head eagerly.

He smiled, then bent to press his lips against hers. At first contact, she let out a gasp of surprise, but soon she relaxed and slowly began to experiment, pushing against him with more pressure. Then, when he moved his hands around her waist and pulled her a fraction closer, she threw her arms exuberantly around his neck and attached herself to him like a snail on a cistern.

But she sure didn't feel like a snail. Paulie might look like a stick figure, but her body felt rounded and warm, womanly. He ran a hand down her back, feeling each gentle swell of her vertebrae beneath the soft flesh underneath her cotton shirt. In response she nestled herself even more tightly against him.

Will groaned at the desire she was so unknowingly stirring up in him. He hadn't expected that, but there was no mistaking the tingling sensation below his belt she had so guilelessly created.

He pulled away and looked down, smiling stiffly. Her own eyes, once they fluttered open, were wide and luminous as she stared dreamily at him. There was no mistaking that this must have been her first kiss.

"Well," he said, relieved. "I guess Trip isn't the wolf I worried he was."

Paulie's dreamy gaze turned to a gawk. "What?"

He grinned. Poor thing. She was still too embarrassed to admit the truth. "You don't have to be timid about it. I know your secret, Sprout."

"What in tarnation are you talking about, Will?"

"About you…and Trip."

Her mouth dropped open, and her eyes grew buggy. *"Trip!"* she said in a voice that would have been a shout if her throat hadn't been so strangled. She looked anxiously over at the sleeping man to make sure she hadn't awakened him by yelling his name. "How on earth… What made you guess…?" She didn't deny it, though.

So it *was* true.

He shrugged. "I suppose it would be obvious to anyone who has eyes."

She looked horrified, and he guessed he could understand. She was probably afraid people would say mean things about her falling for such an older man. Like all the talk he'd heard about Mary Ann and Oat. And in Paulie's case, people probably would say she had snatched Trip away from Tessie Hale.

Her hand flew to her lips, and she continued to stare at him, stunned for a few moments.

"I won't tell," he promised her.

"No!" she cried insistently. "You can't! I mean, please don't!"

"But I want you to know, if you need to talk, you can come right to me."

"Oh…thank you," she murmured. Her cheeks looked so dark, they were probably ablaze. "I'd better…better get back to the fire."

He sent her a sideways grin. "You sure it's the fire you want to get back to…and not Trip?"

Her face crunched into a mortified expression, and she twirled on her heel and scampered off toward their makeshift camp.

Will chuckled softly as she retreated. He was sorry she was so embarrassed; still, he was glad they'd had the conversation. He wouldn't want to think that he had abandoned Paulie in a time of need. The only trouble was, his little kissing demonstration was lingering in his mind—and in his senses—longer than would seem proper for such an innocent little lesson.

He went back to his own bedroll apart from the others and sighed, leaning back and looking up at the stars for a while. He supposed it was just all this business with Mary Ann that was making him feel so restless. And yet, when he closed his eyes, it wasn't Mary Ann's face that he saw. It was Paulie's, her green eyes round and moist. Such pretty eyes—it didn't seem he'd ever really noticed them before. He remembered holding her body against his. He'd expected her to be all pointy bones and awkwardness, but instead all the awkwardness had been his as he'd found himself holding a woman with soft feminine curves in his arms.

Suddenly, Will shot up to sitting, his heart beating like thunder. He took a deep breath, and shook his head as if to clear it. What a crazy day this had been! And now, he was beginning to think that *he* was crazy. It was almost as if he…as if he found Paulie desira—

He swallowed, not even completing the outlandish thought.

That couldn't be so. It just couldn't.

Could it?

Chapter Four

"Got any more coffee, Paulie?"

Paulie yanked the little pot off the fire and handed it to Trip. "I'd like to know who elected me cook," she sniped good-naturedly.

Trip laughed. "You're the only one 'sides Will who's got provisions."

She threw up her hands in mock exasperation. "And where *is* Will?"

Trip looked at her keenly. "That's the fifth time you asked that this mornin'. I told you, he woke me up early and said he was gonna do a little scoutin' before we head out."

Paulie ducked her head. "I only meant that I wondered why he'd been gone so long." She sighed regretfully. "I should have woken up earlier. Then I could have gone with him."

But darn it, whose fault was it that she'd slept till practically sunup? All night long, the memory of Will's lips pressed up against hers kept playing through her mind, making her feel hot and shivery all over again. There was no way to get any shut-eye when a body was so keyed up. She'd tossed and turned on the hard ground half the night, unable to sleep, unable to think about anything besides that kiss. Unable to find relief from the letdown after he let her go and so arrogantly pronounced her to be in love with somebody else!

How could Will possibly think she was in love with Trip Peabody! Not that Trip wasn't perfectly nice—but have a romance with him? That idea sidled right up to the outrageous. Besides, the whole world south of the Red River knew Trip was in love with Tessie Hale. Will hadn't been gone to Kansas so long that he should have forgotten that longstanding state of affairs.

And did Will think she went around kissing just anybody? To her, it seemed that all the feelings she'd had stored up for Will all these long years had come rushing out during that kiss, almost as bold a declaration of her love as if she'd just told him so flat out. She could have held on to him forever. But Will hadn't sensed her feelings for him. He hadn't sensed anything at all, apparently.

Trip sat back on his heels and took a long drink from his tin cup. "He didn't look like he wanted company, Paulie."

She threw a glance to the tree under which Oat sat, snoozing. "Probably Will wanted some time to daydream about Mary Ann," she said, trying not to let her sore feelings seep into her tone.

"Probably," Trip agreed. "Love requires a heap of brooding, I've found."

She had firsthand knowledge of that fact, too. "Only when it goes wrong, Trip. I dare say there are some romances out there that go off without a hitch." Oh, how she wished she and Will could have one of those! Unfortunately, things had already turned so odd between them, she doubted they would ever have a normal relationship.

Or any relationship. Not when he could kiss her without

feeling anything more than he would if he were kissing a rock. And not while he was so obsessed by Mary Ann that he had to go tearing out at the strike of dawn by himself.

"Well," Trip said philosophically, "I guess it's like my old daddy said. Anything worth havin' is worth fightin' for."

Paulie dropped the pot back on the fire and crossed her arms. "Your daddy said that when he was marching off to war in sixty-one, Trip. Brooding about Tessie Hale all day isn't exactly the equivalent of a pitched battle."

"Maybe not, but it sure wears me out sometimes."

After her sleepless night, she could vouch personally for the exhaustion brought on by unrequited love. She poured herself another cup of coffee and drank down half a cup in one swig.

"Ain't you goin' to eat anything, Paulie?"

"I can't eat," she said, staring at the biscuit she'd been holding in her hand since she'd made the batch and feeling almost queasy at the thought of actually swallowing it. Lovesickness seemed to have caused her heart to swell overnight, forming a physical barrier between her mouth and her stomach.

Trip shook his head, misinterpreting her digestive woe. "Whether you eat or not won't make much difference whether we run into Night Bird."

At the sound of the dreaded name, Oat jolted into wakefulness. "Night Bird?" he said, his hand reaching for his gun. His rheumy eyes were wide with fear.

"We were just talking, Oat," Paulie assured the older man. Lord only knew what he would do if Night Bird ever did come riding over the hill.

Lord only knew what any of them would do!

"Then what's that I hear comin'?"

It wasn't until Oat mentioned them that Paulie heard the

hoofbeats thundering toward them. She scrambled for her rifle, as did Trip, who stood on wobbly legs, but with a cool head, watching. How could he be so calm? She wasn't sure what was coming at them, but it didn't sound good.

Just as she was readying her gun for a battle, the rider crested the gentle hill in front of them. It was Will, riding as if Beelzebub himself were nipping at his heels. Paulie waited, looking to see what was following him, but nothing appeared to explain the crazed way he had galloped into their calm little camp.

He brought his horse to a quick stop just a few feet away from them and quipped, "Thought I might need to wake you all up."

Paulie put her hands on her hips, half in anger, half to steady herself as she stared into his whiskey-colored eyes. Heavens, Will was a handsome man! Of course she'd known that already, but now she had the additional bonus of knowing how it felt to be in those strong arms of his. And with his dark hair wild from his ride, and his eyes shining as if lit from some internal fire, he was even better-looking than he'd seemed the night before, when he'd kissed her. She felt dizzy from the mere memory of it—light-headed and weightless.

It was hard to keep her thoughts straight, being so close to him. She just couldn't allow herself to think about that kiss, not right at the moment.

"You've got a lot of nerve, riding in like that and scaring us half to death!"

Will swung off his horse. "Good morning to you, too, Sprout." He seemed to look right through her, as though he didn't want to deal with her at all. Like last night had meant nothing to him!

Well, he would soon find out she wasn't so easy to ignore. "Do you realize we were poised to shoot whoever was coming? You could have got yourself killed just now!"

He turned on her, eyes flashing. "If you can't keep a cool head, you shouldn't be here."

Her blood shot from hot to the boiling point in nothing flat. "*You're* the one who's been flying off the handle all the time, Mr. Hothead," she said. She almost added that it was his jumping to fool conclusions about his lady love's abduction that was leading them off on this crazy mission to begin with, but decided to refrain, for Oat's sake.

Will turned to her with a retort on his lips, but was cut off by Trip.

"Any sign of Night Bird?"

Will pivoted toward Trip—dismissing Paulie as easily as he would swat a bothersome gnat away. "No," he said, shaking his head.

"Where are we goin' today?"

"I thought we could head into Vinegaroon."

Paulie's ire evaporated at the mention of that town. "Vinegaroon!" she cried. "There isn't anything there but a saloon."

"You'll be thirsty by the time we get there," Will told her with a wry smile.

The reply poised on the tip of Paulie's tongue was interrupted by Oat, who was nodding in agreement with Will. "Roy Bean'll know if Night Bird is crawling around."

"That's what I'm counting on," Will said.

"Judge Bean, you mean!" Paulie had heard about Roy Bean, but had never met the man. He had a reputation for running a hell of a saloon, and, since being appointed judge, or appointing himself—no one was ever quite sure which—he'd also become known for doling out swift justice. She wasn't sure she would like him. "I've heard of innocent men wandering into that place in the morning and ending the day swinging by a rope.''

Will looked at her, really looked at her for the first time that morning, and she could have sworn there was laughter in those brown eyes. ''Well maybe if you mind your manners and keep your mouth shut, we won't have to waste time cutting you down at sunset.''

Then he turned, missing by inches the hard biscuit that Paulie sent whizzing past his ear.

If Trip wanted Paulie Johnson, he was welcome to her. And good luck to him!

Will snorted to himself and spurred Ferdinand just a little faster, knowing that the others would keep up, no matter what. Paulie would die before she let out a whimper of complaint about their pace, or her hunger, which she was probably feeling keenly by now. The fool girl should be eating more food and throwing less of it. Trip said she hadn't eaten a bite at breakfast. Probably just more evidence of her lovesickness, he thought, feeling a now familiar prick of unease at the thought of the pair of them.

The whole affair was none of his business, and he'd already spent far too much time thinking about it. Brooding about it, almost. Bad enough he hadn't been able to sleep almost all the night, but the minute his bleary eyes had opened this morning, he'd started thinking about that kiss again, and how surprisingly soft and warm Paulie had felt in his arms. And then he'd remembered that Paulie belonged to Trip. He'd ridden out and had been unable to think about anything else. Night Bird could have jumped on the back of the horse with him and he wouldn't have known it.

He was determined not to give Trip and Paulie—or that kiss—another thought.

He rode on for a few minutes, trying to concentrate on the landscape around him. Scrubby hills surrounded them, providing perfect hiding places for bandits.

Will sighed, unconsciously giving up his internal struggle. He just couldn't even begin to guess why a sensible man like Trip Peabody would choose an ill-tempered waif like Paulie Johnson to sacrifice his long-held bachelorhood to! It didn't make sense. Especially when everyone had always thought he would marry Tessie Hale.

Tessie Hale... Now *there* was a woman! Tessie was tall, pretty and even-tempered. Sure, she was a little long in the tooth—seasoned, you might say—but so was Trip. And she was a widow, which was about the perfect thing for a woman to be, when it came to a man's choosing a mate. It meant that she'd already had some measure of matrimonial success. Will frowned. Or maybe it just meant that she'd nagged her husband into an early grave.

Paulie's laughter startled him out of his thoughts. "Trip, you chucklehead!"

Her voice travelled forward, a husky whisper on the light dry breeze. There was something soothing and friendly about the teasing sound. He remembered now that sometimes when he was going up to Kansas, he'd think back on his silly conversations with Paulie. Paulie could chatter on for hours about nothing and still manage to be entertaining. Now that he considered it, he couldn't remember thinking back on a single conversation he'd had with Mary Ann while he was on his way to Kansas. Maybe that was why he'd written Mary Ann that damn letter—the epistle that had seemed to cause the whole world to turn topsy-turvy.

If so, that was a fool reason. It was ridiculous to compare Paulie and Mary Ann anyway—like comparing a fig to a daisy.

He couldn't help glancing back at her. At just that moment, she tossed her head back, laughing at something Trip had said. Or maybe she was laughing at one of her own jokes. Even from this distance, he could almost see her eyes sparkling with humor. Her head was tilted as it always did when she found something particularly funny.

He quickly turned back, sighed again, and shook his head, clearing it. Trip Peabody? It just didn't make sense. But neither sometimes did his wanting to honor the pledge he'd made Mary Ann's father. Especially now that she was married to Oat. But he felt it just the same, and maybe it was that feeling of being bound to someone against all reason that had brought Paulie and Trip together. If so, he knew he couldn't talk her out of it.

Not that he wanted to, he assured himself for the millionth time. It was none of his business who Paulie Johnson set her heart on.

Galloping hoofbeats closed in on him, and he didn't have to turn around to guess whose horse they belonged to.

"Look, Will!" Paulie cried with more enthusiasm than he would have thought any one of them would have the energy to muster. "There's the saloon!"

"You'd think you'd never seen one before," he said, making fun of her excitement over a mere wooden building—one he apparently would have missed, his mind was so preoccupied.

Sure enough, there it stood on the horizon, looking sturdy, almost fortresslike on the bare arid land surrounding it. A horse was tethered out front, and a pair of men sat on the porch. They were dwarfed by a brand-new sign running the length of the saloon's roof that read The Law West of the Pecos.

"Roy Bean sure seems to take his job seriously," Paulie said.

"His job, his liquor and his woman," Will agreed.

"Woman?" Paulie looked at him in some confusion. "I didn't know he was married."

Will smiled. "Married to an idea, you might say."

She didn't look like he had clarified the situation for her any, so he simply rode on, deciding it was best to let her discover for herself Roy Bean's odd fascination with Lily Langtry, a woman he'd never met—and probably never would, considering that famous English actresses didn't make it around to South Texas very often. Oat and Trip caught up with Will and Paulie in the final stretch, both men looking very excited to be within spitting distance of the inside of a building again. A building with liquor in it, too.

"Think I might have me a sarsaparilla," Oat said, looking about as animated as Will had seen him.

"Me, I'm gonna have a whiskey." Trip almost licked his lips. "Seems like forever since we've had that, hey, Paulie?"

The two looked at each other and smiled—an exchange Will tried to glean for any kernel of meaning. But of course the intent, if not the meaning itself, was clear. From this peculiar couple, a shared grin was the equivalent of a lovey-dovey simper from a more traditional pair of lovers.

"It seems forever since I've *sold* any, I know that," Paulie agreed. "But you never did care about sellin' so much as drinkin', Trip."

Will winced. Hearing them talk about the mundane go-ings-on at that saloon of theirs, he felt as if he were listening in on the most intimate of conversations. Oat didn't look the slightest bit uncomfortable…but perhaps he just didn't know the truth. Yet. The way Paulie and Trip were carrying on, everyone was bound to start suspecting sooner or later.

"What about you, Will?" Paulie asked. She reached

over and nudged him in the arm—at her merest touch, he nearly shot right out of his saddle.

"Good grief!" Trip exclaimed. "From the way you reacted, Will, anyone would have thought she'd poked you with a bolt of lightning!"

Will shook his head to clear it. "What were you asking, Paulie?"

"I asked, what's your poison going to be?"

"I'm not here to socialize," he said tightly. "I'm here for answers."

He spurred his horse and rode on, loping into Vinegaroon just ahead of the others. He needed to put some distance between himself and Paulie and Trip. Their relationship was just none of his business. He needed to get a hold of himself.

Roy Bean, a tough wiry old cuss if ever there was one, pushed out of his chair and leaned against the porch railing, looking bemused by the approaching party. "Well, if it ain't Will Brockett!" he said in his signature terse, wry voice. He tugged at his handlebar mustache. "I heard you'd gotten back from Kansas, Will, but I wasn't expecting you to come callin' so soon."

Will dismounted and tethered Ferdinand at the post in front of saloon. "I just came by to—"

"Well, well!" Roy cried, too focused on the company Will was keeping to care about why he had come around. "This is a ragtag band you got riding drag! Oat, Trip Peabody and some whippersnapper I ain't never seen before."

Before Will could make introductions, Paulie was off her horse.

"I'm Paulie Johnson, from Possum Trot," she said excitedly, pumping Roy's hand a mile a minute. A while back she had seemed reluctant to meet Roy, but now she was greeting him as though he were her long-lost uncle.

"Johnson?" he asked, his beady eyes sparking with interest. "That girl that runs the Dry Wallow?"

Will folded his arms and felt the corners of his lips tug into a frown. Paulie, apparently, could charm men more ably than he had ever given her credit for. At least rough types who hung around saloons.

"I imagine you folks want to come on in and wet your whistle," Roy said. "I was just about to set myself down to lunch."

Paulie practically licked her lips. "Lunch?"

Roy eyed Will. "Man, are you leading these folks on some sort of starvation trail?"

It seemed as good an opening as any for telling Roy why they were really there. "Actually, I'm—"

Roy didn't wait for his explanation. He was too enraptured by his other newcomers. "Well, come on inside and help yourself," he told Paulie. "I don't know if the vittles is what you're used to, but I've got plenty of 'em."

The judge led Paulie, Oat and Trip into the saloon, leaving his companion on the porch unintroduced. Will turned to the man, a mean-looking character who didn't even bother to glance up at him. He just kept staring at the dusty planks that made up the saloon's porch, pivoting once to spit off to the side. Frankly, the stranger gave Will the shivers, but he couldn't say exactly why that was. He was a regular-looking fellow with sandy blond hair peeking out from under the brim of his hat. Only he had a hardness in his eyes that made Will uneasy.

After a few more moments of the silent treatment, Will followed the talking and laughter into the saloon and found the group of men nursing drinks around Paulie, who was seated at the head of a long table, stuffing herself with a plate of some sort of concoction of rice and beans, with a few hunks of nondescript meat mixed in for good measure.

They all glanced up at him when he took a seat nearby, then looked quickly away again, focusing all their rapt attention on Paulie.

She swallowed down a gulp of food and said, savoring every syllable of what apparently was a punch line, "...And so I told the man, 'I don't know about your wife, Mister, but you sure could use a new horse.'"

The men roared with laughter. Even Oat. Roy was all but slapping his knee, and of course Trip was laughing so hard there were tears in his eyes. He had probably heard the silly joke about a thousand times already. People in love certainly did make fools of themselves, Will thought, crossing his arms sourly.

Roy took note of his demeanor and turned to him for a moment. "Well, Will, I keep expecting you to come out and tell me what it is you're doing here any minute now."

As if he hadn't already tried to tell the man twice already!

"Why so closemouthed, Will?" Roy went on.

Glad for the opening to finally get down to business, Will took a breath.

Paulie downed another heaping spoonful of that unappetizing mash of Roy's and blurted out, "We're looking for Night Bird. That's why we've come. Everybody thought maybe you'd heard of his whereabouts."

At this explanation, Roy looked almost startled. His narrow eyes widened and he rubbed his stubbly jaw in wonder. "Night Bird, huh?" he asked, looking at Will as if he'd just gone plumb crazy. "You got a death wish, Brockett?"

Will opened his mouth to defend his mission, but Paulie once again beat him to the punch.

"That's what I said!" Paulie exclaimed. "But the trouble is, we suspect Night Bird ran off with Oat's wife."

They suspected? Will thought. The last time he'd checked, Paulie considered the Night Bird theory to be nothing but pure flapdoodle. Now she was almost making it sound as if chasing the renegade had been her idea!

"That pretty Redfern girl I heard so much about?" Roy asked, uninhibited in his shock. He didn't have to mention that he'd heard so much about her precisely because she had married Oat, either. Despite her beauty, Mary Ann hadn't gained any real notoriety until she'd made a surprising choice of husband.

"That's the one," Paulie said.

"I lost her," Oat added, still as puzzled as ever.

"Good Lord!" Roy exclaimed. Then he called out to the porch. "Cal, you hear that?"

When they looked up, the man with the cold gaze had it fixed on Will, as if sizing him up for the task of chasing Night Bird. "I heard," he said curtly.

"What do you think, Cal?"

The man shrugged.

Roy looked at his assembled guests. "You all have something in common with Cal here. He's been hired by the family of one of those men Night Bird killed to catch him dead or alive."

A killer. That would explain his demeanor, Will thought. One glance at the man was enough to know that he didn't give a fig about whether his quarry was alive or not when he laid him at the feet of the family who hired him.

"Do you know where Night Bird is?" Will asked.

The man spat on Roy's floor, then shrugged. "Mexico."

"Are you going after him?"

The bounty hunter shook his head. "Nope."

"It's foolhardy to chase a bandit into Mexico, Will," Roy said. "He'll get more trigger-happy the closer he is to the border—and the farther away from American law."

Will shook his head, feeling the weight of his responsibility more sharply the worse the news became. "I can't just let him go," he explained. "Not while he's got Mary— I mean, Mrs. Murphy."

"I promise you one thing, Oat," Roy said. "If that damned renegade comes within smelling distance of this place, he's a dead man."

No one gathered around the table appeared comforted by that pronouncement.

Will crossed his arms. Truth be told, he'd prefer to go alone—or with one other person, maybe. But by themselves, none of the others seemed substantial enough help to be of much use to him. He needed somebody like the man named Cal. A man accustomed to chasing killers. But even Cal wasn't willing to chase the murdering bandit onto his home soil.

He had to take what he could get. He still didn't like the idea of dragging Paulie into this. And now that he knew about Paulie and Trip, he didn't feel much confidence in that man, either.

Somehow, his prospects had never seemed so grim. But there was no changing the way things were. The best he could do was try to make everyone realize they weren't duty-bound to follow him into Mexico.

The first chance he had, he pulled Trip aside, leading him away from Paulie and Roy's spirited conversation and onto the front porch. Cal was nowhere to be seen, although his horse was still hitched out front.

"Something wrong, Will?" Trip asked.

"No…not yet, anyway," Will answered, not sure how to begin. Trip wasn't a man to wear his heart on his sleeve, and he was too honorable to ever say on his own that he had changed his mind about going into Mexico. "The thing is, Trip, I'm trying to see that things don't go wrong."

Trip nodded, but the confused look in his eye as he squinted out over the broad horizon let Will know that he hadn't made his meaning clear.

Will took a deep breath. "What I wanted you to know is that I'll understand if you stay behind."

The man looked stunned. "Behind?" he repeated, swaying a little. "You mean, here at the saloon?"

Will nodded. "Or if you and Paulie went back to Possum Trot, I wouldn't hold that against you, either."

Trip blinked. "Oh, Paulie's not going back. I'd bet money on that, Will."

Stubborn kid! "But if I can convince her to," he insisted, "I would understand if you stayed back with her. In fact, I would feel better knowing she had you to look after her."

"Well of course I'll look after her, Will. But as for us stayin' here, or goin' back to Possum Trot, you can put that idea right out of your head. Neither one of us would feel right doin' that. We'll be right behind you all the way to South America, even, if that's where you reckon we should go."

The man's loyalty moved him. In fact, from the anguished look on Trip's face, Will saw that he was on the verge of tears himself. He thought regretfully of how he'd kissed Paulie last night—how he'd enjoyed it. It wasn't right, especially if she was Trip's girl.

He patted Trip's arm. "Still, see what you can do to convince Paulie to stay back, will you?"

Trip shook his head. "It was her idea to come along, Will. It ain't my place to talk her out of it. You can try, but it won't do you any good. Paulette Johnson's got a head like a mule's."

Will knew he was right—but he couldn't help thinking that Trip had just given the most unflattering description he'd ever heard a man give of his sweetheart.

An hour later, he tried to take heart in the looks of his crew as they poured reluctantly out of Roy's saloon, their spirits bolstered by food and drink. He didn't see evidence of Cal's gloomy warning on any of their faces anymore. Not even on Oat's.

Roy and Cal appeared at the door, ready to take up their positions on the porch again. "Hope we see you all soon," Roy called out. "You give that bandit a big kiss hello for me."

But sandy-haired Cal had no words to bolster them. He merely shook his head and spat as he watched them mount up.

Paulie noticed a distinct increase in tension when the Rio Grande came into view. Will looked more alert than ever. Oat, riding behind them, slowed to a snail's pace. And beside her, Trip was uncharacteristically silent, although he managed to clear his throat every ten seconds. And every time he cleared it, he made a hitching sound—*heh-hmmhmm.*

"Lord, I hate crossing rivers," Paulie said.

Trip didn't answer. And then... *Heh-hmmhmm!*

The sound was beginning to get on her nerves. "What the heck's wrong with you, Trip? For heaven's sake, take a drink, or spit, or do *something* to clear that darn throat of yours once and for all. Or better yet, why don't you just tell me what's got you so tied up in knots?"

He looked away, and then, unexpectedly, brought Feather to a halt. "I guess I been thinking about something Will told me."

His words made Paulie tug Partner to a quick stop, too. Just the mention of Will's name was enough to make her heart cease beating. "What about Will? What did he say to you—was it about me?"

She tried not to sound too eager, but from the surprised look on Trip's face, she could tell that he noticed the way she was champing at the bit for any smidgeon of Will gossip—and that she had hit the nail on the head. Will *had* been talking about her!

"As a matter of fact, he did mention you, Paulie. It was the strangest thing."

She nodded encouragingly to Trip, just keeping herself from taking hold of his shoulders and shaking the information she wanted out of him.

"He said that if I wanted to, I could stay back with you."

This was not what she'd expected to hear.

"Back with me?" she asked, confused. "But I'm going with him!"

Trip shrugged. "I know. That's what I told him."

"But he didn't say anything to me about it!" Paulie exclaimed, looking ahead as if she could get a clue concerning this new mystery from Will's straight back. Just looking at him made her throat go bone dry. No man looked as proud or handsome sitting atop a horse as Will did.

"He told me I should talk to you."

"You know that's pointless."

"Well sure…" Trip's words trailed off like mavericks from a herd before he could gather his thoughts and round them back up again. "What I don't understand, though, is why Will would think *I* should be the one to try to convince you to stay."

"Oh!" Paulie exclaimed, sucking in a breath.

Suddenly, she understood Will's thinking. He didn't want her and Trip along if he thought their being in love would interfere with the manhunt.

But that was just plain ridiculous!

"Can you figure that one out?" Trip asked.

She didn't want to lie to her friend—especially when he

was coming all this way on her account. Besides, it wouldn't do to have Trip in the dark, considering that Will thought they were sweet on each other. "Well, I guess I can. You might say Will's suffering under a...a... misconception."

Trip's gray eyebrows rose. "What kind of misconception?"

Paulie felt awkward. How could she explain to Trip— good, kindhearted Trip who'd probably never told a lie in his life—what she had done? Deciding it was best just to plunge in, she blurted out, "Well, I guess you could say in a way that he sort of thinks that you and I are in some way, you know, a little bit...well, in good company together."

She took a deep breath. There. She'd said it. Surprisingly clearly, too.

"What?" Trip asked, not nearly so impressed by her verbal skill.

"He thinks we're in love," Paulie clarified bluntly.

Trip, who had been leaning towards her as she blurted out her news, appeared as if he would fall right over if she didn't do something to stop him. The man was in a state of shock.

"How could you have told him that?"

"I didn't," she said, reaching out to brace his chest with a hand. "He just sort of guessed."

"Guessed?" Trip recoiled. "But it's not true!" he exclaimed, swaying back the other way.

"I know!" she said, reaching out to grab his hand so he wouldn't topple right off Feather. "But Will didn't seem to realize that...and for some stupid reason I didn't correct the misunderstanding."

"But everybody knows I'm in love with Tessie Hale!"

Trip cried, growing more alarmed. "What if Tessie should hear about this?"

"She won't," Paulie promised. "Just as soon as we find Mary Ann, I swear I'll tell Will the truth."

"Mary Ann? What she got to do with it?"

Paulie couldn't bring herself to admit her feelings for Will, or her jealousy of Mary Ann, which seemed incredibly petty now that she thought of confessing it in the cold light of day. She simply insisted, "I swear, Trip, Tessie will never know."

The man looked like he was going to have heart palpitations. "But you and me?" he asked. "That's just plain silly! Will ought to know that!"

Paulie tried not to be offended—to no avail. *Why* did everyone seem to think that her being in love with anyone was "just plain silly"? She abruptly let go of Trip's hand, and felt herself reel backward, off balance.

"Oh!" she exclaimed.

In an attempt to save her as she had saved him, Trip automatically reached forward, and for a moment the two of them, atop horses that were growing increasingly agitated, danced a strange, off-balance gavotte. And then Feather reared, breaking their hold, and as Paulie darted to the side to once again grab hold of Trip's arm, she grasped nothing but air. To her shock, she slipped and found herself toppling as she had feared Trip would, shoulder-first to the ground.

Chapter Five

"How a body can fall off a horse while it's standing stock-still sure beats the hell out of me," Will said, unable to keep the wonder out of his voice. If this had happened to Trip, he wouldn't have been quite so surprised. But Paulie?

"It happens," Paulie muttered through gritted teeth. Her face was set in a permanent wince.

"Are you hurt, Paulie?" Trip asked her, concern written all over him. "It looked like Partner kicked you."

She stared up at him, her complexion pale and clammy, and attempted a smile. "Nah, I'm okay," she boasted. "Just a little banged up, that's all." Even as the words came out, she clutched her side.

Will had seen cowboys "banged up" from falls before, and the damage could be pretty bad. "Did the horse kick you?"

She ducked her head. "Nicked me, maybe. It's nothing to worry about."

Even a glancing blow from a sharp shoed hoof could break a rib. "You better let us take a look," Will said.

"I told you, I'm fine!" He poked her ribs gently, and she let out a howl.

"Is that why you sounded off like a sick coyote?"

Resigned, Paulie reached for her shirt. "Oh, all right," she said. "I'll show you wh—" Her words stopped the moment her movements did, so that her elbows were hitched up just as she was pulling her shirttails out from her jeans. Suddenly, her face reddened. "Don't look."

Will tossed up his hands. "Good grief, Paulie! You want Trip to take a look at you?"

That thought seemed to horrify her even more. "Heck, no!"

Trip didn't look too comfortable at the prospect, either. Some pair of lovers they would make, Will thought disgustedly.

Deciding that they couldn't spend all evening simply deciding whether Paulie could ride or not, he took matters into his own hands. As fast as he could, he reached out and pulled Paulie's shirt up, stopping when he saw an angry red slash across her side. She wasn't bleeding, but the bruise was already beginning to turn blue.

Paulie had screeched out a short protest that died the minute she saw the damage Partner had done. "My word!" she cried out, even as Oat let out a long low whistle.

"Bruised rib," the old-timer said curtly. "I'll betcha."

Will strode back to his horse, pulled out an extra shirt and began ripping it into thick strips. He tried to blot out the memory of the horrible roil that had occurred in his stomach when he'd first seen that bruise slashing across Paulie's white skin. He'd seen worse. But he'd never seen a bruise like that on anyone so delicate. Paulie always seemed so brash and tough, he had been unprepared for the sight of her soft, feminine skin, or the outline of her ribs being visible. She had no defenses at all…at least not from a sharp kick to her side. That she wasn't rolling on the ground moaning was a tribute to her strength, or her will.

"Make a fire, Trip," he said. "We'll stop here till to-morrow morning."

As Trip went about his business, Paulie glanced franti-cally toward the river. "But Will, we've got to keep go-ing."

"Not with you in this shape, we don't."

"Just give me a minute, I can ride."

"Pull your shirt up again," he said.

Her eyes became round as saucers. "Why?"

"I'm going to wrap these rags around you, in case you busted something."

"Oh," she said. To his surprise, she turned her back to him and dutifully obeyed. "Do you think I'd be able to ride then, once you're finished?"

Will suddenly felt awkward doing the wrapping, though it wasn't the first time he'd performed the task. The mem-ory of how small she'd seemed in his arms the night before came back to him. Delicate. She was delicate. Paulie John-son—who'd have thought it!

"We'll see."

The way she shook her head told him she was agitated. "You can't stop here, Will. You need to go after Night Bird."

"I can't go without you," he said, tying off the last strip. "Not now that you've come this far."

"Shoot, I hate to be the cause of problems." She ducked her head. "I especially don't want to make trouble for you, Will."

He smiled, feeling that odd hitch in his throat again. Of course he didn't want to leave her, he thought. Friends didn't desert each other, no matter what the circumstances. Trip wouldn't have been the only one distracted if he'd decided to push on across the border without Paulie.

"You're no trouble, Sprout." He grinned. "Long as you keep your mouth closed."

She blinked, then in her anger picked up a handful of sand and tossed it at him.

Will laughed. "That's a fine thanks I get for saving your life."

"My life!" she hollered. "My life wasn't in danger till you decided to drag us all across Texas."

"I warned you not to come," he answered, feeling much more comfortable now that they were bantering again.

"And as for *saving* me," she said, managing to put her hands on her hips with a wince, "*squeezing* me to death is more like it. I can barely breathe after your kindly ministrations, thank you very much."

"You're just spoiled." He tilted his head. "If you dressed like you're supposed to and wore a corset every now and then, you wouldn't be making such a fuss."

"A corset!" She hooted at the very idea. "If I'd been wearing one of those durned things, a whole herd of horses could have stampeded over me and I probably wouldn't have suffered so much as a bruise. But I don't recall you exactly handing out compliments the last time I tried to deck myself out all female-like."

Will turned his mind back to that moment two days ago when he'd seen her prancing around in her mother's wedding dress. Considering all that had happened since, it seemed a long time ago, but the humor of the sight was still fresh in his mind. "It wasn't the clothes so much as the way you wore them."

His smirk was not appreciated. Paulie pursed her lips. "Well, I haven't had much practice."

Her dander rose so predictably that teasing her was hard to resist. "I would keep working on the hair." Even now, a day after the debacle, she still had locks askew from her unfortunate efforts.

She patted her head self-consciously. "I don't see what the point is anyway. It's not like there's any man wandering loose around Possum Trot who I want to impress!"

Will flinched, surprised by her words. "Oh no? What about Trip?" he asked, cutting off whatever insult she had planned for him.

Her mouth dropped open, and he could have sworn a blush crept up her face. "Oh…well, naturally." She bridled for a few moments, then looked up at him through narrowed eyes. "But Trip accepts me as I am. I don't have to turn myself inside out for his benefit."

Will crossed his arms. "Then why did you?"

"Because I *wanted* to. Haven't you ever just wanted to try to change for somebody, Will?"

He considered her question for a moment. Now that he thought about it, he never had considered altering himself to suit someone else's taste. All those years when he'd been assuming he would marry Mary Ann, he'd been waiting for *her* to change. Her youthful shallowness, her seemingly bottomless interest in life's trivialities—these were things he kept waiting for *her* to grow out of. As if he would ride over to the Breens' one day and discover that she'd become a serious, mature woman overnight.

Naturally, that had never happened.

Strange to think how opposite Mary Ann and Paulie were. While he had been waiting for Mary Ann to place less emphasis on trivialities and appearances, Paulie had been trying to place more on her own appearance. But she did say that she and Mary Ann had become friends. Maybe her stab at duding herself up was a result of Mary Ann's influence.

"Who are you thinking about?" Paulie asked.

"Mary Ann, mostly."

She looked down, her expression unreadable. "Oh."

He reached out and lifted her chin. "I know you two are friends, but I wouldn't let her change you, Paulie."

She gulped and shook her head. "I wouldn't do that. Mary Ann's pretty and all, but…"

"Mary Ann's beautiful," Will corrected. Beauty was about all there was to her. But as he looked down into Paulie's eyes, the memory of Mary Ann's beauty wandered into some dusty recess of his mind. That woman's eyes were never so expressive as Paulie's, nor had her lips seemed half so inviting…

Will captured his wayward thoughts before they got completely out of hand. What the hell was he thinking about Paulie's lips for? He dropped his hand and stepped back, looking away from her confused, blinking eyes. "Tell Trip I'll be back in a little while."

He quickly put as much distance between himself and Paulie as he could.

Paulie sat in practically the same place she had fallen, watching a brooding Will disappear on another of his walks. It didn't take a genius to know who he thought of while he was ambling around the countryside, either.

"Mary Ann's beautiful…" Well, that fact was undeniable. Naturally losing a woman like that would prey on a man's mind.

And yet… Paulie couldn't help but balk at the unfairness of life. How beautiful was it to turn your back on a man like Will Brockett to marry a man like Oat? Not that there was anything wrong with Oat, all by himself. In the past two days, she'd discovered that he was a good travelling companion, amiable and knowledgeable. She even began to feel a little sorry for him for being saddled with such a wife. She still couldn't imagine why he'd married her. It had probably been less Oat's doing than Mary Ann's.

Mary Ann wasn't above using people. Hadn't she led Will Brockett on all those years and then just dumped him without so much as a word of explanation? She'd left the poor man brokenhearted, and Paulie bet Mary Ann didn't feel a smidgeon of guilt. *Beautiful!*

"Good Lord, Paulie, are you feeling all right?" Trip asked.

She straightened, ignoring the pain that shot up her side when she moved. "I'm fine. Everybody needs to stop worrying about me."

"I wasn't worried so much as wondering why you had that thunderous look on your face."

"Oh. I was just thinking about Mary Ann," she explained, not even bothering to hide her feelings from Trip.

Trip let out a sour chuckle. "I never will understand why you're going to so much trouble to rescue a woman you've barely spoken two words to in your lifetime."

She frowned. "It's a matter of principle."

"How's that?"

"Can't just let people go around kidnapping Possum Trot women, can we?"

He scratched his head. "Guess not. But if you ask me, your bein' here has got a lot more to do with Will than Mary Ann."

For the first time, someone had a glimmer of a notion of her feelings for Will Brockett, and Paulie wasn't comfortable with the discovery. She felt a flush creep up her neck, and was very glad it was already dark so that perhaps Trip couldn't see how close he'd come to the truth. "I couldn't let him just ride off alone," she argued, "especially with only Oat for backup. Especially running after an Injun who's killed—"

He nodded and lifted a hand to interrupt her. "The preacher doesn't have to convert me, Paulie. I'm a mite more fond of Will than Mary Ann myself, you know."

"I'd be torn up if anything happened to you, either, Trip."

He shrugged. "I'm sturdier than I look. The only thing that's bothered me so far is what you said about Will thinking that you and me...I mean, that we was..."

Unable to find the correct words, he let his stammer trail off into the growing dark.

"That we're sweethearts?"

"I can't imagine what would have led you to tell him such a thing!" Trip exclaimed, amazed anew at the very idea.

"I told you, I didn't tell him. He guessed...and I just let him keep guessing, is all." She ducked her head, suddenly embarrassed at her unexplainable lie by omission.

"Gol-darn it, Paulie, we gotta do something. I can't have it gettin' back to Possum Trot that you and me is..."

"Well we aren't, so it won't."

"But with Will thinkin' it..."

"Will's no gossip. Besides, goodness knows when we'll be back in Possum Trot."

"But if Tessie should ever find out..."

Paulie remained silent. She could see how the widow Hale would be sorely disappointed that the man who had *not* been able to propose to her for twenty years would be *not* proposing to somebody new. But somehow, she figured Tessie Hale was a little more mentally agile than Will Brockett when it came to detecting a fish story. She and Trip being suddenly in love didn't exactly have a ring of authenticity to it.

"Besides, I don't like Will thinkin' such a thing, me bein' so much older and all. How does that look?"

"Don't worry, Trip. After Oat and Mary Ann, people aren't scandalized by anything."

Despite her assurances, Trip looked glum. "I'd feel awful if Will thought worse of me 'cause of something that ain't true."

Put that way, Paulie wasn't quite so complacent about misleading Will. Maybe she should have thought a little more about Trip's feelings...but how could she have? Will had been standing there looking so darn handsome, and she was just plain old Paulie, like she'd always been forever. Suddenly she'd wanted him to think she was somebody who other men might desire even if he didn't.

"I'm sorry, Trip. I guess I wasn't thinking of the thing from your end."

He shrugged. "Nothin' to get too wound up about, I guess."

Somehow, his being so agreeable now made her feel all that much worse. But she couldn't let him know that, or he would feel worse, too, and then there would be no end to the guilt going around.

She shifted on the hard ground, attempting to push herself up. The effort caused enough pain to make her think twice about going to find Will right away. But now that she had her mind made up to set things straight, she wanted to get it over with. The sooner she faced up to the humiliation of telling him the truth, the sooner she could start living it down.

"Where you going?" Trip asked. "You ain't goin' to see Will now, are you? I'll go with you to talk to him if you want," he offered.

She couldn't imagine anything worse than having to admit her untruthfulness with two men instead of just one. "No, please—I'm not going to talk to him right this minute. I'm not even sure where he rode off to."

"Then why don't you sit here and rest. I'll bring you some water if you need it."

"Uh, no…" She thought fast. "I just wanted to…well, you know."

It was dark, but she knew even an oblique reference to a call of nature would bring a blush to his cheeks. He helped her to her feet. "Sure you're okay?"

She nodded and began to walk away, slowly. Once she got moving, she found that her side really didn't hurt much, as long as she stayed straight and upright. She headed for the hill she'd seen Will disappear over not long before, and looked around for him. Naturally, now that she was ready to come clean, the man was nowhere to be seen.

Maybe that was just as well. She would never in a million years tell Will that she was sweet on him, so she wasn't quite sure what excuse she would give for leading him on about her relationship to Trip. She would have to think of something, of course—hopefully something plausible.

The crunching sound of grass nearby made her stop. "Will?" No answer came, and she felt her hair stand on end. Something definitely wasn't right. Someone was out there, in the darkness.

"Will?" she repeated, her voice a feeble tremor.

The silence made her more nervous than the crunching had. She whirled to head back in the direction of camp when she heard Trip's strangled cry.

"Paulie, run!"

She stopped again, unsure of what to do next. Panic shot through her. Someone had Trip—and probably Oat, too. Where was Will? With Trip's shouts one direction and crunching footsteps in the other, her venues of escape were limited. And how could she leave the others when she wasn't even sure which way to go for help? How could she leave Will?

Her only hope was that he was still out on his walk, safe. If she was careful, she might be able to find him. Deciding that she had to do something, she peered into the pitch blackness around her, took a deep breath, and ran swiftly away from the crunching sounds she'd heard. She bent slightly to make herself feel as if she were moving more stealthily, but the position caused a sharp pain to shoot up her side.

She straightened again, but felt an even greater pain as she smacked face-first into something hard, tall, and definitely human. She gasped in surprise, hoping this being she had bumped into was Will. But looking up into the expressionless face lit only slightly by the moon, she knew immediately that her luck had run out. This wasn't Will. This was someone she'd never seen before at all—but she knew who he was as surely as if they had been acquainted for years.

This was Night Bird.

His parents had named him well. The gaze he levelled at her was as sharp and cold as a hawk or an owl's—and in his cool line of vision, she felt just as small and defenseless as a rodent. The first feverish thought that went through her brain was that he looked young, maybe not much older than herself. He wore a loose shirt, a leather vest, and buckskin breeches. His raven-black shoulder-length hair hung down limp and straight. Somehow, she had expected such a notorious killer to look older. Lord knows, he couldn't have possibly have looked meaner.

Her second feverish thought was to run like hell. She turned and ran only about three strides, however, before an ironlike hand grasped her shoulder. The force and suddenness of her stop nearly sent her reeling backwards again. Shocking pain shot up her side.

"Walk," he instructed her, his voice as clear and insistent as a schoolmarm scolding a small child. "Not run."

There was no way she *could* run, not with the renegade's paw clamped down on her shoulder. Her mind raced frantically to decide on some course of action—how could she warn Will of the danger he was about to step into? What could she do?

She considered briefly doing as Trip had done and shouting out a warning. But if Will was safe, she didn't want to alert Night Bird to there being another person in their party. Keeping silent, she stumbled ahead to their camp, praying she would find the others alive. Night Bird couldn't be acting alone. Trip had yelled out his warning after she had heard someone nearby. That someone had to have been Night Bird.

Unless it had been Will... Through her fear, that small hope sparked and kindled. Will might still be out there somewhere, safe. And as long as he was alive and they were alive, he might be able to save them. He could go for help, or he could bust in on the camp and—

In a split second, her hope died. Night Bird pushed her forward into the light of the campfire that Trip had built, and Paulie saw what she thought then was about the grimmest sight she'd ever seen. Three bandits stood loitering about the edges of the light, the barrels of their guns glinting in the firelight. Their charges, with hands tied behind their backs and legs bound at the ankle and thrust straight ahead of them as they sat upright on the ground, were Oat, Trip, and Will.

Will's gaze met hers. She could read the anguish and disappointment in his face so clearly she felt as if someone had stabbed her in the heart. She had let him down. She had been the only one free when she'd heard Trip's warning. Maybe if she had taken another second and run the other way, she could have helped them all.

The thought made her angry. Angry at herself, and angry at the man behind her, who had outwitted them all, waiting for precisely the right time to ambush them. Oat, who looked surprisingly cool now when face-to-face with his dreaded nemesis, had been right after all. Night Bird had crept up on them silently, even with his three colleagues. She might have been impressed if she weren't so mad.

But she was mad. Madder than hell. And suddenly, she knew she had to strike a blow for their ill-fated search party, no matter how insignificant it might seem. She turned and did something she never would have done if she'd been thinking clearly.

She glared at Night Bird, the most notorious renegade roaming the Southwestern United States, and with all her might, she kneed him, hard, in the groin.

Chapter Six

Will gritted his teeth and glared at the bandits hovering around the fire. He and his friends had been tied up for hours. For the fifth time the three Mexicans were counting the money they had emptied out of their hostages' pockets, while Night Bird stood a little apart, frowning at his men as if he were above actually caring how much they had stolen.

It wasn't that Will minded having his money taken—although that was indignity enough. What really bothered him was this feeling of helplessness, and his knowledge that he had let the others down. He had thought he was the most adept of the four of them at survival, but while he had been out patroling, supposedly for the protection of the people he was leading, Night Bird had walked right into camp and taken them with no trouble. Now they were all in dire straits, and the only thing Will was certain of was that Night Bird would have to kill him first before he harmed one of his friends.

A glance at the others told him they were in various stages of panic, all except Oat. The old man just looked resigned. As well he probably should. So far there had been no sign of Mary Ann, which couldn't be a good omen. Trip appeared frozen in his panic, almost as if he hoped that if he didn't move or make a sound his captors would forget that he was there. Though her face betrayed her nervousness, Paulie stared straight at her captors, studying their faces and trying to understand what they were saying. Only occasionally had she met Will's eye, but those few moments caused him more anguish than he had felt in a lifetime.

He was frightened for her, and cursed the moment he had given in to her demands to come along with him. Now he not only had to worry about Mary Ann's fate, he had to worry about Paulie, too. So far, none of the men had guessed that *"el niño"* was actually a girl, but there was no telling how long that would last, especially since several times he had caught Night Bird looking as curiously at Paulie as she looked at him. Of course, his pride probably still smarted from allowing himself to be kicked in his private parts by a captive. At the memory of the howl that the renegade had let out, Will was hard-pressed to hide a smile.

It was a dumb, foolhardy, incredibly brave thing to do. The bandit had been so furious, it was a wonder that Paulie was still alive. Once he'd recovered, Night Bird had pushed Paulie into camp and had her trussed up especially tight. And Will still worried that he would seek extra retribution from Paulie for her insulting act of defiance.

It was hard to believe that it was just this afternoon that they had been at Judge Bean's, laughing and drinking. Or that just the night before that he had taken Paulie into his arms and kissed her—a kiss he couldn't seem to forget, no matter how hard he tried, no matter what worries should have displaced his peculiar preoccupation with her soft lips. He had been thinking about her when he discovered the three Mexicans in camp, too. Actually he'd been brooding over what a strange position he found himself in, being jealous of Trip Peabody.

Will had had plenty of reasons not to want Paulie to come along with him on this ride. But never in his life would he have thought that it would be because she might cause tension because she was of the fairer sex. He still couldn't believe it. And yet, he knew in his gut that at that moment he would do anything to get her out of there, and if they ever did get free, to convince her to go home.

That would be no easy task. Paulie was ornery, but sometimes that stubborn streak could be used against her. For instance, if he could make her so mad that she wouldn't want to be around him anymore...

As Will brooded over precisely how he was going to dispense with Paulie—if he ever had the luxury of that opportunity—Night Bird broke away from his men and walked toward her. Paulie's eyes rounded as the renegade came closer. Will's heart, which was already pounding a mile a minute, leapt to his throat.

Deciding the best course of action might be to divert the Indian's attention, Will straightened. "Where is Mrs. Murphy?" he demanded.

Night Bird stopped, and tilted his head. The others, too, surprised by Will's dictatorial tone, stopped counting their ill-gotten American greenbacks and turned to view the confrontation. Even Oat turned his head. Blessedly, Night Bird veered away from Paulie and came closer to Will. But not too close. Everything in his stiff stance said that he was a man who preferred to stand apart.

"I do not know your Mrs. Murphy," Night Bird answered, his voice raspy and low.

Will, surprised that the man was actually talking to him at all, smirked. "Surely you don't kidnap so many women that you've forgotten her already."

The renegade's eyes narrowed dangerously. "I do not know her."

"You wouldn't forget her. She was the only thing blond and beautiful in Possum Trot. Does that ring a bell?"

Night Bird rattled off something in Spanish to one of the Mexicans standing nearby.

The man nodded, looking around the circle curiously. "Ah, *la bonita*," he said.

The pretty one. A cold chill shot down Will's spine. So they *had* seen her.

The Indian nodded, but said nothing.

"Where is she?"

Night Bird shrugged. "I do not know your Mrs. Murphy," he repeated.

Will wasn't buying the stone wall routine. "One of your partners seems to," Will pointed out.

The Mexicans began rattling off Spanish so quickly that Will could understand nothing more than a repetition of the name *la bonita* and San Antonio.

"They know nothing," the renegade said. "This woman was your sister?"

Was? "No," Will told him. "She is this man's wife." He pointed to Oat.

Night Bird stared at Oat for a moment, uncomprehending. Apparently, his memory of Mary Ann didn't square with the idea of her being the wife of an old whiskey trader. Oat, Trip, Paulie and Will exchanged edgy glances, wondering what could be going through their captor's head.

After a minute more of his strange contemplation, the renegade turned his head and rattled off some more Spanish to his *compadres*. The group of three threw back their heads and laughed—and laughed and laughed and laughed.

"I don't see what's so funny!" Paulie cried.

Will frowned; if he hadn't been trussed up like a chicken

he would have gone right over and throttled her. Here he was trying to divert the renegade's attention, and she insisted on scolding him!

"Oat's a good man," she insisted belligerently, "better than a skunk like you."

Night Bird turned. Despite the peals of mirth he had set off among his cohorts, his face was as blank, expressionless and cold as ever. "*La bonita* is better off now where she is."

"Where is that?" Will asked, knowing the answer.

Dead. Maybe it would have been better if Night Bird had kept denying seeing her at all. Having Night Bird tell them the truth about Mary Ann's fate was going to panic the others for sure.

The renegade looked at him through clear eyes. "San Antonio."

San Antonio? Will looked at the Indian skeptically.

"*La bonita* wanted to go to San Antonio." Night Bird nodded toward one of his men. "Francisco was willing to take her."

I'll just bet! Will thought heatedly, giving the man called Francisco another quick look. Despite a rather shabby appearance, he didn't have the look about him of a man who would turn down the opportunity a damsel in distress presented. "So why didn't she go with him?"

Night Bird's lips set into a taciturn line. He said nothing, but jabbed a finger at his own chest.

"Because of you?" Will asked.

Night Bird nodded.

Paulie's mouth dropped open in astonishment. "You mean she was willing to ride to San Antonio with a bunch of *banditos* but she decided not to when she discovered you with them?"

Night Bird nodded curtly. "But I want the white man's money. I do not want his women."

Paulie shot a glance at Will. "It's just like I told you all along, Will. Mary Ann went to San Antonio."

Will levelled a gaze on her with more than a share of doubtfulness in it. "*If* she made it there."

Paulie thrust her chin forward stubbornly. "If she didn't, I bet it was her own fault, not this fellow's." She nodded toward Night Bird.

"You're talking about him as if you two were old friends."

"Well, you have to admit what he says makes sense. Everybody said Mary Ann was scared of Night Bird on account of her hair." She looked up at their captor, then asked, "Do you really prefer blond scalps to other kinds?"

Night Bird flinched at the blunt question. "I do not take the white man's women or his hair."

"You see?" Paulie told Will. "He just wants money, like he said."

Trip's gaze darted anxiously between the pair of them. "Maybe you two should have this discussion sometime later."

Night Bird continued to stare at them blankly, though the Mexicans behind him remained perplexed that the four hostages could be infighting at such an insecure time in their perhaps soon-to-be prematurely short lives.

Will looked at Night Bird and demanded, "If you aren't interested in anything but the white man's money, what more do you want with us? You have every cent we had on us, you took our guns, and you've scattered our horses to the four winds. You might as well let us go."

Paulie nodded vigorously. At least they still agreed on something, Will thought with the last ounce of humor left inside him.

"You had not much money. Lucky. Now I will not kill you."

Paulie seemed to relax—something Will wasn't about to do just yet. "I see," he said. "You only turn murderer when the stakes are high."

Night Bird looked at him with a blankness that either indicated disdain or a complete lack of comprehension.

"You have to admit, it's a wise policy," Paulie said. "Nobody's going to care if a bunch of scrub-bums like us get a few dollars stolen. It's not like the railroad payroll."

As Will watched, Night Bird's head snapped around, and immediately Paulie seemed to realize her mistake. This was no time to be reminding him of past triumphs. Her eyes as wide as two full moons, she stared back at the renegade helplessly, looking smaller and more vulnerable than Will could ever remember.

Night Bird took another step toward her. "I not want white man's woman. But a smart boy…might be help." He waved his hand toward his followers behind him. "You are smarter than these grown men. Brave, like the badger who battles the bear."

Will wouldn't have thought it possible, but Paulie's eyes grew even wider as she looked in surprise at the Indian and took in his astonishing proposition. He himself had a hard time believing his ears—or knowing what he would do if Night Bird threw Paulie behind him on his saddle and rode into Mexico. The thought of learning that Mary Ann had escaped Night Bird only to have Paulie kidnapped instead was too terrible to contemplate.

But apparently, that troubling thought hadn't even occurred to Paulie. Though she herself was facing the prospect of being carried off into oblivion as an unwilling recruit of a band of murderous thieves, her mind was focused on a completely separate issue.

Her eyes dark with rage, she raised her chin and glared at the Indian with all the venom her tiny body could contain. "I am *not* a boy, you ignorant galoot!" she yelled hotly.

So much anger and exasperation flooded through her that Paulie simply couldn't hold it in any longer. When she had yelled at Night Bird, it was like a dam bursting after heavy rains.

Bad enough that they were on this fool's mission, especially now that Night Bird confirmed that she had been right all along and that Mary Ann had just been running after that shady gambler fellow. Bad enough that she was *always* playing second fiddle to Mary Ann in Will's mind. But now to have a sorry criminal announce to the world that he thought she was a boy, and spout off about how she reminded him of a badger...well that just took the cake!

She glared across the fire at Will, who was shaking his head and trying to mouth something at her. In response, she shook her head back at him—back at all of them. After a few seconds of vigorous head movement, her hat slipped off, allowing her long hair to spill down her back.

Night Bird took a surprised step backward, looking almost offended by her suddenly more feminine appearance.

"That's right—I'm a girl, you numbskull!"

"Paulie..." Trip grumbled warningly.

But she had already thrown caution to the wind. How on earth was she supposed to win Will's heart away from Mary Ann when everyone was always acting as if she were no different than a bowlegged cowpoke? "I guess you'd have to be about blind not to be able to tell a hen from a rooster!" she shouted. "And I didn't appreciate that badger comment, either."

Night Bird and his cohorts gathered around her curiously now, staring at her incredulously. The Indian fingered her long hair but still looked skeptical. He muttered something to the man called Francisco, and suddenly Paulie found two men attempting to lift her to her feet by the armpits.

They didn't get very far. After a split second, shooting pain in her side overwhelmed her and she let out a cry a banshee would have been proud to produce. She'd been so frightened, she'd forgotten about her damaged ribs entirely. Now the injury came back to her with the force of a red-hot poker being jabbed into her side. The Mexicans were so startled by her howls that they dropped her back to the ground, which caused her to emit yet another piercing wail.

"What're you trying to do?" she thundered, "cripple me?" She sat back on her rump and tried to ignore the sharp pain in her side.

Night Bird looked doubly startled now—first that she wasn't a boy and second that a mere girl should be capable of making a noise to rouse his ancestors from the happy hunting grounds.

"What is your name?" he asked her.

Paulie tried to concentrate on the question, and whether she should answer it. She still wasn't completely used to hearing the renegade speak English. Somehow before, when she'd envisioned him in her mind's eye, she had him pegged for such a murdering thieving heathen that she hadn't considered the possibility that he would actually be able to communicate with anyone. Heck, he could spit sentences out with more proficiency than old Oat.

"Paulie," she said. "Paulie Johnson."

He continued to stare at her for a moment longer and then opened his mouth. Paulie was prepared for anything— mostly a command to his men to kill her. Instead, nothing came out for a few moments. Just air. Then, slowly, a wheezing sound began, which soon turned into a raspy kind of laugh. Finally, he let out something that sounded as if it were probably as close to a belly laugh as they were likely to hear from this man.

"Paulie Johnson!" he repeated, his "J" coming out as a "Ch" sound, so that it sounded as if her name were Paulie Chonson. "The girl sells whiskey."

Paulie brightened. This was the second person in one day who put her name together with the Dry Wallow's. She must be doing something right, businesswise. "That's me!"

"I steal your liquor."

She smiled wryly. "I know."

He continued to eye her as if she were an odd kind of animal he'd never seen before. She looked over at Will, and for the first time in her life, she saw fear in his eyes. Fear and rage. He glanced between her and Night Bird, and she couldn't tell who he was angrier with, Night Bird, or herself for talking to the outlaw.

Finally, after a breathless, interminable amount of time, Night Bird barked something to the men still standing around Paulie. As they scurried to do his bidding, he continued to give orders in choppy Spanish and gesticulate with his arms—commands his men seemed to understand well even if none of the hostages did.

Paulie knew that this was the moment. If they were going to be killed, this was the time. She glanced at Will once more, memorizing his face as if its every contour wasn't already embedded permanently in her mind, then closed her eyes, hanging onto the image. She could have pinpointed the exact shade of brown of his eyes out of a whole palate of browns. She could have matched the texture of his hair strand by strand, and she'd only run her hands through it a few times in her life. And his lips…she would never forget those, or how warm and masterful they'd felt against hers. At least she'd experienced that before the end. And when it came right down to it, she supposed she would rather die here, with Will Brockett, than as an old woman all alone in Possum Trot.

Suddenly, the earth beneath her seemed to quake as the Mexicans mounted their horses and shouted at each other. Then they were riding away, leaving their four hostages on the edges of the dying fire. In all the activity of the Mexicans breaking camp, Night Bird disappeared just as quickly as he had arrived.

The four of them sat in silence, listening to the retreating hoofbeats in stunned disbelief. Paulie could hardly swallow the fact that they had just had a run-in with the most notorious killer in the Southwest and were actually still living to tell the tale.

"Do you think they'll be coming back?" she asked.

She, Trip, and Oat turned to Will in unison. He tilted his head to capture the last whispers of their captors' horses' hooves travelling back to them on the night breeze. "I don't see why they would."

"Maybe they just want to kill us in a sneak attack," Trip suggested, not quite willing to accept their good fortune at face value.

"They already got us in a sneak attack," Paulie reminded him. "You can't get much more sneaky than ambushing us all at once and tying us up snugger than an old maid's underwear."

She and Will and Trip looked down at their bonds and considered their dilemma. The renegade might have left them alive, but how long would they remain that way if they weren't able to free themselves?

"Damn!" Trip said, wriggling his wrists and ankles against the bonds. "They got these ropes tight."

His words reminded her of the hemp biting into the soft flesh around her wrists. In fact, she was sore all over. If she ever did get out of this mess and back to Possum Trot, she was going to fill up her tub and do nothing for an entire day but soak in hot water.

"What should we do, Will?" she asked, thinking that he surely would have devised a plan by now. Instead, he stared at her almost as coolly as Night Bird himself had.

"What's the matter?" she asked. "Is something wrong?"

Will rolled his eyes up to the sky as if seeking patience from the stars above them. "You are the darnedest girl on this planet, Paulie Johnson! Don't you have the sense God gave a gnat?"

"For your information, yes I do," she said, refusing to start a screaming match at this juncture. "May I ask what brought on such an absurd question?" She couldn't imagine what had gotten under his skin. His anger seemed to come out of nowhere.

He had to take a few breaths to hold in whatever demon had taken hold of him. "Your announcing to Night Bird that you were a girl, that's what!" he said. "Why on earth would you say such a thing?"

If only she could have crossed her arms, she would have found it a lot easier to hold in her anger. "I *am* a girl, if you haven't noticed."

"Did you want to get yourself kidnapped?"

"You know what your trouble is, Will Brockett? You don't listen to anyone. If you did, you would realize that not only did Night Bird *not* kidnap Mary Ann—just as I always suspected—he also was not going to kidnap me after he discovered I was a girl. I was in more danger as a boy."

Will frowned. "You couldn't be sure of that."

"And I don't think he was really going to take any of

us along with him. Why would he? Mr. Bird just wanted our money.''

"If you ask me, you were getting awfully cozy with the man there at the end.''

"When?'' she asked. "When I started screaming my head off?''

Trip laughed. "That was a good move, Paulie.''

"That was real pain!'' she corrected.

"It still probably saved your hide,'' Will pointed out.

Maybe so, Paulie thought, though she wasn't about to concede the argument. Will was just trying to make her look silly because he'd never wanted her following along. And now it galled him that she had been right the whole time. They had gone all the way to the Mexican border and risked their lives for no reason at all. Mary Ann and her gambler were probably as thick as thieves in San Antonio already, and now her so-called rescue party was stuck on the banks of the Rio Grande.

She lifted her chin. "If it makes you feel better to think so, then be my guest,'' she said, unable to keep the smugness out of her tone.

He looked at her warily. "What's that supposed to mean?''

"You obviously don't want to give me credit for anything,'' she said coolly. "But don't worry. It doesn't bother me.''

Will looked hotter than the embers simmering in the fire. "Name one thing I should give you credit for and I will.''

That was easy. "You said that I shouldn't have come along.''

"I still say that.''

"I haven't been a hindrance,'' she argued.

"You haven't been a big help, either,'' he said.

"Well if you'd listened to me in the first place, we wouldn't even be in this mess!" she argued heatedly.

Will shook his head stubbornly. "All right, so I was wrong about Mary Ann's whereabouts. But there was no way of knowing that for sure until we started hunting for her."

"If you'd listened to me we would have started hunting in San Antonio, and might have found her by now."

"Maybe, maybe not."

He was so infuriating! Even Trip was looking at Will as if he weren't quite running on full steam. "You gotta admit, Will, she did say Mary Ann had gone chasin' after that gambler fellow."

Will shrugged. "Was I supposed to take the word of one girl?"

Paulie's jaw dropped open. She couldn't believe this was Will Brockett talking. Sure, he had always had a headstrong streak, but now it was almost as if he were being obtuse on purpose, trying to anger her. If so, it was working!

"Let me tell you, Will Brockett, if you don't want to listen to what I have to say, I'll be just as glad to save my breath."

Will smiled. "Miracles do happen after all, then."

She had sworn she wasn't going to start shouting at him, but now she couldn't help it. "For your information, I'd be just as happy right now to be warm and snug in my bed in Possum Trot, so if you don't want me around, I'll be happy to go back there! And furthermore—"

Her throat caught. She was surprised to discover that not only was she shouting, she was actually almost crying. She bit her lip to try to stem the flow of liquid to her eyes.

Will's eyebrows rose on his forehead, and then he nodded curtly. "Fine. Just as soon as we get free, I'll escort you back to Possum Trot."

"Don't worry about me," she snapped, "I can find my own way."

His tone gentled. "Then I'll send Trip with you."

Trip again! She had forgotten that this all started back when she'd been on her way to disabuse Will of the notion that she and Trip were sweet on each other. Now she couldn't muster enough energy to care either way. If the whole world wanted to think she was in love with Trip Peabody, that was fine with her. Her days of tagging after Will were over. Completely over.

Trip looked worried at being included in this argument. "Where are you plannin' on goin', Will?"

Will stared at him as though his answer should have been obvious. "San Antonio."

Paulie bit back a groan. "San Antonio!" she yelled. "What are you planning to do there?"

He glared at her. "What does it matter to you? You weren't going to follow along, the last I heard."

Trip looked from one to the other anxiously. "Of course we'll follow you, Will. We'd follow you clear up to Canada, if that's where you were headed."

"Ha!" Paulie cried. "I wouldn't follow Will ten feet—especially to chase some flibbertigibbet—"

"That's a nice way to talk about your friend," Will said.

Oat cleared his throat. "If'n we don't get these ropes off, ain't nobody gonna be followin' anybody anywheres—'cept maybe to an early grave."

Paulie felt her cheeks heat from the battle and the embarrassment of being so presumptuous as to believe she would actually manage to live through this ordeal. Will and Trip looked equally abashed.

She couldn't figure out how to get out of the ropes. Her wrists were bound so tightly that her fingertips were beginning to go numb, making her hands as good as useless.

And there were no implements around the camp that would be of any use to them. Still, she kept scanning the area with her eyes, trying carefully to avoid Will's gaze as she glanced about her. She was only partially successful in this last endeavor. It seemed everywhere she looked, Will was looking there, too. And whenever his gaze met hers, her pulse would race just as it always did. Only now her excitement was tempered by a sharp stab of disappointment. He didn't even want to be around her anymore. He couldn't even wait until they were freed before he told her to go back to Possum Trot!

In an attempt to avoid him, she turned slightly—just in time to see a miraculous thing happen. There before her very eyes, Oat slipped his hands through the rope and freed himself.

"Jumpin' Jiminy, Oat—you're free!" she exclaimed.

He nodded curtly. "Figured I could do it."

"What are you, a magician?" she asked, trying to scoot over to him as fast as possible so he could free her now, too.

He shook his head. "That Mexican fellow went easy on me—I could feel give in the rope from the very beginning. So while he was tyin' my hands, I tried to keep them separated a little."

"You mean you could have wriggled free the whole time?"

"Most likely," Oat agreed.

"Well, heck," Trip said. "Why didn't you?"

"Didn't seem safe. As long as the man promised not to kill us, figured it was best just to stay tied up. If I'd tried to escape, that only would have made him mad, anyway."

Within fifteen minutes, Oat had Paulie and the other two untied. It was such a relief to be free, Paulie found herself on the verge of tears again. For a moment she had thought they were going to starve out in the wilderness, bound and helpless. But they were saved from that terrible fate, and they had Oat, of all people, to thank.

"I guess that leaves us our horses to round up," Will said, standing and stretching.

He didn't look at her, but he didn't seem to be avoiding her, either. As if he didn't care what she thought at all. Paulie still felt fitful and shaky from their argument. How could he just toss her aside as if she were some troublesome pest? She couldn't believe it—especially when she had been right concerning Mary Ann's whereabouts. It just wasn't like Will not to give credit where credit was due.

She was about to sail right past Will as if she didn't have the time of day to give him when he hooked his hand around her arm and sent her spinning back around to face him. "Ouch!" she cried, surprised by how much her side could hurt from such a simple movement…and how a simple touch from Will could send her insides into a flurry.

His eyes darkened. "Are you all right?"

"I'm fine."

"You won't be able to ride tomorrow."

"Yes I will," she answered quickly, trying to pull her arm out of his grip.

Will held fast. His gaze was so intent on her that she looked down at her feet. How could those brown eyes of his seem so callous one minute and so caring the next? "I wouldn't want you trying to keep up with us just because you've got a point to make. There would be no shame in your going to Vinegaroon and staying at Judge Bean's for a spell."

His voice had softened, and would have sounded almost tender if she hadn't known better. The only reason he wanted her to stay in Vinegaroon was to be rid of her. "I want to get back to Possum Trot as soon as possible,'' she said. "I can't leave the saloon alone forever."

She stubbed her toe into the dirt, as if that would tamp down the rising despair in her heart. She hadn't even had to ask what Will intended to do next. He would go on searching for Mary Ann. Maybe forever if that's how long it took to find her.

She looked up into his eyes. Behind him, the sun was beginning to peek over the horizon, giving the sky a deep-red glow. Will had never looked so dazzling to her as he did at that moment, still clutching her arm. She dreamed of him pulling her to his chest for another kiss. What a perfect moment that would have been like something out of a book or a poem.

Blushing furiously, she looked away. It was absurd to imagine her life as anything half as romantic as a poem. Her existence was about how much whiskey she could sell. But, oh, it was fun to dream sometimes, to let her imagination run wild!

Will followed her gaze. Both their lines of vision stumbled onto Trip, who had found Feather but was having a little trouble catching the horse, which shied away from him when he made a grab for her mane. The movement sent Trip stumbling in the half light, and he fell face forward to the ground.

Paulie smiled. But Will, still looking at Trip, dropped her arm, his face solemn.

"For a minute I forgot," he said, his voice sounding almost disappointed as he walked away.

Paulie took a few moments to take his words in. Why, Will had seemed almost jealous that she cared for Trip.

Jealous, she thought, a smile touching her lips again. In a few seconds it seemed as if the world had become a million times brighter—which in fact it had. The sun had risen enough to cast its first rays over the land, and she stumbled forward again to look for her horse, feeling as suddenly hopeful as if there were rays of sunshine sparking out of her fingers and toes.

She knew Will was still intent on finding Mary Ann, and heaven knew what would happen between him and Oat after they reached San Antonio. But there was something in him that was envious of her relationship with Trip. Maybe he was used to being the one she joked most with, or looked to for advice. He seemed to resent that she would look more to another man—and that another man would have more influence over her than he did.

If so, his attitude toward her wasn't nearly so clean cut as he tried to make out. He wanted to be the one who was most protective of her, which might explain a lot of his peculiar behavior. His bossiness, for instance—and the way he'd insulted her until she was ready to turn tail and run back to Possum Trot.

Not that she would be going back there now. Her smile broadened.

A man who cared that much for her couldn't *really* want to be rid of her, could he?

Chapter Seven

"**T**he road to Possum Trot's that way," Will said, nodding toward a horizon filled with little else but hill after hill of rock and scrub brush.

Paulie nodded and grinned. "Is it?"

Partner curved his neck as he bent gracefully to drink of the water in the creek where they had stopped for a midmorning break. After they had found their horses, they had decided it would be most prudent to sleep for an hour or two before setting out again. Will worried about Paulie's ribs, and especially about Oat, who was looking more haggard than usual after their ordeal. His skin had had an almost gray cast to it, though the catnap had put a little color in his cheeks again.

Despite his worries, Paulie was obviously feeling as fit as a fiddle again, even after riding three hours with her ribs wrapped. She was also smiling as if she were harboring some devilish little secret.

"We can swing by and drop you off," Will offered.

"There's no need for that."

Will tilted his head, feeling a premonition of trouble at her alarmingly vague response. Did she mean that he didn't need to drop her off because she could remember the way…or because she had no intention of being dropped anywhere?

She hummed a jaunty tune to herself, answering his question for him.

"Oh, no," he moaned, burying his forehead in one of his hands.

Paulie flashed him a dazzling smile and tossed the simple braid she'd fashioned her hair into over one shoulder. "Don't be so glum, Will. You'll be glad to have me along, I swear it."

"You mean you're not going home?"

"Nope."

He tossed up his hands in frustration. "I distinctly remember you being madder than a wet hen and announcing that you couldn't get away from me and back to Possum Trot soon enough."

She shrugged negligently. "I was just mad."

He sighed. "Usually you're a little more adept at staying mad."

Her green eyes flashed at him in their old good-natured way. "I've grown up, Will. Now when I'm mad at someone, I try to look at things from the other fellow's point of view."

"Uh-oh." He didn't want to imagine the motives Paulie could start ascribing to him if she was in a mood to be analytical.

"You're not so hard to figure out, Will," she told him, plunging right in despite his lack of encouragement. "Once I started examining the situation, it all became clear. You were *too* eager to be rid of me."

"That's right!" he agreed, jumping in before she could go any further. "I was hoping you'd go back to Possum Trot so I wouldn't have to put up with you anymore."

She crossed her arms. "But only because you were worried about me after our encounter with Night Bird. You just wanted me out of harm's way. You knew I would never agree to give up the search while you all were still at it, so you tried to insult me into going home."

He couldn't speak. He was stunned at how quickly and completely she had found him out.

Paulie beamed triumphantly. "You're pretty sneaky, I'll grant you that."

And she was pretty crafty when it came to figuring him out.

Her smile slowly dissipated. "But you didn't need to be *quite* so insulting, you know," she said, more hotly. "I only wanted to help you."

He shook his head. "I know. You always just want to help."

"Well, heck—it wasn't my fault that we got caught. And you can't say that I hurt things any by being there."

No, except that the thought of something happening to her scared the hell out of him. "Well, I suppose we're out of danger now, mostly."

Her face brightened. "You mean you want me to stay with you?"

"No, I just realize that I can't stop you any more than an ant could stop the transcontinental railway."

She laughed. "You might say you couldn't stop me any more than I could stop you from going to San Antonio."

His smile faded. "If you've got reservations, you'd better tell me about them now."

She rubbed her hands together uncomfortably. "Well, you've got to admit, Will, Mary Ann hasn't been kidnapped. Have you ever stopped to think that you're looking for a woman who doesn't want to be found?"

He bit his lip, considering. He hadn't ruminated too much about what Mary Ann had up her sleeve when she left home. He assumed she was just tired of living with Oat and regretted marrying him. Was it so hard to understand her running away under those circumstances?

"I'll bet she doesn't know what she wants."

Paulie shot him a doubtful stare. "Mary Ann was born knowing what she wanted. Why should you waste your time going after her because she ran off with some good-for-nothing?"

Will's jaw clenched in response to her assertion. "We aren't certain that's what happened."

"Night Bird said—"

He nearly howled. "You're willing to take the word of a criminal?"

"What reason would he have to lie?"

Her question didn't hold much water with Will. "I'm going to San Antonio to find her, whether or not you and Trip and even Oat want to come along."

"Okay, don't get your dander up," Paulie said. "Of course I'll come along—I'm not saying you're right, but I'm coming along."

"Sometimes people need to be saved from their own stupid decisions," he said. "It's no shame to make a mistake. If Gerald were alive, he'd try to find her."

"Yeah, but it would have been his place to. He was her father."

Will felt his jaw tense. "I made a promise to Gerald that I would look after her, and I intend to keep it. Besides, we don't know for sure that she's with that Tyler fellow."

Paulie kept silent on that question. "I guess we're going to San Antonio, then," she announced.

Paulie took great comfort that the rest of the party was as skeptical as she was about their mission. No one argued with Will about chasing after a woman who didn't want to be caught, but then again, he made it pretty clear that his mind was made up.

Surprisingly, the one most resistant to the next leg of the trip was Oat. As they stopped that night, weary after their long day of uninterrupted riding, he collapsed by their fire, a blanket wrapped around him, and contemplated finding his wife.

"Could be the Injun was right," he said, recalling Night Bird's observation that Mary Ann was better off in San Antonio than back in Possum Trot with Oat. "Maybe it's best."

"You mean you want to give up on her?" Will asked sharply.

Oat's bloodshot eyes widened. "No. Heck, no. But if she don't want to come home... Well, it ain't like we had a real marriage anyways."

Three heads snapped to attention and turned from the fire to focus solely on Oat. "What do you mean?" Paulie asked. Will shot her a sharp glance, but she didn't care. If Oat was going to come out with such tantalizing assertions, he had to expect a little prying.

The old man wrapped the blanket a little more tightly around his shoulders and shrugged. "Well, it ain't like we was a real husband and wife...in that way, you know. Mary Ann wasn't interested in affection."

Trip blinked in confusion. "Well heck, Oat, what was she interested in?"

Oat sighed. "Dunno."

For all his scolding her for questioning the man on the nature of his marriage, Will seemed too frustrated by Oat's vagueness to let the subject drop. "What exactly brought you two together?"

"Mary Ann did," Oat said quickly, as if there were no doubt in his mind. "Not that I cared. She's a right pretty girl. Used to pass her house and think to myself, 'Now that's a right pretty girl.' Then I'd move on, 'cause it always seemed she wouldn't look twice at an old whiskey man. She never did, that I can remember. Till that one day.''

Paulie, Will and Trip leaned forward, waiting to find out precisely what events occurred on *that one day*. Unfortunately, Oat chose that juncture to fill his pipe, which took all of his attention for a few minutes.

As soon as he had the darn thing lit, Paulie jumped right in. ''So what happened?''

Oat shrugged. ''Well, I'll tell ya'. I just drove right by her house one day, and a few minutes later I heard someone yellin' after me. And when I turned around, there she was, runnin' down the road after me. Called me Mr. Murphy. Looked real pretty, too. Naturally, I stopped the horses and stepped down to see if there was any little thing I could do for her. But she said no, she just wanted to talk.''

Paulie tried not to be judgmental, but the woman's behavior already sounded fishy. ''What did she want to talk about?''

'''Bout my route.''

Even Trip seemed surprised by this answer. ''You mean your whiskey route?''

''Yeah,'' Oat answered. ''Mary Ann has quite a head for business. Right off she was askin' how much territory I covered, and how many days I was on the road, and how much money did I make and all. Was real interested.''

His words sent a chill through Paulie. ''Did you tell her how much money you made?''

''Why, sure,'' Oat said. He looked a little abashed but admitted, ''I guess I was flattered by her suddenly takin' notice of an old coot like me. I know I ain't much to look at, so I figured I needed to catch her fancy some other way.

So I started braggin' a little, you know, tellin' her about all the money I'd saved up and how I could stop sellin' whiskey altogether if I had a mind to.''

Paulie blinked. "You could?" She started rethinking the commission she'd always paid him on that whiskey!

"Well, I ain't rich, but I ain't poor, neither. I got some put by."

Paulie, Will, and Trip exchanged glances. She didn't have to worry that only she was having doubts about the honesty of Mary Ann's motives. It was written all over Will's face, even, and he never seemed to want to hear the least bad thing said about her.

"Your savings..." She cleared her throat. "Do you still have them?"

Oat looked at her, surprised. "Why, sure."

"So you counted your money after Mary Ann left?"

"Oh, I ain't got the money in the house," Oat assured them. "I got it all in government bonds back in a bank."

"In Fort Stockton?" Paulie asked.

He shook his head. "In San Antone."

Paulie didn't want to think the worst of Mary Ann, she really didn't. But it was so easy.

Oat looked from one face to the next, speculatively. "But it wasn't for my money that she married me," he said. "She lost all interest in the money the minute we were married and I told her my savings were in San Antone. Said she didn't give a hoot about a bunch of old bonds, that cash was better."

Better to steal so she could run off to find her lover, Paulie thought, feeling irate for Oat's sake.

"Then why do you think she married you?" she asked, throwing tact to the wind to ask the question that had been perched on the tongue of every person within fifty miles of Possum Trot.

Oat's simple nod indicated he didn't mind her inquisi-
tiveness. "Said she wanted someone to take her away from
her troubles. Said she'd marry the first man who offered
'to take her out of this place.' That's how she put it. I
thought she meant she wanted away from the Breens.
Didn't know she wanted to go clear to San Antone."

Paulie didn't want to push Oat for any more answers.
Mary Ann had obviously headed for the big city the moment she realized that marrying Oat wasn't going to offer
her any kind of financial rewards.

Oat looked tired, and what's more, he was growing more
agitated with every mention of San Antonio. "I guess I've
got to defend her honor no matter why we married."

Will cocked his head. "What do you mean, 'defend her
honor'?"

"Well…this Oren Tyler fellow. I guess I'll have to take
care of him," Oat said.

Paulie bit her lip to keep herself from laughing at the
idea of Oat getting into fisticuffs with the gambler. If memory served, Oren Tyler was the size of two Oats. He wasn't
anybody she would want to grapple with. But then, he
hadn't stolen her wife.

Only, according to Oat, Mary Ann hadn't been much of
a wife anyway.

"Durn, Oat. Maybe you should just talk to Mary Ann
first, and see what she says."

"She'll probably just want to call the thing off, anyway," he said, his shoulders sagging in defeat. "I guess
it's for the best."

"You can't be sure of that," Trip assured him. "Maybe
she'll be glad to see you."

Oat didn't look convinced. In fact, he gave his shirt and
britches a cold assessing stare and definitely found them

lacking. "I ain't got much to recommend me," he observed. "You say that Oren Tyler is a real dude?"

Paulie nodded regretfully. "But Trip's right," she said. "Maybe she's already tired of the gambler. Women are funny, you know. Besides, you shouldn't sell yourself short. I bet you clean up pretty neat."

Will shot her a quelling glance, but she couldn't help herself. It was as seductive to dream about Mary Ann rushing into Oat's arms as it had been to dream of herself rushing into Will's.

She smiled and gave Oat a friendly punch on his arm. She hated to see him looking so blue. In the past days she had developed a fondness for the old codger. He had a dry, sometimes almost imperceptible wit, but he could tell a good yarn, which was important when days on the road got long. And if it hadn't been for him, they might all be still trussed up on the banks of the Rio Grande.

"Don't worry, Oat. First thing when we get to San Antonio, we'll run you by a barber and get you so fixed up that Mary Ann'll wish she never left Possum Trot."

Oat shrugged bashfully. "Don't think that's likely."

"Well why not? She might be sittin' in a hotel room up there, just waiting for you to show up. You'll want to look your best."

Her words seemed to latch on some stray wispy feather of optimism floating lost in Oat's crotchety old soul. "Well, I guess maybe so. Maybe if I look like something, that Tyler fellow won't want to duel."

Paulie laughed. "I don't think there's been a duel in San Antonio for a few decades, Oat, so you can put that out of your mind."

He smiled at her and actually caught her hand. "Just might take you up on the barber bit, Paulie," he said. He let go of her hand and rubbed his scraggly, furry chin. "Guess I could use a shave at that."

Paulie felt a lump form in her throat. In all her years, she couldn't remember Oat Murphy calling her by name. Now, as she looked into his light blue eyes, she could almost imagine her rosy scenario coming true. Oat wasn't so bad. Once somebody shaved and washed him, and maybe treated him to a clean shirt, he might actually appeal to some women. Taking into account all that and those bonds of his, who was to say that he wouldn't win Mary Ann back?

"Just you wait, Oat," she promised him. "Everything'll work out."

Embarrassed by Oat's expression of gratitude, she lifted herself off the ground with effort and decided to take a short walk. "I think I'll stroll before turning in," she announced, yawning.

She hadn't strolled twenty yards, however, before Will caught up with her, his face about as cheery as a thundercloud. He fell into step beside her, his hands clenched behind his back. "Just what do you think you're doing?"

"Stretching my legs," she said, trying to work the kinks out of muscles sore from being in a saddle all day long.

He scowled. "I meant, what did you think you were accomplishing by the load of hooey you were handing Oat back there."

She lifted her chin. "I was only trying to cheer him up. Goodness, is that a crime?"

Will bristled impatiently. "Maybe it should be," he said. "You heard him describe his marriage. Do you honestly think Mary Ann is going to jump in his arms the minute he knocks on her door?"

"You're the one who's always saying that we shouldn't think the worst of Mary Ann," she reminded him.

"I don't think it's unrealistic to accept the fact that Mary Ann shouldn't have married Oat in the first place."

His words finally managed to bring reality crashing back onto Paulie's head. It had been so nice to imagine Oat and Mary Ann living happily ever after. But of course there was about as much hope of that as there was of Trip Peabody becoming a tightrope expert. And naturally, it would suit Will to a tee if Mary Ann *did* get an annulment.

Didn't anything Oat had said make Will rethink his devotion to a woman who clearly didn't deserve him?

"I won't argue with you about that," Paulie agreed. "If you want my opinion, the woman should be kept in a cage until she either grows up or grows some sense."

She caught Will's smile before he did himself and managed to sober his expression. "Anyway, all those promises you were making Oat were out of line. How do you intend to pay for the works at a barber's when we're travelling to San Antonio without a dime? Night Bird cleaned us out."

His question brought a gleeful smile from Paulie. "Ha!" she cried triumphantly, taking off her hat to show him her ace in the hole. She reached into the ripped lining and pulled out twenty-eight dollars, which she waved in front of his stunned eyes. "He didn't clean *me* out," she bragged.

Unthinking, Will snatched the bills and counted them. "I'll be switched!" he exclaimed. "How did you think to hide money in your hat?"

She laughed. "You forget, I'm a businesswoman," she said. "I never keep all my money in one place. It's safer that way."

He shook his head good-naturedly and handed the dollars back to her. "Well, if you want to throw all your money away playing fairy godmother, I can't stop you."

She thought of Oat and how hopeful he had seemed and knew without a doubt that it would be money well spent.

They returned to camp, where Oat was sleeping sitting up against an old tree stump and Trip sipped water in front of the fire. Will wasted no time telling Trip about the money Paulie had squirrelled away, and Trip immediately wanted to see the evidence.

"By gum, Paulie, I always knew you was resourceful," he said, inspecting her loot.

She flaunted her dollars and laughed as she pranced proudly in front of them. "Too bad Night Bird has such a low opinion of women. I would have made an excellent *bandito*."

"Bandits are supposed to steal money, not hide it," Will pointed out.

"True, but I would have been excellent at knowing where to look for things to steal."

The three of them laughed at her joke on Night Bird when suddenly Paulie looked over at Oat, snoozing soundly. "The thought of being in that barber chair must have calmed old Oat," she said. "This is the first time in three days that the mention of Night Bird hasn't jolted him awake."

Trip laughed. "Maybe he just figures the worst has already happened."

Paulie giggled as a devilish idea took hold of her. Before she could think better of it, she tiptoed over to Oat and whispered close to his ear, "Is that *Night Bird* standing over there by the fire?" She emphasized the name, hoping for a dramatic reaction.

When her words brought no response, she punched him lightly on the upper arm. Then she recoiled. Something was wrong—terribly wrong.

Her heart in her throat, she turned and beckoned Will with her eyes. "Something's happened," she said.

Will and Trip scurried over and Will knelt next to the man, lifting his arm to feel for a pulse. It didn't take more than a moment to see the situation was hopeless. A lump the size of an orange formed in Paulie's throat.

"Oh, Will," she moaned. "Can't we do something..."

He looked at her sympathetically, but shook his head. "He's dead, Paulie. Oat's dead."

Chapter Eight

Oat was laid to rest under the canopy of an old live oak tree in the spot Will estimated to be right in the center of his one-time whiskey route. All three of them agreed that it was an appropriate setting for his final sleep, for if there was anything that Oat enjoyed more than his old route, it was finding a cool shady place to take a long snooze.

They all did their best to make the service memorable, reciting what prayers they knew by heart and singing one of the many hymns they had learned from years of Dwight's serenading them from the mercantile. In eulogy, none of them forgot to mention to God that they owed their lives to the gruff old man, to whom no one had given much consideration before he'd married Mary Ann Redfern.

"I guess I've seen Oat Murphy most every week of my life since I moved to Texas with my Daddy," Paulie said, shaking her head. "You might say I took him for granted, even. When he married Mary Ann and gave up his route, I realized how much I depended on him. Then, when he decided to go along with us to find Mary Ann, I came to like him, like an old uncle you might say. Oat couldn't have been feeling well these last few days, and Lord knows we were all scared, but he never once complained."

Will nodded along with Trip as they stood on either side of Paulie over the newly turned earth, waiting for her to finish. After a moment of prolonged silence, though, Will saw Paulie's shoulder's shaking. He reached out and put a bracing hand on her back, touched by her effort not to lose control before she said what she had to say. In all the years he'd known her, he couldn't remember seeing her cry. Her face was red from fighting off tears, and any moisture in her eyes she dashed away with the back of her hand.

"I guess I just want to finish by saying that Oat was a good friend." She continued brusquely, but her voice was hoarse with emotion. "I'll admit I fibbed to him a little, right there at the end, but I think it made him happy to think he might clean himself up and get his wife back. Leastways, I'm sure he's content where he is now, where a body can rest all day, and knowing he won't ever have to duel Oren Tyler."

"And he won't never have to face Night Bird again," Trip added.

A smile touching her lips, Paulie looked at her friend. Will thought it odd that Trip wasn't a little more comforting to Paulie when she was so upset, but he supposed Trip wasn't one to show affection publicly.

Will and Paulie recited the Twenty-third Psalm, joined in by Trip on the bits that he could remember. After that, each said a final silent goodbye to Oat and then they walked back to their horses, their hearts still heavy. They tethered Oat's mare, Beulah, behind Feather, and then started on their way again.

None of them felt much like talking, which wasn't odd for Will, except that he was accustomed to hearing sound coming from Paulie's direction. Usually she chattered like a magpie—especially when she was upset. No tears filled Paulie's eyes now, but she appeared pensive and sad. They no longer rode in their old diamond formation, since they were missing the bottom point, but trundled silently along three abreast, with Paulie in the middle. It seemed odd not to have Oat lagging behind them.

Will shook his head. The funny thing was, when he'd first heard about Oat and Mary Ann's marriage, he'd blamed Oat for taking a wife half his age. Really, he'd been ready to strangle the old rascal. And that day that he'd come into the Dry Wallow to announce he'd lost her…well, it was a miracle Will had managed to rein in his temper long enough to form any kind of plan at all. No wonder he had ignored Paulie's advice and run off half-cocked for the border, seeking out the first culprit he could think of.

But after hearing Oat's side of the story last night, he understood the old man's motives a little better. And Mary Ann's.

Will wasn't used to thinking of Paulie Johnson as the voice of reason, but he had to admit now that she'd been right from the start. Mary Ann hadn't been snatched away from her home. She'd been seduced away, lured to San Antonio by an unscrupulous rake. Oren Tyler. He gritted his teeth even as he thought the name, and cursed his own hardheadedness.

His trip to the border had cost them precious time. A lot could happen to a girl like Mary Ann in San Antonio in a week. And this time if something terrible had befallen her by the time they arrived, he would have no one to blame but himself.

One thing was painfully obvious. He was thinking about Mary Ann.

As hard as she tried not to, Paulie couldn't help tossing sidelong glances at Will. He hadn't said a word since Oat's funeral, and it wasn't hard to guess why. Paulie knew he was sad; despite the fact that he blamed Oat for Mary Ann's disappearance, Will had never been anything but respectful to the old man. She would even bet that he had taken a grudging liking to him. But Oat's death also opened up an opportunity for Will. His rival was out of the way now. There would be nothing to stop Will from marrying Mary Ann, just like he'd always intended.

So much for feeling elated that he seemed protective of her. Or jealous of Trip. She stared straight ahead, expressionless. All during their search so far, she had been fairly secure in knowing that even if they did locate her, Mary Ann was another man's wife. Will might have said he wanted to steal her away, but when it came down to brass tacks, Paulie knew that he would never have been able to do anything so underhanded.

At least while Mary Ann was out of the way, Paulie had a sliver of a chance with Will. Now that chance had dwindled to a possibility so minuscule she was angry with herself for still tagging along after him, and making her coming heartbreak that much more difficult to bear. Yet as often as she told herself to give up on Will and go home, she couldn't force herself to leave his side. Though she was just a banged-up, saddle-sore scrap of a thing, he needed her. He just didn't realize it yet.

A sigh travelled through the air, and Paulie looked up in surprise. She knew the mournful sound hadn't originated with her. And Will wasn't the sighing type. She glanced over at Trip, who was staring dewy-eyed into the horizon.

"Say, Trip, are you feeling okay?"

"He doesn't look good," Will observed. Which was true. Not to mention, he was weaving in his saddle.

Trip shook his head. "I'm all right. I was just thinkin'…" Paulie and Will leaned toward him, and he ducked his head self-consciously.

"Thinking's not a hangin' offense," Paulie joked.

He nodded in appreciation of her attempt at levity, but his face remained somber. "Well, I guess with all that's happened—with us being caught by Night Bird, and then watching poor old Oat die—it's made me realize that I've been squanderin' a lot of time."

Paulie could see what he meant. Those hours being tied up with a renegade Comanche manipulating her life and death as if she were nothing but a puppet on a string made her feel as if she had never appreciated her freedom.

"Anyways, I've been thinkin' that from now on out I can't waste my time like I have in the past."

"Carpe diem," Will said, nodding once.

Paulie and Trip turned to him questioningly. "Beg pardon?" she asked.

Will smiled. "It's a Latin phrase Gerald taught me. It means 'seize the day,' or like Trip said, don't let life pass you by."

Trip nodded vigorously. "That's just it. From now on I'm going to *carp...carp...* Well, whatever it was that you said."

"I guess that makes sense," Paulie agreed. *Carpe diem.* She liked the idea better the more she thought about it. "There are several things I've been puttin' off that I've been wanting to do. Like getting a new pump for the well. That sure would be a big help." She turned back to Trip. "What were you figuring on rushing out and doing now that you've discovered this new zest for life?"

"Gettin' married."

Paulie stared at Trip in surprise, but her expression couldn't have been as stunned as Will's. "Married!" he exclaimed.

Paulie chuckled. "Trip Peabody, you've been sayin' you're going to get married since I've known you."

"But now I *know* I want to get married," he answered decisively. "Immediately."

She looked into his eyes and saw that he was dead-on serious. "Lord, Trip—I think you mean it!"

"'Course I mean it. Would I have said so if I didn't?"

Paulie shook her head in wonder. "Well, this is a change. I've never seen you in a hurry to do anything before—especially not to run to the altar."

Beside them, Will cleared his throat. He'd been so quiet since Trip's announcement, Paulie had almost forgotten he was there. "You know…" He hesitated, as if weighing his words carefully. "There's such a thing as being too hasty…"

Paulie hooted. "Hasty!" she cried. "The man's been a bachelor for forty-three years."

"Forty-*two*," Trip corrected with pride.

"Well all right, but the world would hardly say you hadn't had time to give the matter of matrimony sufficient thought," Paulie argued.

"Naturally *you're* eager for him to make up his mind…" Will said testily to Paulie before locking a sobering gaze on Trip. "But marriage isn't something you can just rush into. If you're thinking of running off tomorrow—"

Trip's eyes widened to the size of wagon wheels, and as he swallowed his Adam's apple bobbed laboriously up and down his throat. "Tomorrow?" he asked, his voice a raspy squeak.

"Wasn't that what you intended?" Will asked him. "You said immediately…"

Trip glanced nervously between Will and Paulie, drumming his fingers against his saddle horn. Apparently marrying a woman in his imagination was an entirely different matter than actually marrying her in person. In his eyes,

Paulie could see the wheels of procrastination beginning to turn once more.

"Well now, when I said immediately, I didn't exactly mean *immediately* immediately."

Paulie drew her brows together, trying to understand just what that word did mean to Trip. "So what's your plan?"

Trip's busy fingers moved to the gray stubbling his chin, which he rubbed anxiously. "Well you can't expect a man to propose to a woman lookin' like I do. I'd definitely need a new suit first, and maybe get cleaned up like you told Oat to do."

Will drew back, looking as if the whole conversation confounded him. "I wouldn't think you two would have to stand on ceremony."

"That's another thing!" Trip said, grasping at every straw he could get his hands on. "There's the ceremony to plan. A woman wants her wedding day to be something she can remember. And I wouldn't want it to be just like any old day, either. Not after all this time."

Paulie chuckled. "Trip, you're a case."

The plan solidified in Trip's imagination. "Since I'm goin' to San Antonio anyways, it'll be no trouble to get myself outfitted with some new duds."

"You don't have any money," Paulie said.

Trip looked annoyed. "Well, there ain't no harm in shoppin' around, is there? Not like I could buy Tessie a ring in Possum Trot, you know. I can look. And like Will said—I don't have to be too hasty. Once I'm sure I can find the right suit and a ring, *then* I can go immediately back to Possum Trot and ask Tessie to marry me."

"Immediately, finally," Paulie said with a laugh.

"*Tessie!*" Will shouted, as if he'd never heard the name before. He gazed incredulously at Trip. "Tessie Hale?"

"Well sure," Trip said.

Paulie looked at Will and suddenly understood his confusion. Trip had apparently forgotten that their friend was under the delusion that they were sweethearts, and for a short while, so had she. Will probably thought Trip was on the verge of proposing to *her,* which, now that she thought about it, was some progress. A few days ago back in Possum Trot, he'd acted like no man in his right mind would even consider her a female, much less a marriageable one. Still, she didn't want Trip to know that she'd never put Will wise to the deception she'd played on him.

"Of course Tessie Hale," she said, gazing pointedly at Will. "Who else could he mean?"

Poor Will stared back at her with brown eyes that were completely perplexed. "I—I don't know," he mumbled, as confused as an actor who found himself saying lines from the wrong play.

"Tessie will make a beautiful bride, Trip," Paulie told him.

Trip's lips curled into a blissful grin, and his gaze was faraway and misty again. "She sure is a peach."

"More of a peach than those scraggly things she grows in her backyard," Paulie said, unable to resist a dig at the woman's ill-fated hobby.

Will turned to Trip. "Well," he said, snapping back into the flow of the conversation, "If your mind's so made up, Trip, I'd think you'd be so excited about marrying Tessie you wouldn't want to put it off for another single day."

Trip looked alarmed. "Well, it would be just a week." He swallowed. "Or thereabouts."

"Yes, but—"

Trip held up a hand palm-out and insisted, "After I get back from San Antone will be immediately enough for Tessie and me."

"Or maybe you should send for Tessie while we're in

San Antonio and get married there,'' Will suggested help-
fully.

Paulie frowned at Will's erratic advice. A minute ago
he'd been telling Trip that he shouldn't rush into things.
Probably he was hoping now that they could have a double
wedding. Trip and Tessie, Will and Mary Ann. And she
herself would be there, too. In the exciting role of witness.

Swerving off the mental path he'd set for himself clearly
made Trip anxious. "No...I think we'd like to be married
right there in Possum Trot,'' he said. "Soon as we can
convince a preacher to come out."

"But that could be a month!" Will told him.

Trip shrugged. "It ain't like we got to rush into anything."

So much for seizing the day, Paulie thought. Will was
right about one thing. If Trip waited another month, he
might forget all about his resolution to not waste his life
away putting off marrying Tessie Hale. Given the fact that
the man had been stuck in the same rut for his entire adult
life, it probably wouldn't be difficult for him to jump right
back into it. After all, what were six hours of fear as a
renegade's captive weighed against forty-two years of
bachelorhood?

"You put on a brave front this afternoon."

Paulie looked up, startled out of her reverie by Will's
coming to sit close to her by the fire. Too close. The
warmth of his body had double the impact of the flames of
the fire they had built. She looked nervously around for
Trip, who was over by the horses, checking that they were
secured for the night.

She swallowed, hard, and scooted away from Will.
"Brave front?" she asked, confused.

Will gestured in Trip's direction. "His sudden announcement that he was going to marry Tessie Hale," he explained. "I thought you handled it like a real trouper."

Paulie blushed. "Oh, that," she said with a false bravado. If Will wanted to see her as a martyr for love, she was willing to play the part to the hilt. She'd read too many of her father's books about women who suffered exquisitely for love, some even expiring from the ailment of heartsickness, to shy away from the opportunity this presented. "I suppose deep in my heart, I expected it."

She turned away slightly and added with a melodramatic quaver, "Maybe it wasn't meant to be."

Will scowled in the direction of the horses. "It was sort of callous of him to announce it that way, right in front of me."

She sniffed. "It's true, he didn't seem to care much about my feelings."

Will crossed his arms. "That's all right. You're better off now anyway."

"Yes, you're probably right," she admitted truthfully. How long could she have gone on allowing Will to believe that she and Trip were in love without his discovering her falsehood?

Not that the switch in Trip's affections would mark any change in Will's. All his talk about seizing the day wasn't lost on her. He probably intended to seize his own day the minute he clapped eyes on Mary Ann. Now that he'd nearly lost her forever to Oat, he wouldn't want to waste time before whisking her away to the nearest preacher, just like he'd suggested Trip do with Tessie.

She sighed a genuinely forlorn sigh at the thought.

Will moved closer to her again, and that odd fluttery feeling inside her made another sudden reappearance. Heavens, the man affected her in ways she'd never dreamed. Who would have thought love would feel so much like a queasy stomach?

He cleared his throat, causing her to turn and look into his brown eyes. Her insides felt like they just might melt. "You know," he said, "back when I was a little kid, before my parents died, I remember our neighbor had a pony—a little paint. I was nine years old at the time and had decided that it was time I had my own horse. My father had other ideas, but I was determined, and I begged for an entire year, and did double chores to convince him that I would be able to handle the responsibility of an animal of my own."

Paulie nodded, uncertain where this discussion was headed.

"Wanting that horse nearly ate me up. All winter I passed him every time I walked to school. Then finally, on my birthday I walked past the field and he wasn't there. I ran the rest of the way home, thinking how happy I would be when I got my first ride atop that beautiful pony. And when I ran into the barn, there he was."

Paulie smiled, remembering the elation of a childhood dream come true. As Will described saddling up the little paint, she could just imagine how giddy and happy he must have felt.

"And then it was time to take my first ride. And you know what happened?"

Paulie stared at him in anticipation.

"He threw me."

She laughed. "How many times?"

"Every time I rode him," Will admitted, smiling broadly. "That pony was a menace. All those months I had stared at him, wanting him, never guessing how miserable I'd actually be with the object of my desire."

Paulie blushed, suddenly realizing why he was telling her this silly story. He was trying to explain why she shouldn't be upset over losing Trip—but of course he had it backwards. What would Will have thought if he had known that *he* was the ornery painted pony in her life, not Trip?

Then again, the story could work both ways. What if he was right? Maybe she and Will *would* make a terrible pair. They might fight, just like they always did now. Then their funny little arguments might not seem so humorous anymore. His poking fun at her for being a homely tomboy wouldn't be funny, either. She got up and paced a few feet away.

"You understand what I'm telling you, Paulie?" he asked, following her.

She frowned. "Unfortunately, I do."

He put an arm around her shoulder and squeezed. "You shouldn't worry about losing Trip."

Trip was about the furthest thing from her mind when Will had his arm around her. Paulie squirmed uncomfortably. Being so close to Will made her heartbeat race way ahead of her reason, yet she couldn't force herself to pull away. She tried to hide her face, which she was sure was pink with embarrassment. Here she was getting all worked up over being close to him, and he'd just been trying to offer her a little neighborly advice. Will had no way of knowing his very touch made her feel as if she could leap over the stars.

"You're young," he observed.

"I'm not *that* young!" she blurted out. Heaven knew, she was old enough to know that the tempest tossing inside her meant that she wanted to wrap herself around Will and kiss him like there was no tomorrow.

He chuckled patiently. "You'll find someone else. There's more than one fish in the sea, you know. Believe me, someday soon you'll wake up one morning and forget all about Trip."

"Have you been able to forget about Mary Ann?" she challenged.

His face became an unreadable mask. "What does that have to do with anything?"

She folded her arms. "It doesn't seem that you have gotten over her. You're going all the way to San Antonio to find her."

His jaw clenched, and his eyes began to burn with a fire she couldn't understand. "That's different."

Paulie laughed bitterly. "Everyone thinks they're different! Maybe my feelings are different, too. Have you ever stopped to consider that? Have you ever noticed that I'm not a girl anymore, but a woman over the age of twenty-one?"

He stared at her for a few moments, surprised by the vehemence of her outburst. Paulie knew she should have held her tongue, but she couldn't help herself.

"I didn't mean to sound condescending, Paulie," he answered, his tone chastened.

She felt embarrassed now, especially when he kept staring at her that way, as if he were trying to see right through to her most secret thoughts. What a shock he would be in for if that were actually possible!

She attempted to shrug away, but he held her fast.

"Will you forgive me?" he asked.

"Oh, sure," she mumbled hastily. Anything to get him to let her go.

But he didn't. Instead, he brought his face closer to hers—his lips were tantalizingly close. She was surprised at the brazen urge she felt to simply tilt her head a little and press her lips against his.

"I keep underestimating you, Paulie," he whispered gruffly.

His voice sent a shiver through her, and that was all it

took. Suddenly, she was the trout in front of the baited hook. The kid with his hand on the cookie jar. The mouse spying a hunk of cheese. Nothing short of natural disaster could have stopped her from tasting his lips.

There was nothing tentative about kissing Will this time. The minute their lips touched, she felt fireworks shoot off inside her, and there was no keeping her arms from snaking around his neck. Nor could she have managed not to press herself as close to him as humanly possible. He felt so warm, so strong, so sure of himself. He made her feel as if everything she was doing were perfectly right.

He tilted her head and drank more deeply of her mouth, and his hand moved up and down her spine, causing little explosions wherever he touched her. She felt dizzy from all the sensations happening at once, but she would have never forgiven herself if she'd chosen that moment to faint. Not for anything would she have missed a single moment of being this close to him, of smelling the strong male scent of him, of their playful fencing with their tongues.

She intended to hang on forever. It didn't matter to her if she never ate or drank or even breathed ever again. As long as she remained attached to Will, he was all the nourishment she needed. And she needed him with a fever she never knew existed. She felt a heat build deep inside her, a desire she couldn't begin to comprehend. She only knew that Will was the only man who could stoke the flames— or put them out.

But put them out, unfortunately, was what he intended to do.

All of a sudden, Paulie felt a different kind of pressure, and she realized with a horrified shock that it was Will, trying to unpeel her arms from around his neck. She pulled her lips away, and looked into his shocked face, her own surprise mirrored in his dark eyes. Her lips were also reflected there, and were positioned in such a comically perfect O that the sight would have been funny, if she weren't so ashamed.

Had she really lost control so completely?

"Lord, Paulie…" Will muttered huskily.

She looked down and was further mortified to discover that her hands were attached to his forearms like leeches to an invalid. "Oh!" she cried. She let go of him and stepped quickly away—reeled away, almost.

He looked repentant. For her, heartbreakingly so. "I should never—"

She cut him off, not caring to hear his regrets. "Oh, no, *I* should never—"

He agreed, nodding vigorously. "This was the wrong time. We both know…"

She nodded with him, their heads bobbing up and down in unison like floating ducks on a stormy pond. She couldn't begin to describe the hurt she felt, especially when he was so obviously sorry that the kiss happened at all. But it had only happened because she had attacked him— thrown herself at him as if she'd been launched from a cannon!—and now she wanted to escape.

She waved her hands in front of her face, cutting off any further examination of the topic. "I had better go check on Partner," she said. "It's been a long day, and…"

Before she could get another word out, or look another moment into his perplexed eyes, she turned tail and dashed over to the horses.

"Lord-a-mercy, Paulie," Trip whispered over Feather's back, "what was *that* all about?"

Even as her mind roiled with shame, heat and desire burned hot inside her. "You didn't see, did you?"

"How could I help it? You two were standing right there in the moonlight!"

She closed her eyes, remembering how it was partly the moonlight illuminating his face so close to hers that had made her want to throw herself at him.

"Do you want me to talk to him, Paulie?"

She blinked in confusion. "About what?

Trip frowned. "I don't like him taking advantage of you like that. Especially with all this business about Mary Ann still up in the air."

"No thank you, Trip." It was too humiliating to admit that Will had already apologized to her for kissing her when he still cared for Mary Ann. Or that *she* was actually the one who had taken advantage of Will.

"Well, all right," Trip said. "But you know I'm here if you need me to deal with him." He snorted in disgust. "A man ought to know better!"

She ought to have known better. "You don't have to play big brother for me," she assured him.

It was Will's big-brotherly feelings that had gotten her into so much trouble to begin with. And the fact that she had misinterpreted his closeness for an invitation, which was the only lame excuse for her brazen behavior that she could grasp on to.

But oh, what she wouldn't have given for Will to feel something besides big-brotherly toward her!

Chapter Nine

"My goodness!" Paulie exclaimed, her eyes bugging in amazement as she looked at the town around her.

Trip laughed. "I told you the place had changed."

But San Antonio wasn't just bigger than the last time she had made her way out here four years ago, it had an entirely different ambiance. The dusty town was bustling, impersonal. The sight of the three of them riding through old Market Street with their riderless horse turned not a single head—except, Paulie noted with dismay, the heads of a few ladies who craned their bare elegant necks to get a second look at Will. Even after untold days straight in the saddle, the man was still a sight for female eyes to behold.

Some of these ladies were a little overly enthusiastic with their smiles, which made Paulie stare back in astonishment. Though the sun was still high, the fancy ladies were out in full force, plying their trade—and within spitting distance of the Alamo, that almost sacred monument to the Texans' fighting spirit. Will didn't seem to notice the inviting glances of the women, but Paulie caught Trip actually winking at one of them.

She harrumphed loudly. "You aren't forgetting dear old Tessie, are you, Trip?"

"No, no," he said, coughing self-consciously. "I was just...just wonderin' if maybe one of those ladies would know where we could find Mary Ann."

"I'll bet!"

Will turned to them. "I thought we could stop here and ask around." He nodded toward a bright pink stucco building with a sign proclaiming it to be Las Tres Reinas. The Three Queens. "If we find Tyler, we'll most likely find Mary Ann."

Las Tres Reinas was by far the most fancy-looking gambling establishment they had passed on their way through town, and appeared just the place that would appeal to a man like Oren Tyler. There were plenty of men of all descriptions trundling through the black bat-wing doors, both coming and going.

"I'll bet Oren Tyler's been through here, all right," Paulie observed.

Will laughed sharply. "Half of humanity's been through here." He got down from Ferdinand and tethered him to the post in front of the saloon. "Trip, you come in with me."

"Okay, boss," Trip answered with a mock salute.

Paulie stared slack-jawed at the brim of Will's hat. Was he insinuating that she wasn't supposed to go inside? Quicker than Trip could blink, much less move, she swung to the ground and tied Partner next to Ferdinand. Will looked at her and rolled his eyes.

"You watch the horses, Paulie," he said.

After coming this far, she wasn't about to be left out in the cold. Especially not when things were just about to get interesting! "Trip can watch the horses." She pivoted and shot a cunning smile at Trip, who was still perched atop Feather. "Can't you, Trip?"

He was as yet mulling over the speed with which she had pounced to the ground. "Why, sure..."

Will's jaw clenched, and he pinned her with a stern glare. "The Three Queens isn't a place for a girl."

Just then, two women with red hair a vibrant shade never meant to appear in nature, except perhaps in parrots and cactus flowers, let out a laugh and pushed right through the double doors. Paulie nodded at them. "Looks like they're welcome," she pointed out.

"I believe they're going to work," Will replied.

She planted her hands stubbornly on her hips. "I work in a barroom, too."

He smiled patiently. "Yes, but I don't believe you all share the same occupation."

Paulie shrugged. "Well I don't care. I'm going in."

She began to march past him, but he caught her by the arm and whirled her around to face him. "Suit yourself, as long as you keep your mouth closed and let me ask the questions. Is that a deal?"

She hopped impatiently. "You make it sound like I talk too much!"

He didn't reply to that. "Deal?"

Paulie pursed her lips, annoyed. "Deal."

She let him lead the way into Las Tres Reinas, which wasn't quite as fancy on the inside as it was on the outside. In fact, Paulie felt a little disappointed with her first glance inside a real big-city drinking and gambling house. Somehow, she'd expected ornate crystal chandeliers and fine carpets from the Orient; instead, the place resembled nothing so much as Judge Bean's on a large scale. The long bar was magnificent, carved of a fine oak and shined to a high gloss, as were the several bevelled mirrors hanging behind it. Yet the rest of the establishment was furnished with the same plain oak tables that one might find in any barroom west of the Mississippi. There were just a lot more of them.

What really struck her about the place was the clientele. She didn't spy Oren Tyler among the patrons enjoying cards at the tables, but she did see many men who could have passed for his likeness. Several of them were duded up like a mayor on meeting day, with enough brass and silver ornamenting their hats, suspenders and belts to keep a munitions factory going for a decade. And the women who lounged around the tables like living furniture were just as dazzling as the men; all sported brightly colored gowns and more face paint than Paulie had ever seen in one place.

She tugged on Will's sleeve. "What do we do now?"

He studied the room carefully, searching the tables for an opening. "You stick close and say nothing. I believe I'll play some cards."

She gave him some of their precious money to stake him, then nodded, strolled across the room behind him as he approached a table playing stud poker. Paulie was always up for a game of cards, but even so, she wouldn't have picked these men to play with. One had a long curly mustache that looked like it would take at least an hour of daily grooming to keep in presentable condition, and his partner wore a ten-gallon hat so bedecked with silver stars that it probably weighed more than she did.

"Mind if I join you?" Will asked the men.

The star-studded fellow looked Will over with a cold assessing gaze, but when he glanced to his partner for affirmation, the man nodded curtly without so much as a squint at Will. Paulie had the idea that he had probably pegged Will as an honest man the minute they had crossed the bar's threshold.

Star man dealt the cards, and for a few minutes, the men

studied their hands in silence. Seeing a new man settling in for a game drew one of the ladies from a nearby table, who sidled up to Paulie. "Aren't you playing?" she asked, looking Paulie over from head to toe.

Paulie, unnerved by the woman's even gaze, shook her head. Maybe Will was right to tell her to be wary of this place.

"You're too late for a game, Iris, but you might as well set for a spell," the mustachioed gentleman told the fancy lady. He drew a card and added it to his hand without expression crossing his face. If she hadn't seen his lips moving, Paulie would have doubted that the man had spoken at all.

"Thanks, Henry," Iris said, sinking her bustled behind into the chair next to his. "Been a while since I seen you around here."

"Just come back from New Orleans," he answered, as if he weren't the least interested in the cards the other men laid down in front of him.

"New Orleans?" Will said in the same nonchalant manner. "I know a man who's there now, too." Just as Paulie was about to ask who that could be, he finished by adding, "Oren Tyler."

The woman named Iris raised her brows. "Tyler? In New Orleans? Not the last I heard!"

Will shot her a look so surprised that even Paulie would have believed the man was certain Oren Tyler had been in New Orleans.

"Why, just yesterday he was sittin' where you're sittin' now," Iris went on, not so schooled in the art of discretion as the men at the table.

"Tyler? Here?" Will asked as if amazed. "Perhaps he had my cousin with him?"

She shook her head emphatically at that notion. "Not

yesterday, he didn't. He was alone. For a while he had a gal taggin' 'round him, some girl who'd rode into town with a patent medicine man, but that didn't last.'' She laughed. ''They never do with Oren.''

Will was hard pressed to keep his eyes on his game. ''This woman wasn't by chance a blond woman, with blue eyes?''

Iris nodded, and gestured broadly with a long-nailed hand. ''Oh sure, a real cute thing. She was Oren Tyler's girl, all right.'' Her painted lips turned up in a sly sneer. ''Or that's how she fancied herself.''

The past tense of Iris's reply didn't escape Paulie, and she could tell by the way he stiffened that it hadn't gone unnoticed by Will, either. Oren was still running around San Antonio, but he had apparently had his fill of Mary Ann.

So where was she?

Paulie could stay silent no longer. ''Will, if your cousin's in town, maybe we should try to find her. Do you know where she is, ma'am?''

Iris beamed a radiant smile at her, her teeth appearing stark white against her red lips. ''Sure don't, honey.''

Paulie frowned. Then, when Iris stood up and sidled up close to her, Paulie positively scowled down at Will, and pulled the brim of her cap self-consciously over her eyes. Did this woman actually see her as a potential customer? Did Iris, like Night Bird, actually think she was a *boy?*

''Say…'' Iris cooed seductively. ''You're just a young 'un.''

Paulie swallowed. She was beginning to feel sick to her stomach. ''Gosh, Will, maybe we should go try to find your cousin *right now.*''

He laid another card down. ''No hurry,'' he answered breezily.

"What's your rush, pumpkin?" Iris asked. "You aren't sweet on the man's cousin, are you?"

Paulie was certain her face was beet-red. Though she had never harmed another creature in her entire life, if the woman said one more thing to her she was going to receive a hard clip to her powdered jaw. Will had told her not to gab with the people in the saloon; he hadn't said a thing about hitting them.

Still, she aimed for patience. "No." She glanced pleadingly at Will, pointing her head toward the doors. "Will…?"

He appeared all caught up in his card game. Or else he was having fun watching her squirm. "Hold your horses, Paulie."

Iris giggled. "Paulie? That's a sweet name."

The whole place could probably hear Paulie's teeth grinding. "Thanks," she muttered.

"Don't mention it. And since you're such a nice kid, I'll give you a tip. I saw that girl you were askin' about headed for Maudie Worthington's the other day. I wasn't going to mention it to your friend there—even a snooty gal deserves to be left alone sometimes if she doesn't want to be found. But you seem like a nice kid."

Paulie tried to keep her mind on business, not on how much she wanted to murder Will. "Who's Maudie Worthington?"

Iris shrugged. "She owns a house." She mumbled a street name that meant nothing to Paulie.

Paulie wondered just what kind of "house" Mary Ann had gotten herself installed in. She cleared her throat and slanted an anxious glance at Will, who ignored her as he studied his cards.

Iris grinned at her coyly and scooted so close that Paulie thought she would be knocked out by the stench of the woman's pungent perfume. Was *this* what men found so appealing? "You interested in seeing my room, little Paul?"

Iris batted her long eyelashes, and finally Paulie could stand no more. "The name's *Paulie,*" she corrected heatedly, doffing her hat and letting her braid spill down her back. "As in Paulette!"

The shock in Iris's eyes was no less than it had been in Night Bird's two days before. Silence was a shroud over the saloon as all eyes pinned on Paulie and the painted lady, whose red cheeks had by this time flushed crimson naturally.

"Look there—he's a girl!" the old man behind the bar crowed.

Another man nearby hooted with laughter. "Say, Iris, hadn't you seen enough men to get that part of your job nailed down yet?"

Suddenly, Paulie realized that Iris's face wasn't heated with embarrassment, but anger—and all of it directed straight at her. Her tricking the woman hadn't been on purpose, but it hadn't been smart, either. She scrambled to one side, but too late.

Iris reached forward and clutched Paulie's shirt in two bunched fists, nearly lifting her clear off the ground. Paulie struggled like a perch dangling on a hook. Her bruised ribs still smarted. "Why you little cheap rascal chit—"

In a split second, Paulie felt another set of hands at her back, tugging her away from Iris. It was Will—and about time!

"We're just going, ma'am," Will told the angry woman, attempting to pry Paulie free.

"I oughta rip her little throat out!" Iris bellowed, holding fast. Her cry brought more peals of laughter from the card players and women at the tables around them.

Paulie feared she was about to be ripped in two in front of the laughing, jeering crowd when Will finally loosened her from Iris's talons and steered her speedily toward the exit. He thrust her through the bat-wing doors and onto the dirt walkway. Iris's outraged shrieks still rang in her ears even as she saw Trip gaping at her from atop Feather with wide surprised eyes.

"What the—"

Paulie didn't even wait to answer the question evident on Trip's tongue. She wheeled around and poked a finger into Will's chest. "What were you doing in there—trying to win enough to buy a homestead?"

Will smiled and lifted his shoulders innocently. "Just having a friendly game."

"At *my* expense!" Paulie cried, her voice now almost as shrill as Iris's. "You saw what was happening. Why didn't you get me out of there?"

"I did."

"Not before I was almost clawed to death by that creature!"

Trip's eyes rounded in horror at her words. "What the heck happened?"

Will shook his head. "Just a little argument between Sprout here and one of the ladies." At Paulie's angry sputtering, he lifted a hand to calm her. "How could we leave when you were doing so well at information gathering?"

Paulie's mouth stopped in midprotest. Was he actually giving her credit for finding out where Mary Ann was? Why, that was almost like a compliment! She looked up into his light brown eyes and found her anger melting away like an ice floe in El Paso.

Then he smiled that devilish, smug grin of his. "Besides, I warned you to stay outside with the horses."

She stomped over to her horse and mounted with a resentful scowl. "Well, just don't you forget I *was* the one to find Mary Ann."

His eyes twinkled wryly. "I don't expect you'll let me."

From the tone of Paulie's conversation with Iris, Will had mentally braced himself to find Mary Ann installed in a bordello. Instead, Maudie Worthington's turned out to be a boardinghouse on a very respectable-looking residential street set back from the river, far from the bustle and noise of the town. So respectable was the place, in fact, that Maudie Worthington thought twice about talking to the ragtag trio of strangers who arrived at her doorstep that afternoon.

The widow Worthington, who met them on the porch of her two-story house, was pleasantly plump, wore a black serge dress with a neckline practically reaching her lower lip. Her hair, a baffling cross between blond and silver gray, puffed elegantly around her face and was gathered neatly at the crown of her head in a perfectly round bun.

"We've come looking for one of your residents, Mary Ann Murphy," Will announced to the woman. Her gaze narrowed first on Will, then Trip, then Paulie—lingering longest on Paulie. "Incidentally, the three of us could also use a place to stay while in town, if you have a vacancy."

A large placard sign on the front door of the house announced plainly that there was, but the woman didn't appear to give that fact any credence. "Mary Ann isn't exactly living here," she said.

"She's not?" Will held back a sigh. He'd feared all along that this had been too easy. He wondered what Mary Ann was up to now.

"No sir," Mrs. Worthington replied. "She's working for me."

"*Working!*"

Will couldn't say for certain who had let out the exclamation or if all three of them actually had. Everybody knew that Mary Ann hated to do chores around her own farm. He couldn't imagine her coming to the city to hire herself out as a servant girl.

Loudly, a second-story window was thrown open, and there, after all these days, appeared Mary Ann herself. Will sucked in his breath at the sight she created. For so long now he'd feared some terrible fate had befallen her, but here she was, looking as pretty and pampered as ever. Her blue eyes were framed by the same riot of blond curls as she leaned out the window and stared down at them in shock. "Why, it's Will Brockett!" she exclaimed. A smile that could have lit up all of Texas spread across her face. "Will! Wait there—I'll be right down!"

Mrs. Worthington harrumphed. "This is dusting day, and the girl took half the morning just to drag a rag over a banister. I hope you all can pay for these rooms you want, because I can't be making up more chores so I can take in more people who can't afford to stay here otherwise. Heaven knows, having Mary Ann is already like having no servant girl at all."

Will nodded, feeling strangely comforted by her words. Same old Mary Ann, all right. "We can pay."

The woman didn't seem to doubt Will, but she again shot dubious looks at both Paulie and Trip, who Will had to admit did look a little frayed around the edges after their hard travelling.

Paulie, though, lifted her chin as if she were Queen Victoria of England and looked down her pert nose at the venerable Mrs. Worthington, something which would have been impossible for the diminutive girl to manage had she not been atop her horse. Then, with much ceremony, she doffed her hat and produced her stash of money. "I have here the sum of twenty-eight dollars," she announced to the older woman. "I assume that's enough to cover our lodgings for a week?"

One glance at the money was enough for Mrs. Worthington to be won over. "More than enough," she agreed, nodding. She turned and beckoned them toward the front door. "If you'll just follow me, I'll show you—"

Her words were cut off when Mary Ann came racing through the door. Although he had been preparing himself, Will nearly gasped in surprise at the sight of her, more beautiful than ever. Her blond curls were pulled back from her face but spilled down her shoulders in a dazzling display. Her blue eyes shone brightly, especially set against the cornflower-blue of her long-sleeved dress. She wore a white pinafore over the garment, giving her a domestic look she didn't normally possess.

She seemed overly enthusiastic, almost agitated, to find this group of Possum Trotters in her San Antonio hideaway.

"Well, my word!" she exclaimed, just standing there breathlessly and drinking him in. "Will!" Finally able to stand no more, she laughed gaily and ran into his arms, practically exploding off the porch at him in a flurry of blue and white. He couldn't help smiling as he held her for a moment.

"You don't know how glad I am to see you!" she said. "You don't know—" A half-choked sob bit off her words.

He looked down into her blue eyes, which were dry of tears but filled to the brim with troubles. In the last few moments, he had almost forgotten the bad tidings he had come to San Antonio bearing. Now he dreaded telling her about Oat's death all the more.

Mary Ann's eyes focused on a point behind him, and Will turned to see Trip beaming at the pretty sight Mary Ann created—and Paulie scowling like a mad hound dog.

"Oh," Mary Ann said. "I guess I didn't see you, Mr. Peabody, and Miss...I mean, um, Paulie."

Will frowned, glancing between the two young women. It seemed almost as if Mary Ann could barely remember her friend's name.

Paulie's lip propped itself up into a lopsided smile. "How are you, Mary Ann?"

"Fine, thank you," Mary Ann answered stiffly.

Mrs. Worthington, her hands propped on her ample hips, shook her head. "Mary Ann, you take a moment to visit before you get back to your chores," she said, as if she were the very soul of generosity. Then she turned to Trip and Paulie. "I'll go ahead and show you two the rooms."

Paulie and Trip dismounted, hitched their horses and followed Mrs. Worthington into the house, leaving Mary Ann and Will by themselves. Will felt uncomfortable, and fidgeted with his hat as he listened to the squabbling of two blue jays in an elm tree nearby. For days he'd been expecting to find Mary Ann, yet since he'd had so many people along with him, he hadn't reckoned on facing her alone. He wasn't sure how to begin voicing all the things he had to tell her. Mary Ann's gay, almost hysterically happy mood didn't allow much room for bad news.

She glanced up at him, her blue eyes dancing slyly. "You don't have to say it, Will," she said. "I know what you're thinking. I've been bad. You've come here to scold me." Long black lashes fluttered demurely. "You always were a scold." Lord, she was pretty. Pretty and manipulative. He wondered why that fact had never seemed so clear to him before this moment.

She lifted her small shoulders and let out a sigh. "Oh, well, I guess I should be happy that it's you who's come to find me, not Oat Murphy."

"Mary Ann..."

Her eyes filled with anguish. "Oh, Will, I can't tell you how horrible he was to me!" A hand lifted to her breast, just as Will had seen an actress do once up in Kansas.

He kept a level stare on her. "Oat's dead, Mary Ann."

She sucked in a breath. "What?"

"He *did* come looking for you," Will told her flatly. "Only he died trying."

A progression of emotions paraded across her pretty face, none of them too hard to keep up with. Surprise, guilt, relief. Guilt didn't last very long. "He was *so* old, Will," Mary Ann said, folding the ruffles of her apron with her hand. "I'm terribly saddened by your news, of course, but it hardly comes as a shock."

Will folded his arms. "His looking for you probably didn't do his constitution any good. Before he died, he had a run-in with the renegade Night Bird, and a group of Mexican bandits. I suspect you know just what bandits I'm talking about."

Mary Ann glanced up at him anxiously, and her little pink tongue darted out to lick her lower lip. In an instant, Will saw that the Comanche had been telling the truth. She *had* tried to get the Mexicans to bring her to San Antonio. Now she resembled nothing so much as an anxious little bunny rabbit. Before he could question her further on her misdeeds, however, her eyes filled with tears.

"You blame me for all that's happened," she said, sniffling. "But don't you understand how desperate I was? All right, I made a mistake—but was I supposed to pay for it the rest of my life?"

Will continued to study her, torn by his desire to believe her, and logic, which told him that she was overplaying her martyrdom. Her small shoulders were racked with sobs. She turned to him, her hands open in supplication.

"What was I supposed to do after that letter you wrote me, Will? I'd always just assumed that we…"

A wave of guilt washed over him. *The letter.* In all the events of the past two days, he had nearly managed to put that infernal thing out of his mind. Now his own action came back and hit him. So the letter *had* sent her into despair—and into the arms of an old man she didn't love. Which meant *he* was the one who had set the unhappy course of events that had led to Oat's death into motion.

"Mary Ann, I'm sorry."

A lone tear trickled down her cheek. "It's all right," she said, her lip lifting into a brave little smile. "You were right. If you don't love me, then there's certainly no reason on earth why we should have gotten married…"

Regret as sharp as a butcher's knife sliced through him. "Mary Ann…"

She shook her head. "No, Will. Don't say you're sorry. You have nothing to be sorry for. I'm the one who should be sorry. You're right. I've behaved abominably."

"It's not as bad as all that," Will told her gently. "You're young."

She sobbed. "I'm a widow!"

Softly, he placed a hand at her elbow and found himself repeating the same words he'd told Paulie. "You'll find someone else to love someday. And in the meantime, if there's anything I can do for you…"

Mary Ann turned, and at once he saw the determined glitter in her eye that even the welling of tears couldn't mask. "There *is* something you can do, Will."

He gaped at her, stunned by her immediate response to his offer. "What?"

"There's a man. I need someone to talk to him for me. Tell him I'm a widow now, that everything would be different."

Will dropped his hand away from her. "Tyler," he said in disgust.

She drew her brows together, confused. "That's right. How did you know?"

He snorted in derision. "It took most people in Possum Trot exactly five minutes to guess that you had gone running after Oren Tyler, Mary Ann." That wasn't exactly the truth; only *Paulie* had been that quick to guess. But it would do Mary Ann good to learn that she wasn't as cunning as she thought.

Mary Ann lifted her head proudly. "I love Oren."

"You can't go running after a person just because you think you love them."

She grinned. "You came after me."

He felt his cheeks heat. "I felt an obligation. Because of your father."

"My father wouldn't have wanted me married to that old whiskey man!" she cried. "Especially when he found how stingy Oat was. The man had a thousand dollars in government bonds, and he had no intention of letting me hav—"

Her words broke off abruptly, and she grabbed Will's hand. "The bonds!" she said, a light dawning. "They're mine now, aren't they? All mine!"

Will took a deep, steadying breath. Just before he died, Oat had told them of Mary Ann's interest in the bonds. "I guess they are."

She clapped her hands together. "I could sell them. Why, I don't have to work this silly job anymore—or won't once I find them. And if I'm rich, Oren will *want* to take me to Denver. He'll…" The thought trailed off as a look of worry crossed her face.

Will folded his arms across his chest. "What's the matter?"

"He won't see me," she said. "He won't even look at me to talk to."

"Nice beau you got for yourself."

She shot him an annoyed glance. "Oh, he just got mad 'cause I was married and because... But I'm not married now." She looked up at Will and smiled her prettiest. "You said you would help me, Will."

"Oh, no." He shook his head frantically. "This is your business."

"But if you'll just *talk* to him. Tell him that I'm a widow now—that I'm rich. Or will be, once I find out where Oat put his bonds," she said. "Just go talk to him, that's all I ask. Tell him that he needs to marry me."

Despite his disgust with her, Will had to chuckle at that notion. "A man doesn't usually need to be told who he needs to marry."

Two splotches of red appeared in Mary Ann's cheeks. "It's not just that I want to marry him, Will," she said. "I *have* to. Do you understand?" Instinctively, her hand drew up to the apron covering her belly. Her figure was only slightly swollen, but Will understood immediately.

In contrast to Mary Ann's healthy color, he could feel his own face turn white as the blood drained out of it. He looked at her almost as if for the first time. Beautiful. There was no doubt about it. She was the daughter of Gerald and Nancy Redfern, the girl he had known and admired for years. But he saw something else now, too—something his gut had sensed all along but his head had never wanted to put a name to. Trouble. He'd come here to help her, and ever since she'd seen him, she'd been attempting to twist him around her little finger, using every turn in the conversation to lead him to this point. To his agreeing to talk to Oren Tyler on her behalf, because she was carrying the gambler's child.

Will bit back a sneer of disgust at his own gullibility. She didn't care for him, and probably never had. The letter he had written her was probably forgotten as fast as she could read it. She'd cared even less about Oat. Just used him.

"Don't you see?" she asked, a pathetic look in her eyes. "Back in Possum Trot I was so lonely and bored. And after your letter came, I just went a little mad. So I married Oat. And then when I found out there was a baby on the way, I felt trapped. I panicked. So I came here, and then I ran into Oren…"

Will bit his lip. He couldn't believe she was still trying to lie to him. "That's a fine story, Mary Ann. Except that I happen to know that you and Oat didn't have husband-wife relations."

She stared at him, stunned. "Oat told you that?"

He nodded curtly.

She licked her lips, appearing almost feverish at having been tangled in her own lie. "All right! I was desperate, so I married Oat, but I couldn't go through with it. Is that so terribly hard to understand? I realized I had made a terrible mistake and came here to look for my baby's real father!"

Will shook his head sadly. Mary Ann's duplicity almost made him lose his faith in women. It was a good thing he had brought Paulie along. She'd had Mary Ann pegged from the start—and she'd been dead right. But Paulie, though she recognized feminine wiles, didn't seem to know much about using them herself, which was refreshing—and a good antidote to Mary Ann.

"Go back to Possum Trot, Mary Ann."

She looked even more horrified at that thought than she had at the idea of having conjugal relations with Oat. "I couldn't go back there!"

"Why not?" he asked. "It would be easier than working for Mrs. Worthington, less humiliating than begging a man to marry you. No one in town will know your baby isn't Oat's."

"Of course they will!"

"How?"

"He told you, didn't he?" she said. "Who else did he tell?"

Will remembered that Paulie and Trip had also been present when Oat revealed the details of his marriage. "Your secret's safe," he assured her.

"I can't be certain of that," she said. Her face had turned blotchy, and she rubbed her hands briskly against her arms as she paced in front of Mrs. Worthington's home. "Besides, I don't want to go back to Possum Trot. I don't belong there. Don't you see, you *must* talk to Oren for me. You must!"

"Calm down," Will said, grabbing her by the shoulders. The thought of how duplicitously she had acted toward everyone made him almost physically ill, but he still felt a responsibility toward her. The woman had no one to advise her. "I know you're in a bad spot, but we'll figure something out."

"If I can just get my hands on those bonds..." she murmured fervently.

Will decided it was time for plain speaking. "If you don't mind my saying so, I think you should take a few days to think things through. You're a widow now, with responsibilities and a child on the way."

"Of course!" she cried hysterically. "That's why I need you to talk to Oren!"

Nothing he said seemed to penetrate her pretty, thick head. Finally, he took a deep breath, admitting defeat. He doubted he could handle this woman alone. "Mary Ann,

I'm thinking about sending for your stepfather, Mr. Breen. Maybe if you went back to the farm, visited with your ma, and rested for a few days, things would look different.''

He awaited her reaction, which was amazingly swift—and severe. At the mere mention of the chicken farm, her pacing stopped, the fluttering of her hands came to an abrupt halt, and every particle of her appeared to go still. Her pink cheeks drained to a ghostly white, and right before his eyes, Mary Ann collapsed in a heap of blue onto the well-worn path in front of Mrs. Worthington's house.

Chapter Ten

"**A** widow!" Maudie exclaimed when she heard Paulie's stunning revelation about her maid. "I didn't even know the girl had a husband."

"Her name's Mary Ann Murphy. *Mrs.* Murphy," Paulie said, sitting on the edge of the tester bed in the small room Mrs. Worthington had escorted her into. This chamber, with its wallpaper festooned with bunches of tiny violets, cheery yellow ruffled curtains, and fine carved cherry furniture, including a pretty bureau and a matching standing mirror next to it, was the nicest room Paulie had ever seen. And for the reasonable sum of five dollars, it would be hers for an entire week.

"Why, that sly girl! I took one look at her, and I knew immediately that she was hiding something." Maudie sighed. "But I confess, I'm a weak one for a sad story, and that girl spun a yarn the likes of which you've never heard. All about looking for her long-lost brother. Yes, ma'am, my husband always did tell me I was a soft touch." She turned back to Paulie, her hands on her hips. "You like the room, hon?"

Paulie blinked. Maudie Worthington looked so solid, and acted so brusque, she couldn't imagine anyone pinning the word *soft* on her. She nodded enthusiastically. "Oh, yes. Very much. I don't believe I've ever spent the night in such a fine place."

The woman's face bloomed with approval. "I *knew* you would! This was my daughter's room," she confided, coming closer. "The first moment I laid eyes on you, you reminded me of her."

The comparison to the unknown daughter made Paulie swell with hope. If she could remind someone of a girl raised in a roomful of violets, maybe her prospects weren't so dismal after all. "I did?"

"My Abra had a bit of the tomboy about her," Mrs. Worthington said. "But she also had your lithe frame. Delicate, but wiry."

Delicate? Paulie puffed up a little more, and caught a glimpse of herself in the beautiful mirror. What she saw almost made her gasp in horror. A coating of dust clung to her skin and clothes, and her hair hung limply down her back. She looked puny, not delicate. But maybe that was because the shirt and britches she wore were dirty, and hung on her thin frame like old worn rags.

"Where is your daughter now?" she made bold to ask, praying nothing had befallen her fellow delicate creature.

"She married a farmer in New Braunfels. A German fellow—very hardworking." She let out a laugh. "But he still has a hard time keeping up with my Abra!"

Suddenly, Paulie felt an intense liking for this woman. What would it have been like to have grown up with such a champion? Paulie's father had been the most wonderful person she had ever known, and from what she could remember from her early childhood, her mother was a kind, gentle, beautiful woman. But she had to admit, sometimes during her adolescence and older years, she sorely missed having another woman to turn to for advice.

"Your daughter sounds like a fine person," Paulie said. "I wish there was someone like her in Possum Trot."

Mrs. Worthington pursed her lips knowingly. "If all you've had for company is that Mary Ann character, I can see why!"

"Oh, Mary Ann and I aren't—" She cut her words short, suddenly remembering that she was supposed to be masquerading as Mary Ann's friend.

"That girl's worse than useless. Can't even play cards." Maudie's face scrunched up as she eyed Paulie with renewed interest. "Can you?"

Paulie hesitated. She wasn't certain whether she should 'fess up to owning a saloon. Some women had peculiar ideas about what kind of businesses other women should be allowed to run, but she was beginning to sense Maudie wasn't that way. "I know my way around a deck."

"Good!" Maudie cried. "I haven't had a regular partner since my Abra ma—"

The front door banged open below. "Mrs. Worthington!"

It was Will's voice. The two women ran out to the stairs, which Will rapidly ascended with Mary Ann, unconscious, in his arms.

"Why, what happened to her?" Maudie asked.

Will appeared hesitant to give the reason for Mary Ann's passing out cold, but he looked into Paulie's eyes and saw that she had already let the cat out of the bag. "I told her about her husband."

Maudie harrumphed. "As if an early death couldn't be expected of any man unlucky enough to hitch his wagon to that creature!"

Paulie just managed to bite back a peal of laughter. What a relief to know there was someone else in the world who didn't think Mary Ann Redfern hung the moon and stars both!

Will looked uncomfortable, but Paulie couldn't tell if it was because he disagreed with Mrs. Worthington or because Mary Ann was heavier than she appeared. "If you could just show me where her room is…"

Maudie jabbed her thumb toward the ceiling. "She's got the attic room," she explained, bustling ahead of them and mounting a dark narrow staircase on the right. "She earns two dollars a week, plus bed and board. But considering the amount of work she's done so far, I'm considering turning the tables on her and having her pay me for waiting on her."

Just then, Trip ducked his head out of the room Maudie had designated his and Will's. His eyes rounded to see Mary Ann passed out in Will's arms. "What the heck…?"

Poor Trip. He always seemed to come in on the confusing tail end of things.

But Paulie herself was too amused—and irritated—by Will's playing gallant hero to explain the matter to her friend. "Shall we follow our landlady," she asked Will, who was still standing there with Mary Ann in his arms, "or are you just holding her so tightly because you're thinking of making a wager with Trip about her weight?"

"Very funny," he muttered, traipsing up the stairs with his cargo.

A few moments later Will laid Mary Ann out on the small bed in the corner of the tidy but diminutive room, which consisted of little else but the bed, a washstand with a basin, and a small wardrobe. He patted Mary Ann's cheeks, trying to get her back to consciousness. Seeing that her servant was still out cold, Mrs. Worthington went to the pitcher next to the basin and poured a glass of water.

"Splash some of this on her face," she said, handing the glass to Will. "Pour the whole jug on her if you have to."

Paulie was too curious about Mary Ann to keep herself from opening the wardrobe, especially knowing she might never get another opportunity to go through her things. She threw wide the doors and was amazed to discover an array of clothes there—most of which she could recognize as Mary Ann's from that woman's trips into Possum Trot.

"Oat was wrong," she said. "Mary Ann didn't leave Possum Trot empty-handed."

Will looked up at the clothes, but didn't appear the least fazed. "Does it really surprise you to learn Oat didn't have an eye for women's clothing?"

Paulie shook her head. "You'd think he'd notice that *something* was missing."

"Too bad." Maudie turned slightly so she could angle past Will and get to the wardrobe herself. "Mary Ann will probably be brokenhearted about all these clothes."

Paulie looked at her questioningly. "What do you mean?"

"Why, the poor lamb will probably hate having to dye all her clothes widow's black." She glanced mischievously at Paulie. "I know! Why don't I do it for her and save her the trouble?"

Before anyone could voice an objection to the plan, Mrs. Worthington swept all the clothes into her arms and trotted quickly to the stairs.

Will shot Paulie a bemused glance. "You could stop her, you know."

Paulie shrugged. "I know."

Perhaps sensing the doom that was about to befall her wardrobe, Mary Ann let out a moan and lifted a hand limply to her forehead. Instinctively, Will reached out and touched her cheek.

Paulie moved a few steps closer to the bed, agitated by Will's attentiveness to Mary Ann. He was so obviously touched by the distraught way she had taken Oat's death— having forgotten that Oat most likely died from all the troubles his runaway wife had caused him. He probably wouldn't believe that Mary Ann could be putting on this grief for his benefit. Men had so little imagination!

Mary Ann's eyes fluttered open, and she looked up at Will, almost as if she couldn't see him at first. Then, when she did recognize him, her dry lips mouthed his name and her eyes welled with tears. "Oh, Will…" she finally managed. Her voice was weak, but she circled a hand firmly around his neck, like a spider about to spin a cocoon around her prey. "I'm so glad you're here!"

Will shifted his weight and glanced uncomfortably up at Trip and Paulie. Trip nodded questioningly toward the door, but Paulie wasn't budging. Two things rooted her to the spot—morbid curiosity and protectiveness. She had to see how eager Will was to crawl into the spider's web, and she wanted to be there to try to stop him when he climbed on.

"I don't know what I would have done if you hadn't arrived, Will," Mary Ann said in her thin, wispy voice. "You'll help me now, won't you?"

Will froze, as if he couldn't quite decide what to say.

Paulie didn't hesitate, however. "Don't promise her anything, Will."

Mary Ann lifted her head woozily. "Is there someone here with us?"

"Just Paulie and Trip," Will told her.

She tugged him a little closer to her beautiful face and pleaded, "You said you would help me, Will. You promised."

Paulie rolled her eyes in disgust. If Will had done anything that stupid, he might be here forever untangling the snarled mess Mary Ann had made of her life. She wondered if any of them would ever see Possum Trot again.

Mary Ann fell back against her pillow, her blond hair spilling spectacularly around her across the starched white linens. ''And don't forget...my father loved you so...''

Will stiffened at the reminder, and suddenly Paulie knew they were lost. That *he* was lost.

''All right, I'll help you,'' he said. But from his tone of voice, Paulie could tell that even he wondered just how much he was bargaining for.

Standing in the doorway of the general store, Will shoved his brand-new loaded Colt revolver into his holster and took a deep breath. For better or worse, he was ready to face Oren Tyler and demand that he do the decent thing by Mary Ann.

He'd given the situation a day, hoping that Mary Ann would calm down. But this morning she was still in bed, claiming to be too distraught to move and certainly too upset to do chores. Paulie had helped Maudie with breakfast, and when he'd left the house the two of them had been huddled around the cleared dining table with a deck of cards. He'd told them he was going for a walk, but they seemed so absorbed in their game he doubted Paulie even heard him. Trip had left directly after breakfast to hunt for a wedding ring good enough for his Tessie and cheap enough for himself.

That left Will to hunt down the gambler by himself, which was just as well. He strode across the patch of wooden sidewalk that the mercantile owner had erected in front of his store, passing up the spot where Oat's horse was tethered, minus his saddle and blanket, which Will had swapped for the gun. He would have to repay Mary Ann when he got his hands on some money, but for now he felt safer wandering the streets of San Antonio ready to defend himself. Maybe he would have more luck talking Tyler into matrimony with a gun in his hand, too.

He stopped at the street to let a rickety wagon pass, stirring up a small whirlwind of dust in the cool breeze. At the same moment, he felt the hairs on the back of his head stand on end. All morning he'd had an uneasy feeling he was being followed, and now it quadrupled. A blacksmith's shop stood on the opposite corner, and Will walked toward it, careful to keep his gait easy as he passed its doors then turned left. After rounding the corner, he stopped and waited, leaning his shoulder against the wall of the building, his arms crossed.

Bootsteps hurried past the entrance of the blacksmith's, following his own path. A second later, a small body plowed into him. Paulie jumped back, shocked to see him standing there, lying in wait for her.

"Will!" Paulie shoved her hat firmly on her head. She looked up at him as if he were the last man she ever expected to see. "What are you doing here?"

"I told you back at the house that I was taking a walk," he said, curling his lips into a frown to hide a smile. Paulie really was a very bad actress. "The question I have is, why are you following me?"

She stared at him, wide-eyed. "I'm not following you. Can't I decide to go out for a stroll, just the same as you?"

"That was a pretty brisk pace for a stroll."

She shrugged, not budging from her stance. "I never did care for shilly-shallying."

He pushed away from the wall and gave it to her straight. "I don't want you coming with me. This is a job for one."

She eyed him stubbornly. "I'm sure I don't know what you mean," she said, lifting her nose a few inches higher.

"You know exactly where I'm headed. And I'm perfectly able to handle this business by myself."

Her small booted foot stamped impatiently on the ground. "Darn it, if you're so sure of yourself, what did you go and buy a gun for?"

A grin touched his lips. "You just happened to notice that on your stroll, too?"

Her face heated with a blush that didn't fail to remind Will of the other times he'd seen her face redden. Back when she was a little kid, when he'd tease her about her freckles, or whenever she lost a poker game, or when he kissed her…

He shook his head, dragging his gaze away from her pouty lips.

"All right," she admitted heatedly. "I was following you. Is it such a crime to want to help?"

"Help!" he repeated.

She jutted her chin forward. "I *could* help," she argued. "You've never even seen Oren Tyler. I have."

"How do you know that I'm trying to find him?"

The scowl returned, but somehow, when Paulie scowled, it didn't seem unappealing. "Just a guess," she muttered.

He tilted his head. Once Paulie got a notion in that hard noggin of hers, there was no dissuading her from doing exactly as she pleased. The best he could hope for was to negotiate a settlement.

"You can come point out Tyler if you're so determined," he agreed reluctantly, "but I don't want you taking a step into Las Tres Reinas."

Paulie's brows lifted. "The Three Queens? Why would we go there?"

"*I'm* going there because it's the one place where we know Tyler has been."

Her expression slowly indicated agreement with this

idea. "I see. You could have brought Trip along, you know. I bet you would have let him go into the saloon with you."

Will turned and started walking, knowing she would be right on his heels. "He wasn't available. Besides, a person in love's never the best backup. They tend to be preoccupied."

Paulie stumbled over a root sticking up in their path and pitched forward. Will caught her arm just before she would have lost her equilibrium and brought her back to standing next to him. "You're beginning to resemble Trip in some ways," he observed with a chuckle.

She wasn't laughing. "I just stumbled," she said sheepishly.

Will clamped his mouth shut and continued on his way, kicking himself for saying such a thing. Poor Paulie. She was bucking up so well to Trip's defection that he sometimes forgot that she must be brokenhearted over his decision to finally marry Tessie. He would have to be more careful of what he said to her in the future, and try to avoid discussing Trip.

They continued on in silence, with Paulie openly gaping at the sights of the burgeoning city, until they reached Las Tres Reinas. Paulie bumped against his back when he stopped abruptly a few feet away from the entrance.

"Peek inside," he instructed her. "If he's in there, point him out."

She nodded and stepped forward. Standing on tiptoe, she peered into the saloon. Her gaze soon honed in on something, and after a moment of observation she turned back to him, her lips pursed in disgust. "Wouldn't you know it!" she exclaimed, her hands on her hips. "The devil is having breakfast with *her*."

"Who?"

"Iris!" she spat angrily, the memory of her brawl with the woman still fresh in her mind.

Will put aside the thought of Paulie's hatred of Iris and focused instead on the good news. "That's fine," he told her. "Just wait here while I talk to the man."

As he approached the doors, he was surprised to feel Paulie's hand snake out and capture his arm, stopping him. "Don't go, Will. There's bound to be trouble," she argued quickly. "And anyway, Mary Ann's not worth it."

He shook his head and slowly removed her hand from his arm, thinking of Gerald. "It's a matter of honor, Paulie."

She looked at him sharply. "Mary Ann doesn't care about honor. She's not worth it—you just think she is, because you're chivalrous."

"I'm what?"

She blurted out, "You're all mixed up, just like a Spanish fellow I read about once. He was in love, too, and overly chivalrous, and once when he saw some windmills he thought they were giants and so he started fighting them."

Will looked at her, sure she had gone mad. "What kind of crazy book was that?"

She lifted her shoulders. "It was one of my pa's, about Don Somebody. It's a true story, though."

He leveled a calming gaze on her. "Look, Sprout, you have my word. I'm not going to shoot anything, windmill or man."

"Then what's the gun for?"

"I just thought it might make me look a little more authoritative."

"That it does," Paulie agreed, then she frowned. "But you never were a man to rely on a gun for persuasion, Will."

"I'm just going to talk to the man." He glanced inside, spotting Oren Tyler.

Swarthy. That was his first thought upon looking at the man who was supposed to be Oren Tyler. The man had a head of thick black hair, a dark complexion, and a long, well-groomed mustache that looked like tending it would take more trouble than it was worth. Even from a distance, Tyler had an imposing stature, and his glittering dark eyes as he flirted with Iris bespoke the attitude of a man who was accustomed to getting just what he wanted out of life. No sacrifices. No responsibilities. Just pleasures of the moment. If Tyler hadn't been lucky enough—or cunning enough—to be able to afford fine clothes, society would have deemed him a reprobate.

In short, Will didn't see much to like in the man. Nevertheless, he had made Mary Ann a promise. And before that, he had made Gerald a promise. Will pushed through the bat-wing doors and wasted no time approaching Tyler.

The gambler continued to laugh with Iris, but Will knew he was watching his approach. When he stopped by the table, Tyler glanced up questioningly.

"Is your name Oren Tyler?" Will asked.

"Sure is," the gambler answered, "and if you haven't noticed, I'm having my breakfast."

"I have some business with you."

Tyler shook his head and winked slyly at Iris. "I never mix meals with business."

His blithe dismissal didn't sit well with Will. "I've come to talk about Mary Ann Murphy."

The man looked up at him with just the hint of a sneer. "Are you an outraged relative?"

Will stiffened. "I'm not related to her." But he *was* growing more outraged by the second.

Iris jumped in, leaning close to the gambler's ear. "He's

the one I was tellin' you about, Oren. The man that came here with that queer girl yesterday lookin' for Mary Ann.''

Oren's gaze narrowed. ''What's your stake in the outcome of my little romance with Mrs. Murphy?''

''I was her husband's friend,'' Will said, feeling the words more strongly than he would have ever thought possible. God knows he missed Oat more than he had ever missed Mary Ann.

The man's eyebrows shot up to his forehead. ''Was?''

''Oat Murphy's dead.''

Oren Tyler took in this information for a moment, then, after some consideration, shrugged. ''Then everything should be fine.''

''There's going to be a child,'' Will said in a clipped voice.

''Don't widows ever have children?'' the man asked glibly.

Quaking with rage, Will leaned down just enough to swipe the man by the collar and drag him to his feet. He was surprised at how easy a task it was. Oren Tyler was about his height, but heavier. His anger tipped the scales in his favor, Will decided. ''I should knock your teeth in for saying that. You know whose child it is.''

''Do I?'' Tyler's lips turned up cynically. ''How can I be sure an eager young buck like yourself didn't come along after me?''

Tyler wasn't smiling now. ''I never told her I would marry her,'' he said. ''How could I? She was married already.''

''Then you should have left her alone.''

''I did,'' Tyler said. ''Then she trotted after me.'' His lips turned up cynically. ''A girl who's come all that way deserves something for her troubles, don't you think?''

Will wasn't a violent man—normally. But Oren Tyler

was no normal adversary. Feeling no remorse, Will hauled back and punched the man, sending him flying back into his chair.

"Oren, watch out!" Iris cried. She lunged at Will. "He's got a gun."

But the odd thing was, he *didn't* have a gun. When he reached down to the holster, the Colt wasn't there. Not that he intended to use it anyway. A low-down snake like Tyler wasn't worth the price of a bullet. But when he looked over and saw Iris pointing the gun straight at his chest, Will sorely missed the firearm.

He stiffened, knowing immediately from the glitter in Iris's eyes that he had underestimated the impact that the news about Mary Ann would have on the woman. He should have waited until he could speak to Tyler in private. Or set up a meeting in the boardinghouse. Now he was in a real spot. Iris was probably kidding herself that she had a chance with Oren Tyler—just as Mary Ann had done. And she apparently wasn't going to let him—or the mere matter of Mary Ann's baby—get in her way.

"You step away from him!" she cried.

Will was glad to oblige, but from behind him, he heard Iris's words echoed in a fierce familiar voice.

"Get away from him!"

Will turned in surprise just in time to see a streak of white and brown pass him. Paulie launched herself at Iris with the ferocity of a mountain lion pouncing on a rabbit. Only this rabbit was armed.

"Paulie, stop!" he hollered, but his command was ignored as Paulie and Iris wrestled with the gun. Behind them, he saw Oren Tyler shaking his head, then leaning forward woozily. The gambler watched the women in confusion for a split second, then stood.

"Watch out!" Will said, rushing forward to untangle Paulie from the mass of limbs, flounces and firearm.

But as he took a step, an explosion sounded that seemed to make the very walls of the saloon shake. After a blinding pain that practically doubled him over, Will's world went black.

Chapter Eleven

Will's face was as white as chalk. Paulie knelt over him in the rickety buckboard she had managed to procure for conveyance, and prayed that he wasn't dying. He looked like he was.

Iris's bullet had gone into his shoulder, and the wound still bled profusely. Paulie had never seen so much blood. But then, she'd never actually seen a man shot before. Things like this just didn't happen in sleepy Possum Trot.

She leaned over Will's half-conscious form, brimming with regrets. "Oh, Will, forgive me," she whispered fervently. "I shouldn't have jumped on that woman—I should have stayed outside." He had specifically instructed her to keep out of the bar, and she should have, she knew that now.

Yet the minute Iris had raised that gun, Paulie had known Will's request would prove impossible. Seeing his life in danger, there was no way she would stand outside and simply let the woman gun him down. Of course, that's exactly what had happened despite her blundering intervention....

The wagon rattled up the street to Maudie's, and Trip, who had been sitting on the porch outside, saw Paulie and came running.

"What happened?" he asked, not waiting for the answer. "Is he hurt bad?"

"It's all my fault," Paulie said, as if that answered anything. "Please, just tell Maudie to fetch a doctor—quick. Will's lost a lot of blood."

Trip nodded, turned, and ran back to the house. In a crisis, the man could be surprisingly steady on his feet.

"We're getting help, Will," she whispered, watching as Trip quickly ran out the door and waved to her as he dashed down the street. She prayed he would find a doctor quickly.

Maudie burst through the door next, ran down to the wagon, and immediately inspected Will. Then she glanced sympathetically at Paulie and didn't even raise a squeak at having a man injured by gunplay quartered in her house. Between her, Paulie and the driver of the wagon, they managed to get Will up to his room. Mary Ann was nowhere in sight, Paulie noted bitterly.

Once Will was settled on the bed, Mrs. Maudie explained the woman's absence. "Mary Ann went shopping for a new bonnet," she explained, seeming to know intuitively that Paulie would share her disgust. "Said if she was going to wear black, she at least wanted to look fashionable."

Paulie frowned, telling herself she didn't care. All that mattered was Will, and Will getting better. If only he would live, she thought fervently. If he lived she would try not to mind even if he did marry Mary Ann.

"I'll feel so terrible if anything happens to him," she said, hearing the hysterical edge in her own voice. His face was so pale...so cold-looking. She pulled the woolen blanket on the bed up over him, blessedly covering the deep red patch seeping across his shirt. "He's got to get better...he's got to."

Maudie looked at her with a certainty Paulie wasn't close to feeling. "He will. I can tell—Will's a fighter. 'Sides, when the good Lord makes a specimen as fine-looking as Will, He likes to keep him down here on earth for a long spell and show off His handiwork.''

In spite of her fear, Paulie nodded. Will *was* a fighter. But in this instance, this fight might have been one he could have avoided altogether if he'd had the opportunity to reason with Iris. If she herself had simply stayed put.

Maudie patted her shoulder. ''You did right to bring him here. Dr. Branson is the best in town.''

He certainly must have been the quickest. Though for Paulie the wait seemed an eternity and then some, barely fifteen minutes passed before she heard Trip's bootsteps followed by the doctor's coming up the stairs. ''Thank heavens!'' she said, gratefully relinquishing her seat to the doctor so he could examine Will.

She stepped away, trying not to hear Will's groans when the doctor inspected the wound that the bullet had made. During the extraction that followed, she blindly did as she was told, wishing she had done just that when Will told her to stay outside that barroom. She fetched hot water and bedsheets, ripping the latter into even strips to be used as bandages. The simple task made her feel less helpless.

Finally, as the doctor was wrapping Will in the bandages she had made, Paulie stepped out into the hallway. Trip was there, waiting anxiously for news of Will, trying to stay out of the way.

''The doctor said Will's going to be fine,'' she told him, wiping her brow.

Trip looked relieved, and then frowned, his face becoming almost as pale as Will's had been in the back of the buckboard. ''What did he say about that?''

Paulie looked down at her sleeve, where Trip's gaze was pinned. The material of her shirt was plastered to her arm with dried blood. She gasped. The bullet must have nicked her without her realizing it!

Trip, biting his lip and steering her stiffly back into the sickroom, immediately presented her to the doctor for inspection. Though her wound was insignificant compared to Will's, it stung like the dickens to have it cleaned. Just peeling the shirt off the scrape made her wince.

"I should have gone with Will," Trip said, his tone remorseful once her ordeal was finally over. "He should have waited for me."

"It's no use both of us being full up with regrets over this," Paulie said, brimming with a new determination. "Will's hurt, but he's going to get better. I'm going to make sure of it."

"How are you going to do that?" Trip asked.

Paulie frowned. How, indeed? "For one thing, I'm not going to leave his side till he's able to sit up and give me the devil for the fool way I acted in Las Tres Reinas."

"If I just could have been there…" Trip sighed. "After promising your Daddy I'd keep a lookout for you, too."

Paulie huffed in frustration, and lifted her uninjured hand up to her forehead, almost as if in a salute. "I've had it up to here with men feeling responsibility toward females because of some promises made to their fathers! Do you know what the biggest favor you could do for me now would be?"

Trip hazarded a guess. "Getting you some whiskey to take the sting out of that cut?"

"No," Paulie replied, although that wasn't a half-bad idea. "I want you to go home."

"Home?" Trip repeated. He looked hurt. "Back to Possum Trot?"

Paulie nodded. "And when you get there, tell the Breens to come fetch their daughter."

"To fetch Mary Ann?" he asked. "How's that going to help you or Will?"

"Because I'm not going to leave Will, and we'll never get Will back to Possum Trot until Mary Ann is safe from the clutches of that gambler fellow. And since we can't force Oren Tyler out of town, we'll have to settle for trying to move Mary Ann."

Trip looked at her dubiously. "Does Mary Ann know you're asking me to get her ma and stepfather to drag her back to Possum Trot?"

"No, and I'm not gonna tell her, either. She can just find out when the Breens get here."

"She ain't gonna like it," Trip warned, something Paulie didn't need to be told. "Her folks might not even want to come."

"Make them come. Tell them she's in trouble." She tossed her hands in the air. "Heck, tell 'em she's in jail. Just get them up here."

"Back to Possum Trot," Trip mused. He thought the matter over for just a moment. "I guess it would be good to go see Tessie."

Paulie raised her eyebrows and smiled. "Will said you were off looking at rings. Find anything?"

He flinched. "Just lookin'. I didn't say I was going to do anything rash."

Paulie laughed, surprising herself. She hadn't thought she would ever be able to laugh again. "I wasn't thinking you would, Trip."

Paulie hovered by Will's side all afternoon, watching him drift in and out of consciousness. He never seemed to come fully awake, never seemed to really see her. The doctor had said that he would be fine, but Paulie couldn't bring herself to simply trust his word. To her, Will looked so terrible, so different from his usual robust self.

Terrible, that is, in that he was still pale and clammy in appearance no matter how many of Mrs. Worthington's blankets Paulie piled on top of him. But in another sense, she had never been so free to gaze at Will, and to her eyes he seemed more handsome than ever. She had helped Mrs. Worthington give him a quick bath after the doctor had left, and the fleeting view of his muscled chest had practically stopped her heart. Especially when she saw the rippled muscles covering his stomach, sprinkled with a light dusting of hair that narrowed to a V before disappearing below the bedsheet and out of her sight. At that juncture in the bathing process, Maudie had sent her to the kitchen for more hot water.

But Paulie's imagination was quick to supply what propriety forbade her to see. It wasn't hard to guess that Will was handsome all over, and now that she sat by him, wiping the perspiration off his brow, she felt a little low thinking how physically mismatched they were. He was a perfect specimen of manhood, a man any woman in her right mind would be proud to have at her side, while she…

Well, she wasn't any man's dream. Or if she was, she would have serious doubts about that particular man's sanity. Will could have any woman in the world, in her estimation. Why would he want her? What had ever made her hold out the vain hope that he would?

A shadow appeared from the doorway and Paulie turned, expecting to see Maudie. Instead Mary Ann stood there, watching Will, a stunned look on her face. She came forward in a rush, practically breathless. "What happened?"

"Will went to Las Tres Reinas this morning."

Her blue eyes glittered eagerly. "To talk to Oren?"

Paulie nodded, feeling a familiar surge of dislike for the

woman. For a moment she had thought that Mary Ann might actually care for Will, but her words suggested that Tyler was still forefront in her mind, even while Will was lying near death—or as close to it as Paulie ever wanted him to be. "He took a bullet in the shoulder."

Mary Ann frowned, staring down at the blanket covering Will. "Oren didn't do that!" she exclaimed defensively.

"A woman named Iris did it," Paulie said.

Mary's Ann's tense shoulders sagged in relief. She clucked her tongue. "Oh, poor Will. Is he going to be all right?"

"The doctor says so, but he's so pale—"

Mary Ann didn't even hold her tongue long enough to hear the full prognosis. "I can't wait to ask him what he said to Oren."

Paulie bit her lip. "He went to Las Tres Reinas on your account, I know that."

"Well of course!" Mary Ann said disparagingly, as if pleasing her were the only reason anyone did anything. "I just wonder if Oren's coming here to see me. Were you there?"

Paulie narrowed her gaze on Mary Ann's pinched, worried brow. "I couldn't hear much from where I was." She had assumed that Will was going to the saloon to threaten Oren to stay away from Mary Ann. Could it really be that the opposite was true?

"Then you don't know what Oren said about me?" Mary Ann persisted.

"Not exactly. But I saw enough to know whatever they were talking about wasn't working out very well." Mary Ann's eyes, feverish for a specific answer, took this in without appearing to register the meaning. "It didn't look like Oren was being very cooperative, Mary Ann."

"I was hoping Will would help me!" she exclaimed,

disappointed. The woman was hovering over Will's seriously wounded body—a wound he had acquired on her account—and she acted as though he had let her down somehow. In fact, Mary Ann blinked unhappily, looking like she would gladly have kicked Will's unconscious form. "Oh, what am I going to do now!"

If there was one thing the whole sorry episode at Las Tres Reinas should have taught Paulie, it was to keep her nose out of other people's business. But as she sat looking at Will, with Mary Ann standing fitfully next to her, she couldn't tamp down her need to know one thing.

She tilted a glance at Mary Ann. "Do you mean you're still interested in convincing that gambler fellow to marry you?"

Mary Ann took immediate offense. "Oren wanted to marry me—he just thought there were too many obstacles between ourselves and happiness."

"Like what?"

"Well…like my marriage to Oat." She lifted her pointy chin defensively. "But now that's done with, I'm free to marry whoever I please."

Paulie couldn't believe how mixed up a woman could become in the space of twenty short years of life. She hesitated to point out the obvious to her, especially when it was not to her own benefit to do so, but curiosity demanded she find out what was going on beneath that blond cap of curls. "What do you want to chase after a man like Oren Tyler for? You could just marry Will, couldn't you?"

"Will?" Mary Ann exclaimed in surprise, as if the idea had never even occurred to her before.

"Sure, Will. Hell, he's risked his life for you. That's got to prove he cares for you enough to warrant some consideration."

"But what kind of a husband would he make? He's a cowboy."

"He's always planned on starting up a ranch of his own," Paulie pointed out.

"A ranch!" Mary Ann imbued the simple words with more disgust than Paulie would have thought possible. It was as if the woman were contemplating living in a leper colony. "What would *I* do on a ranch?"

"What have you been doing on that chicken farm all these years?"

"Work!" Mary Ann cried, the simple one-word answer backed by a wellspring of anguish. "That's just the trouble! I don't want to spend the rest of my life doing *that*. Why, everyone knows I wasn't born to do manual labor, or slave over a hot stove all day so some cowboy will have something to eat when he comes in from the outdoors smelling like a farm animal."

Paulie was curious. "So what exactly *were* you born to do?"

Mary Ann frowned in thought, then threw up her hands. "Goodness, I don't know! Nothing in particular, I guess. Is it my fault that I'm a beauty? I'm sure you're very suited to whatever it is you do in that place you run, but you have to admit you might have different ambitions if you had my looks."

Her words made Paulie wince—and then think. Unfortunately, it took only a moment to realize Mary Ann's reasoning was completely wrong. If she were pretty like Mary Ann, she would still want Will. Deep down she knew nothing would ever change that desire. And if she looked like Mary Ann, she bet she would get him. Life just wasn't fair.

"I want to go to Denver with Oren," Mary Ann continued, "and have all the fine things in life I deserve but haven't been able to get my hands on. I'm sure when Oren stops to think about it, he'll agree that we're destined to be together. I've always had a strong sense of destiny.''

What would cause a woman to be so blind? Paulie couldn't understand it. If Will Brockett had just risked his neck for her sake, she would have happily given up everything else to be with him for the rest of her life. ''Aren't you even a little bit grateful to Will?'' she asked.

Mary Ann sighed. ''Poor Will. I guess he's just no match for Oren.''

Paulie thought she might explode like a stick of dynamite. ''Will Brockett is twice the man Oren Tyler is!''

Mary Ann looked at her with faint surprise in her eyes, and a knowing grin touched her lips. ''You certainly have strong opinions, Miss Johnson.''

''You can cut the Miss,'' Paulie said, still feeling her face aflame for revealing so much of her feeling for Will. ''Everyone just calls me Paulie.''

The grin turned to something dangerously close to a sneer. ''Funny, in all the years I've known him, I don't remember Will ever mentioning you by name. He always calls you 'that kid with the freckles.'''

Paulie looked down at Will, certain her face was as red as a sugar beet. ''He likes to tease,'' she mumbled. ''That's just the way we are.''

Mary Ann giggled patronizingly, but she didn't have to say anything more. The implication was clear. Will was like a teasing older brother to her—he would never take her seriously.

''Well,'' Mary Ann said at last. ''Let me know if he gets any better.''

She sashayed out of the room as if she were a royal princess. Just as soon as she left, however, Paulie heard Maudie in the hallway reminding Mary Ann of her rightful place in this particular kingdom.

"Mary Ann, the parlor needs sweeping."

A long-suffering sigh echoed back from the hallway. "But Mrs. Worthington, I'm—"

Maudie cut her off in midwhine. "I always say there's nothing like a good dose of work to take your mind off your troubles."

Without waiting to hear the response to that bromide, the good lady bustled into the room and went straight up to Will. "His color's better," she declared. She put a hand to his forehead and nodded once. "His temperature's down."

Paulie leaned forward and looked at Will more closely. He did have a more normal color in his cheeks. "He was sweating so, I worried that he would die of the fever."

"You were probably watching when his fever broke— before you got tied up talking to Miss Destiny."

Paulie couldn't help smiling.

"All right, I was eavesdropping," Maudie admitted guiltlessly. "That woman gets me as steamed as my old black kettle down in the kitchen! Which reminds me, I've made you a pot of tea."

Paulie looked at her. She hadn't brought a tray up. "But I can't leave Will."

"Certainly you can," Maudie said. "I nursed a child and a husband through much worse than this. The man's sleeping, and he doesn't need your help to do that."

Paulie looked doubtfully at Will, who tossed his head on the pillow. "I suppose not..." Still, she didn't budge.

"Besides," Maudie said, "I have some things I want to show you."

"Things?" Paulie asked.

"Dresses," Maudie explained. "They belonged to my daughter."

Paulie needed no more hints to guess the woman's motives. She shook her head vehemently. "Oh, no," she protested. "Me and dresses are about as compatible as foxes and chickens."

"Now, Miss Paulette, I find that very difficult to believe. A pretty little thing like yourself?"

Flattery would get Maudie nowhere. Paulie continued shaking her head. "I've tried that before."

"And…?"

Did she have to lay bare for the woman the humiliation of her last attempt to impress Will with a skirt and a new hairstyle? "Let's just say it wasn't a success."

Mrs. Worthington planted her hands on her hips. "I refuse to believe it! You obviously didn't have the right woman helping you."

She hadn't had *any* woman helping her, but that was beside the point. "It's not the method that sets things awry, it's the raw materials. I'm just not the type for frills and curls."

"Well, who said anything about frills?" Maudie said. "I'll show you how to do yourself up so's men'll take notice of you—and not because you're trying to be something you're not. I had plenty of practice with my Abra."

In the midst of more adamant head-shaking, Paulie hesitated. She glanced down at Will, who blew out a long, labored sigh that matched a similar sigh building within her own breast. It was so tempting to believe in the miracle Maudie promised she could perform.

"You're in love with that man," Maudie announced.

Paulie flinched at the bold statement, and glanced nervously at Will. He was sleeping soundly, and couldn't possibly have heard Maudie, and yet just having the words said aloud in his presence made Paulie uneasy. "I'm not," she protested. "I just…"

"You just love him so much you would follow him to the ends of the earth," Maudie insisted.

Paulie crossed her arms. "San Antonio isn't *that* far."

"It'll do," the woman said dismissively. "There's no use arguing with me. I've got eyes in my head, and the way you look at that man is exactly the way my Abra used to ogle that German of hers. I managed to get her married, didn't I?"

"Married!" Paulie cried. She had never thought about what the end result would be even if she ever did get Will to like her—any sort of declaration of affection would have been enough for her. But marriage! That seemed about as likely as their taking a romantic stroll to the moon.

"Of course, married. That's what every girl wants, isn't it?"

Paulie sat staring openmouthed at the woman. She just wasn't used to lumping herself in the same category with "every girl." "Maybe so, but every girl doesn't wear britches and run a saloon."

Maudie Worthington folded her arms over her ample chest and slanted Paulie a look of pure determination. "No, and in about thirty minutes, *you* won't be wearing britches, either."

Abra's old dresses fit Paulie to a tee, and Maudie had chosen one that was a simple but pretty white pattern with tiny pink cabbage roses, with a high neckline and simple long sleeves. She also managed to free Paulie's hair from its usual braid and tame the locks into a loose, manageable bundle tied in a chignon at the nape of her neck. Paulie couldn't have been more shocked at the results of the lady's tinkering with her appearance. Why, she didn't look so silly at all! Unfamiliar, maybe.

Or maybe not. In her father's things there was a little drawing of her mother, dressed in a blue gown with a cameo at the neck. Her hair was tied back simply, highlighting her slightly upturned nose and pointy chin, and her green eyes that sparkled with intelligence and kindness that even some unknown artist had seen. Paulie didn't want to be too optimistic, but to her own eyes she resembled nothing so much as that picture of her mother.

"Turn around, Paulie, and let me get a look at you."

She did as she was told and whirled as gracefully as she knew how—which wasn't difficult. She'd never felt as light and feminine as she did now.

Or as much like a sausage encased in a muslin skin. She had tried to convince Mrs. Worthington to forego the corset, but the woman had insisted, even after seeing the bruises slashing across Paulie's middle.

"This'll work better than any bandages," Maudie had declared, lacing Paulie up snugly.

Now the woman nodded approvingly at the fruits of her efforts. "Abra was a little more long-waisted than you, but besides a little bunching, you look as pretty as a flower."

Paulie ducked her head and blushed. A flower! "A goat weed, maybe."

The lady frowned and waved a finger admonishingly at her newly transformed friend. "The first lesson you've got to learn is not to put yourself down. You're a lovely girl, and there's no reason why you shouldn't be perfectly self-assured around people."

"Self-assured," Paulie repeated, feeling much as she did in school when she'd had to learn unfamiliar grammar rules by rote.

Maudie added with a sage nod, "'Course, there's no reason to take that idea too far down the road, like our Miss Destiny up in the attic. You don't want to be considered vain."

Slim chance she had of that! Paulie mused to herself,

although she left the forbidden self-deprecating thought unvoiced.

"Now let me see you walk," Maudie commanded.

Paulie froze. "Walk?" she asked, suddenly feeling anything but self-assured.

Maudie nodded. "Just across the room and back."

She made it sound so simple. But the moment Paulie took two steps, she knew something was terribly wrong. That old awkwardness she had felt when tromping around in her mother's wedding dress returned. She stopped midway across the room and looked at her friend in despair.

"Perhaps if you took smaller steps..." Maudie's suggestion was gentle but firm. "You're not wearing work boots now, you know."

Paulie lifted her skirt and marvelled again at how delicate her feet looked encased in a pair of soft leather shoes with a small but shapely heel. She'd never seen such an expensive-looking pair of shoes—and Maudie Worthington wanted her to simply *take* them, even though she'd only known her a few short days.

"Gracious, don't just stand there staring at the things—walk," Maudie instructed. She even got up and minced daintily across the room for Paulie's benefit.

Paulie attempted to follow suit, but feared her best stab at grace resembled nothing so much as a drunken crane picking its way across a lagoon.

Maudie bit her lip. "That's not a bad start. Now just take your hands off your hips."

Paulie frowned. This directive posed a serious problem. "Where should I put them?"

"At your sides."

"Usually I tuck my thumbs into my belt," Paulie told her, giving a little demonstration of her usual stance, digging her hands into the waist of the pretty pink-and-white dress, and rocking back on her heels. "I feel sort of awkward with my hands just dangling."

Maudie smiled patiently. "What you're doing now looks perfectly *un*natural."

Paulie forced her hands down to her sides, and put one foot in front of the other. After a few more steps, she tossed her fitful hands up in the air in dismay. "Well, it feels perfectly ridiculous." Who would have thought just walking would be so damn difficult?

"You'll get used to it."

But would she ever get used to the strangled feeling she got from being buttoned into a dress that was so tight around her middle? Or to the off-center, tippy feeling she got from wearing shoes other than her sturdy old boots? It was one thing to want to look pretty and feminine, but those qualities weren't particularly comfortable.

She sank down onto her bed in a fit of doubt. "I thank you for what you're trying to do, Maudie, but I'm afraid it won't work. I'm not Mary Ann."

The good woman put her hands on her hips and eyeballed Paulie severely. "In this woman's opinion you should be down on your hands and knees thanking the good Lord that you aren't like that unfortunate girl up there. Maybe you don't have blond curls, but you're pretty just the same, and what's more, you've got something she sorely lacks, and that's a heart."

Paulie blinked. A few hours ago, she wouldn't have thought much of Maudie's assurances. Who cared about hearts and all that blather? Most of the time—especially when she was thinking about Will—her own heart felt like a broken-down wreck. Now things seemed different. She *felt* different, and it wasn't just because she was wearing a dress.

Mere hours before she had sworn that if Will managed

to open his eyes again and get well, she would try not to be upset if he and Mary Ann got married and lived as happy as a fairy tale couple. But that was before she had spoken to Mary Ann. The young woman was so callous, so blind to all that Will wanted to do for her, the sacrifices he was so obviously willing to make for her. Mary Ann *was* heartless.

Will deserved better. Paulie wasn't certain that she herself was any prize, but she loved Will. And if snatching Will's attention meant prancing around in an uncomfortable dress and feeling as if she were being slowly squeezed to death by her underwear, then so be it. With some practice, and a little help from Maudie, she would go on breathing and perhaps even manage not to stumble over her own skirts, and hold her arms at her sides as though they were actually part of her body and not some awkward sticks nailed into her shoulders by an inept carpenter.

And maybe, just maybe, when Will opened his eyes, Paulie could make him see that *she* was more worthy of his affection than Mary Ann.

Chapter Twelve

Will had always assumed Heaven would be a lot more comfortable than this. His whole body felt clammy, and there was a biting throb in his shoulder that wouldn't go away. His head didn't ache so much as it felt like someone had stuffed it full of cotton. And just when he thought things couldn't get worse, somebody rustling around him would pile something on top of him, and his world would become a few degrees hotter.

Perhaps he *hadn't* gone to Heaven, he began to worry. Though he was too woozy to remember with exact clarity, he was fairly certain that he hadn't been a saint in his lifetime. There were things he had handled badly. Like that whole situation with Mary Ann.

And Paulie. A vague memory of kissing her swirled through his mind, along with the remembrance of how it felt to hold her soft body in his arms. She'd been getting under his skin, and to his surprise, he hadn't minded one bit. Even the fact that she was in love with Trip Peabody didn't deter his growing ardor for his old friend.

His sudden romantic urges for her were as wrong as they were unsettling. Trip might be marrying Tessie, but Paulie was still stuck on him. And maybe that was just as well.

Paulie was just too stubborn, too much like a pal for him to be serious about. Wasn't she? That's what he'd always liked about her, what made her safe to joke with and share a drink with. Perhaps his own feelings were just a passing phase, a result of the whole mixed-up situation with Mary Ann.

Maybe he just needed to spend a long afternoon on the second floor of Las Tres Reinas.

That definitely mortal, earthy thought made him groan.

If on the off-chance he ever made it back to the land of the living, he would handle things differently. Especially women. He'd behave with more sense. He would settle things with Mary Ann, and he'd leave Paulie Johnson strictly alone. She was—a friendly sort, not the kind for a man to be fantasizing about.

A second chance, he mused. Perhaps he hadn't died at all—though that hope didn't seem likely. The woman with the gun hadn't been ten feet away from him, and for what seemed like hours, he had felt the life being drained out of him while good old Paulie tried to get him out of that saloon. And then the world had gone black.

Nah. He wasn't alive. Couldn't be. And he *was* in Heaven. He knew that now because there was an angel floating around him. Her shadowy figure flitted about in the twilight around him, first standing close to him, then dancing away, then hovering ever closer to him. He squinted, trying to make her out. He'd always wanted to know what one of those gossamer-winged creatures looked like. His mama had told him a long time ago that the beauty of the angels was almost blinding. He remembered because when he'd first seen Mary Ann, he'd thought of his mother's words. Appearances could be deceiving.

Take this little angel tending him, for instance. Looking at her more closely, he saw that her beauty wasn't anywhere close to the blinding kind—and yet it had a more subtle, alluring quality. Her figure was willowy, framed by a dress fashioned quite like those mortal women wore; it wasn't just white, but white with a little flowery pattern in it. Very pretty. And then her hair wasn't loose, either, as he would have expected, but tied neatly back. But the brown feathery tresses framing her face seemed lit from beyond, creating a delicate halo around her.

No wings, though. Where were the wings?

"Will?"

She knew his name and said it in such a familiar way that bells started ringing in his head. But he supposed bells went with the vaunted territory, too. Harps would probably come later.

"Will, can you hear me?"

Land's sake, she sounded just like Paulie! Will shook his head, trying to get some of the cotton out so he could appreciate the sights and sounds of his new home without his old life horning in. But the clearer his head felt, the more he was certain that he actually *had* heard Paulie's voice. And when his little angel tiptoed closer, he saw that she also bore a striking resemblance to Paulie.

He felt his heart race as he tried to understand the implications of her being there. His only thought was that he had led her into trouble again, and failed to protect her—this time with fatal results.

"Paulie!" he exclaimed, though it sounded as if the word had come out a whisper. "Are you in Heaven now, too?"

Light laughter rang through the room, a familiar sound more welcome to his ears than any trumpets, harps or bells. "I'll agree Maudie keeps a nice house, but Heaven would be an exaggeration."

Will blinked in confusion. Maudie's. Mrs. Worthington's. Slowly, bits and pieces of what had happened in the days before his getting shot came back to him—Mary Ann's disappearance, Night Bird, Oat's death. Finding Mary Ann at the woman's boardinghouse. Will swallowed. He wasn't dead, and neither was Paulie. That was good, he guessed. Except now he would probably have to wait a whole lot longer for the pain in his shoulder to go away.

"Oh, Will," Paulie said, sounding more resoundingly like her old self. "I'm so glad you're feeling better!"

He groaned again. Better? He felt like his body had been stampeded by a herd of longhorns!

"Maudie's making some broth for you, in case you're hungry."

Hungry. He *was* hungry, and attempted a nod to let her know. "Broth," he repeated. Lord, he felt suddenly that he could have eaten a huge plate of steak and potatoes. "Maybe a little bread, too?"

"You must be feeling better," Paulie teased. "But the doc didn't say a thing about stuffing you full of food just yet."

Will shook his head on the soft pillow. "It makes sense that if you were going to turn nurse, you'd decide to become the mean snippety kind."

"Well, I like that!" Paulie exclaimed, her hands on her hips in an old familiar gesture. Although now that Will thought about it, there was something decidedly *un*familiar about it, too. "After all I've done for you. After all I've worried!"

He shook his head. "As I recall, your first deed was running half-cocked into the saloon when I had the situation well in hand."

Her defiant expression fell away, and she rushed forward, practically kneeling at the bedside, her back bowed in contrition. "I know, Will. I'm such a darn fool. You told me to stay outside, and by gum, I should have done it! If it weren't for me you wouldn't be in this condition.''

He stared in some confusion at the back of her head. Was this the old spirited Paulie, apologizing so profusely, without a defensive word to say about his arrogance, his high-handedness? It didn't seem possible.

He reached out and touched the back of her neck, giving it a reassuring rub. His eyes narrowed. Her hair was tied back neatly in one of those doohickeys women sometimes wore. And this getup she had on wasn't what she usually wore, either. A dress—the white one with roses that he'd mistaken for an angel's garb. Good heavens!

She pulled back from him, slowly coming to standing, her hands folded demurely in front of her. ''And I want you to know, Will, that from now on I'll do just as you say. I'll never snipe at you or be bad-tempered or stubborn again.''

He gaped at her, wondering suddenly whether this was all just a dream after all. Paulie was standing before him in a dress saying that she wasn't ever going to argue with him again. This state of affairs certainly had nothing in common with the world as he'd known it when that woman had shot him.

''What's the matter, Will?'' she asked, two little worry lines appearing just above the bridge of her pert nose. ''Are you feeling poorly again?''

He reached a hand up to his forehead, rubbing it to see if he could alleviate some of the achiness, some of the confusion that seemed to stem from there. Back when he'd thought he was dead, he'd almost had things sorted out. But now he was looking at Paulie and she seemed almost, well…pretty. How was he supposed to raise a glass and stay friends with someone like *that?*

''Good Lord, Paulie, what did you do to yourself?''

Her frown deepened. "What do you mean?"

He waved a hand to indicate her sudden transformation. "That outfit you've got on!"

Two splotches of red rushed to her cheeks, and she smiled, twirling lightly, as if he'd just paid her the highest compliment. "Do you like it? Maudie found it for me out of her daughter's things. I think it's the most elegant little dress I've ever worn."

He grunted in dismay, but was unable to take his eyes off the alluring way the dress clung to Paulie's figure. He couldn't remember a woman with such a tiny waistline. "It's practically the *only* dress you've ever worn."

"Well, yes." She laughed. "Takes some getting used to after years of wearing men's duds."

Will attempted to cross his arms but was stopped by the sudden pain in his shoulder.

"Oh, be careful!" Paulie said, rushing forward. She hovered over him, checking the dressing on his shoulder. Her skirts rustled as she moved, and he could smell a light perfume wafting toward him as she covered his forehead with her hand. Paulie Johnson—wearing perfume!

"Your temperature seems to be down."

Will forced himself to take his eyes off the gentle, seductive slope of her neck. The dress's cut was conservative and chaste, and yet hugged her body so closely that a man didn't have to use much imagination about what was beneath those layers of innocent muslin.

What was her game? He thought about Trip, and the possibility that while she had the man here in San Antonio, she was trying one last-ditch effort to win him back from Tessie Hale. How sad.

How irritating. She was a good-looking girl. What did she want to waste her time on a man like Trip Peabody for? She needed someone who was more of a match for her. Someone young and feisty, and reliable. Someone more like…well, more like himself.

He frowned, forcing himself to think about something else. "What are all these blankets for?"

"You had a chill," Paulie said patiently.

Patiently! Her sudden feminine calm agitated him all the more. She'd probably been working on *that* for Trip's benefit, too. "That's no reason to smother me half to death."

"We wanted your fever to break."

"Well, it's broken. And now I feel as though someone had put me on a spit and roasted me for a few hours."

"Goodness!" Paulie exclaimed good-naturedly as she responded to his unspoken command and removed one of the blankets. "Who would ever have guessed you'd be such a cranky patient?"

Her teasing nearly drove him over the edge. "How's a man supposed to feel when he wakes up with a headache and a pain in his shoulder and discovers that the world's turned upside down?"

She stopped folding the blanket and shot him a curious stare. "Everything's just the same as it was this morning, Will. Still right side up as far as I can tell."

He let out a surly chuckle. "Maybe you haven't looked in the mirror then."

Her fingers gripped the blanket with white knuckles. "What's wrong with the way I look?" she asked slowly.

"Everything!" He nodded curtly at the dress that fit her so lovingly and gritted his teeth. Here he was determined to be decent and honorable and treat her like a pal—and what did she do but go and get herself gussied up so that she looked nothing like his old friend at all! "That getup looks ridiculous on you. Why, it's like a chicken wearing peacock feathers."

Her chin raised just a notch—enough to let him know

her vow of agreeableness was being sorely tested. "There's nothing particularly flashy about this dress, Will," she said, her voice frosty.

"Why do you have to wear a dress at all? What happened to your britches and work shirt?"

"You used to make fun of me for wearing those clothes, if you'll recall."

He watched her foot, encased in a pair of kid leather boots, tapping silently but impatiently. "I never knew you to shy away from a little joking," he said, knowing it was wrong to needle her. Yet at the same time, there was something comforting about bantering with her. "If it's ridicule you're afraid of," he said, "you'd better do something about your hair."

Her hand flew to the back of her head, and her cheeks turned from rosy red to angry crimson. "My hair looks fine!"

He nodded. "It would look especially accommodating to a mouse looking for a place to make a nest."

Her eyes narrowed on him, but he could see the fire flashing in their green depths. "You are a sad little varmint, Will Brockett, and if I'd had any sense I would have just left you to bleed to death all over the floor of the Three Queens!"

He laughed. "And you said you would never be bad-tempered again."

She stomped her daintily clad foot and marched over to him. "That was back when I felt sorry for you!" She shook out the blanket in one brittle snap and laid it back over him, raising his temperature in all sorts of ways. "Maybe this will sweat some of the meanness out of you!"

And with that, she turned on her heel and strode out the door, wobbling only once on the unfamiliar shoes before she disappeared from sight.

The minute she left, Will missed her. His smile disappeared, and he closed his eyes. Why did she have to stomp out just when things were beginning to seem a little more regular between them? Maybe he'd been a little too rough with her. Despite her quirks and whims, Paulie had more pride than most women he knew. He wouldn't want to hurt her feelings irreparably.

Also, he realized gloomily, all he'd managed to achieve was to send her fleeing back to Trip's arms. She was probably with him now, crying on his shoulder. Trip never teased her so unmercifully.

Not that it was his business whether Trip married Paulie, Tessie Hale, or both, he amended for his own benefit. It just didn't make any difference to him, when it came right down to it. It was only the lack of logic that bothered him.

If he lived to be a hundred, Will would never understand women. Or why they set their hearts on such improbable objects of affection. Mary Ann and Oren Tyler. Paulie and Trip Peabody. Of course, *he* had spent years thinking he and Mary Ann would be a match, but he had come to his senses. He didn't feel love for her, but an obligation to her family that seemed an even stronger bond than pure affection.

Women, on the other hand, when faced with undeniable facts, seemed never to grasp the folly of their own hearts.

"I hate him!" Paulie exclaimed, setting down the pot with a crash of metal against metal. She looked into the stove and heaped a few more chunks of wood onto the fire, which didn't feel nearly as hot as she did inside. "I only wish Iris had better aim! I should have gone back to Possum Trot with Trip, and left that low-down snake in the clutches of Mary Ann. She wouldn't have raised a finger to make sure he was warm enough, or was sleeping comfortably. She—"

Maudie cut her off. "What are you doing?" she asked, her brow wrinkling.

Paulie looked down at the kettle. "Heating some broth for Will."

The woman smiled. "Should you be going to such pains for someone you hate?"

Paulie tapped her foot impatiently. "It's not just for him," she muttered. "I could use some myself, too."

"I can't imagine what he said to make you so angry so fast."

Paulie brayed with outrage. "What *didn't* he say? The man lobbed so many insults at me I couldn't keep up with him!"

"About your appearance?"

She got angry all over again just thinking about it. "He told me I looked like a chicken in peacock feathers—and that I should just go back to wearing pants because no man in his right mind would find me attractive."

Actually he *hadn't* said that last bit, but the meaning had been implied. At least in Paulie's mind. He had looked at her with such horror and ridicule, it had been worse than the time when she'd dressed up in her mother's wedding dress, even. Maybe because back then she hadn't acknowledged the fact that she was in love with him. That bitter fact burned in her mind now. How could she have lost her heart to such a mean, insulting creature!

"I don't even know what I'm doing here," she said, waiting impatiently for the broth to heat. "He and Mary Ann belong together."

Maudie shook her head, chuckling. "My dear, you're just not thinking like a woman."

"Good!" she cried. "I can't wait to get back home. Back there I did just fine thinking like a saloon keeper."

"You'll never win Will that way."

She harrumphed decisively. "He's no prize."

"You're taking his insults the wrong way," Maudie lectured. "You're forgetting that men tend to be backwards creatures. The male mind is an ornery thing."

"I'll say!" Paulie cried, pulling the pot off the stove, ready or not. She splashed hot broth into the bowl waiting on the table. "If Will wants Mary Ann so much, why doesn't he just say so instead of blathering on about duty and getting my hopes up with meaningless kisses and…"

Her words trailed off at the same moment that mortification filled her. She couldn't believe that she'd just blurted out that Will had kissed her! What would Maudie think?

By the arch of her brows, she could tell the woman thought this tidbit of news was interesting in the extreme. "He doesn't want Mary Ann," Maudie said emphatically.

Paulie, pouring a cup of broth for herself, spilled the brown liquid down the front of her dress. She jumped back, both in reaction to the hot liquid and horror at possibly ruining Abra Worthington's beautiful dress. "Oh, no!" she cried.

"Don't worry about it. I'll show you how to remove a stain like that. Simplest thing in the world."

Paulie felt like crying. Dress or no dress, she was as awkward and clumsy as ever. "Will might not love Mary Ann, but he certainly has no feelings for me."

"There's where you're wrong," Mrs. Worthington said. "And I'll prove it to you."

"How?"

"All you have to do is take that broth up to him, and do exactly as I say."

Paulie wasn't quite ready to face Will again. She lowered

her eyes to her lap and discovered the perfect excuse. "I'll have to change clothes, and I'll be switched if I'm gonna let him think I changed back into my britches on his account!"

"You won't be wearing your pants."

"I won't?"

Maudie shook her head. "For one thing, I'm cleaning them. For another, I've got another dress picked out for you that will serve our purpose quite nicely."

Paulie tilted her head skeptically. "And then what am I supposed to do?"

"Nothing that you haven't done before, apparently. Just let him kiss you."

Paulie nearly jumped out of her skin. Surely she hadn't heard correctly! "Why should I let that varmint touch me?" she cried. Then, realizing how absurdly presumptuous she must sound, she added, "Not that he'd want to."

A knowing little smile touched the older woman's lips. "Ah, but I'm going to prove that kissing you is exactly what Will Brockett wants to do."

Will glanced up and felt his mouth drop open in astonishment. Paulie, looking radiant in a mauve dress that was every bit as shapely as the other one but ten times more revealing, stood in the doorway holding a tray and smiling at him.

He hadn't known what to expect. Truly, after his performance earlier, he hadn't thought Paulie would pay him a visit anytime soon. After his scathing review of her appearance, he assumed she would have changed into her old clothes—not yet another, and more revealing, dress. Her hair was the same, only this time his gaze wasn't drawn to her face. Instead, the cut of the dress drew his eyes to its low, scalloped neckline, and the way it fit snugly over the hips before the skirt flared out. What surprised him most was how at ease she appeared, how naturally the material seemed to suit her. A week ago he couldn't have imagined Paulie in such a creation. Now he wondered if he would ever shake the image out of his head.

She swept regally into the room. "Sorry I stayed away so long," she said. "I forgot that I had promised you some hot broth."

Will licked his lips, and his eyes reluctantly jumped from the creamy white of the skin of Paulie's breasts to the aged white of the china. Food! The thought made his stomach grumble in anticipation, and yet his eyes strayed from the broth to the perfect redness of Paulie's lips. The pink tones of the dress brought out her natural healthy color.

She set the tray down on the table next to the bed, then reached out to him. "Here, let me prop you up." She gently lifted him by his good shoulder and wedged several plump pillows behind his back until he was nearly upright. "We don't want you to get woozy."

But he was almost woozy just from the nearness of her, and that perfume she was wearing. She must have sprayed some more on when she changed clothes. He almost panicked when he saw her turn to walk toward the door again. He didn't want her to leave.

"Wait!"

She turned, arching a brow at him questioningly.

"Aren't you going to stay and feed me?" he asked. "I, uh, don't think I can manage myself."

She smiled. "I'm sorry, I should have thought of that."

"No need to apologize," he said. "In fact, I guess it's I who should be apologizing to you. I was awfully cranky a little while ago. I said some things I regret."

She tilted her head. "Like what?" she asked, all innocence.

He hesitated, not quite trusting that this wasn't a trap. In the old days, just mentioning names he had called her would rile her up all over again. "I shouldn't have compared you to a chicken," he said, testing the words gingerly.

She laughed. "Apology accepted. But don't expect me to say I'm sorry, too. I still think you're a varmint." She lifted a spoonful of broth to his lips. "Why, I was so mad at you that I spilled broth down my other dress and had to put this one on. You like it?"

Will swallowed. The broth quelled his hunger immediately, but there was another niggling ache building inside him, one that grew stronger when Paulie leaned closer to him to give him another spoonful of nourishment.

"It's very beautiful," he managed.

She smiled, and for the first time he noticed what white even teeth she had. What a pretty mouth. What very kissable lips. But of course, he'd discovered that twice before. And he had regretted kissing her both times. He attempted to look away as another spoonful of broth came toward his mouth.

"Yes, I certainly was steamed," she chattered on. "I called you all sorts of terrible things to Maudie!"

He moaned. "She must not think much of me."

"Nonsense. She likes you very much. She even said you were handsome." Paulie laughed. "We had a big argument about it."

Will opened his mouth, only to have a spoonful of broth slopped in, drowning out his question. He choked it down and sat up a little straighter. "If Maudie was saying I was handsome, what were you saying?"

She lifted her shoulders, and he noticed how chiseled her neckline seemed. How pertly her head rested on those strong but delicate shoulders. "Just that you were nothing too special."

He felt his jaw tighten. "You think I'm just an ordinary-looking fellow, do you?"

"Well, certainly." She smiled teasingly. "What do you think?"

He turned his head away stubbornly when she offered him more broth. "I suppose *you're* only attracted to older men. Like Trip."

"Trip *is* handsome," she allowed. "But I'm not incapable of appreciating good looks, young or old."

He couldn't believe he was even having this conversation with Paulie at all, much less that he was coming out so badly. "I haven't heard any complaints from other women," he said, hating how vain he sounded, yet unable to help himself.

She laughed again. "Well, I suppose it's just my unworldliness talking. I just sort of go by instinct, you know. Some men attract me, some men don't." She lifted the spoon again. "More broth?"

"No," he said, clamping his mouth shut.

"Well, there's no reason to be petulant, Will. Lord knows you've got plenty of admirers."

He cocked his head. "Who?"

She thought for a moment. A long moment. Too long. "Well, for instance…" She stopped to think, as if dredging a name from some deep recess of her memory. "Oh! There's Tunia!"

Will drew a blank. "Tunia?"

"Petunia Sweeney, over in Cobb City."

Good Lord! "Petunia the Tuna?"

Paulie rolled her eyes. "Children are so mean! No one's called her that for years, Will. Her family bought a bathtub over at Dwight's back in eighty-one, and now lots of men even say she's a good partner for dancing.''

If Petunia Sweeney was his one admirer, he was in trouble. "'Course, I'm not around as much as I used to be,'' he said, giving an explanation for this deficit of females swooning over him.

"And that most likely explains it,'' Paulie said, misunderstanding. "Tunia probably still remembers how you looked a couple of years ago.''

Wait a second. He frowned. "What's that supposed to mean?''

"Well, you can't doubt that several trips to Kansas and back can…weather a man.''

Weather! "You're a fine one to talk!'' he argued. "You're half gone for a man whose face looks like old boot leather!''

"That's not a very nice way to talk about a friend,'' Paulie said.

Will beat his fist lightly against the covers. "Some friend! I haven't seen hide nor hair of him since my brush with death.''

Paulie clucked her tongue. "My, my. You are feeling sorry for yourself, aren't you?''

He reddened. "Well, where is he? What have you two been doing all day?''

She laughed at him. "For your information, Trip went back to Possum Trot.''

Will perked up at this news. "Did you send him back there?''

"Yes I did.''

Suddenly, he felt hearty enough to do a little jig. "Why?''

"To fetch the Breens.''

This news was almost too good to be true. Someone

would be arriving soon to take the Mary Ann problem out of his hands. "Paulie, you *are* an angel!"

She looked at him skeptically. "You're talking off your head."

He laughed and took a closer look at Paulie. She'd sent Trip away—and back to the same town Tessie lived. All this dressing up wasn't for Trip's benefit, then. And since there was no other man in the house...

A slow, lazy smile spread across his lips, and he reached out and grabbed her with his good arm. Paulie stiffened, and looked at him with guarded eyes.

"What's the matter?" she asked.

"I was just thinking about what we were talking about earlier."

She swallowed, and he saw that a flush heated her neck, bared by her low-cut dress. "Wh-what was that?"

"About your not being attracted to me."

"Oh." She swallowed again. "Well, I suppose if we're going to start repeating ourselves, I'd do just as well to take the tray back down..."

He held fast to her. "I was thinking about when I kissed you."

Her green eyes looked down at him sharply. "You were?"

He nodded. "You didn't seem so unattracted to me then."

She attempted a nonchalant shrug, but he could feel the tightening in her body, and felt his own coiling in response.

"Maybe your instincts aren't as clear-cut as you seem to think they are."

"Nonsense!" Paulie cried, her voice hoarse from tension. "I suppose I know my own mind. Besides, that first time we kissed you were only providing a little demonstration. It would be hard for a girl to be carried away by a kissing lesson.''

''And the second time?''

She tugged at her arm. ''This is silly! I really should be going....''

He nodded. ''All right, but first I propose a little experiment.''

She eyed him warily. ''What kind of experiment?''

''I'll kiss you, and if you don't show any sign of appreciation, I'll have to accept your word that you're simply not attracted to me.''

''That doesn't sound very scientific.''

''Oh, but it would be. We'd have three instances to judge by. If two out of three are tepid responses, then I'll know I should go straight to Cobb City from here and propose to Tunia Sweeney.''

She laughed. ''Oh, all right,'' she said, almost gritting her teeth as she said the words. ''I suppose it can't hurt...as long as it's just an experiment.''

''Just an experiment,'' he repeated.

He tugged her toward him, not at all sure kissing her was wise, but certain it was irresistible. Her lips touched his lightly at first, tentatively. He held his breath, waiting, then realized she was too. Her whole body was tensed, waiting. Defensive. Prepared not to show the slightest response to his touch.

He darted his tongue out to trace the outline of her lips, and she let out a little breathless gasp. It was amazing she didn't faint dead away from lack of air. He pulled her closer, plundering her lips, deepening the kiss. Her own tongue touched his, featherlight, causing his already rigid body to press closer still to hers. Lord, she was a luscious thing. Why had he never seen it? Did he really have so little imagination that he couldn't see how she had blossomed under his very nose?

He couldn't recall when it had happened. Only now, holding her in his arms, did he fully appreciate how the years had changed her, changed both of them. He was no longer clinging to the idea of Mary Ann. Paulie was no longer impossibly youthful. Instead, the sprout he had always teased had blossomed into the woman he had never dreamed of finding.

"Oh, Will," she said on a sigh, leaning into him.

White-hot pain shot through his shoulder, and he let out a sharp yelp of shock.

Paulie jumped back off him, her face mottled red and white. "What happened?"

"My shoulder!"

She gasped. "Oh, dear! I shouldn't have..." Her hand flew to her mouth when she remembered exactly what she had done. "Oh, no, I shouldn't have at all! You wait right here—I've got to talk to Maudie!"

"Maudie?" Confused, Will gritted his teeth as he watched her retreat in a swirl of mauve. "What for?"

"Never mind—I just do!"

"Ask her for some brandy!" he called out before she disappeared. "Lots of it."

He relaxed back against the pillows and tried to think about something besides the pain. Like Paulie. And their little experiment. Right now it seemed to him like a little miracle.

He grinned, and placed one hand behind his head as he looked up at the ceiling. His thoughts were a jumble, but one thing was wonderfully clear. He wouldn't have to propose to Petunia the Tuna anytime soon.

Chapter Thirteen

"Didn't I tell you?" Maudie asked smugly as she folded a batch of newly ironed sheets. "He kissed you, and with you doing nothing but sitting there talking to him."

Elbow propped up on the table, Paulie buried her cheek in her hand and sighed fretfully. She'd come down from Will's room ten minutes ago, but her heart still felt fluttery and jumpy. "Oh, but I went and messed it all up by kissin' him back."

The woman winked at her. "I'm sure he didn't consider the experience messed up."

"He was just trying to prove that I think he's good-looking. He didn't really want to kiss me. Then I went and jumped all over him, losing the bet and embarrassing myself to boot."

"Sometimes a little embarrassment pays off in the end."

Paulie frowned. "How so?"

Maudie planted her hands on her hips and pinned her with her sternest gaze, just like Paulie had seen her do with Mary Ann. "Goodness sakes, Paulette. Did it never occur to you that Will might actually find *you* attractive? That he might have actually have kissed you simply because he thinks you're a pretty girl?"

At the odd sound of someone using the words "pretty girl" in conjunction with her own name, a whiplash moved through Paulie's spine and she sat up ramrod-straight, stunned at the very notion that her attraction to Will might be mutual. The idea seemed dangerous—like stepping off the edge of a cliff. Unrequited love had been her best friend for so long, she didn't know whether she had the heart to bid it farewell.

But he *had* kissed her, she thought, her mind clinging fervently to that single fact. Kissed her three times, all told. Three. That number was comforting. One was so paltry—one kiss might very well be a gamble, or worse, a mistake. Two could be considered a fluke. But three kisses added up to something.

A smile spread across her face, and she was just about to present her triad theory to Maudie, only to discover that the woman's mind had already wandered to more pressing matters. "Now where is that girl?" she fussed, referring without a doubt to Mary Ann. "I swear! Two dollars a week is money thrown away if I'm going to be doing all the work all the time!"

She put the iron back on the hearth and scurried to the door. "Mary Ann!" she bellowed toward the staircase, causing Paulie to wince. There was no doubt in her mind that the sound carried all the way up to the attic. If Joshua had been lacking for a trumpet at the battle of Jericho, he could have just used Maudie instead.

As it turned out, her lung power was wasted. Mary Ann appeared at the back door. "Here I am," she said, her voice unusually mild and pleasing as she sashayed into the kitchen. "I was just coming to help you do the ironing."

Both Paulie and Maudie eyed her skeptically. "Well…good," the older woman said, not quite trusting this biddability in her servant. She picked up an armful of sheets. "I'll just carry these up to the linen closet."

Paulie, suddenly realizing she was about to be abandoned to Mary Ann's company, sprang out of her chair. "Oh, let me—" she begged.

Maudie shook her head curtly. "No, no. Sit down and enjoy your tea."

And then she was gone. Paulie turned slowly and trudged back to her seat at the table, glancing once at Mary Ann, whose lips were turned up in a big but somehow less-than-heartfelt smile. Paulie sat down. The silence between them stretched like India rubber.

"Well!" Mary Ann exclaimed suddenly, breaking up their vocal logjam. "It seems that Will has taken a shine to you."

Paulie's face reddened. There was no telling how long Mary Ann had been standing at the back door. How much had she heard? She shrugged helplessly, wishing herself anywhere else in the world. It was bad enough discussing Will with Maudie, but to have Mary Ann of all people knowing her secret yearnings was simply unbearable. "I'm sure he can't care much for me," she answered modestly. "Not really."

Mary Ann nodded approvingly as she spread a sheet over Mrs. Worthington's ironing table. "It's smart of you to take a realistic attitude."

Her words stopped Paulie cold. "Realistic?"

The other woman gestured dismissively toward Paulie's mauve dress. "It's only natural that he would look at you differently now that you've changed your appearance a bit." Her insincere little smile spread until a dimple appeared in her cheek. "You really do look sweet. Who would have ever guessed?"

Paulie shifted, feeling anger well up inside her. How could a compliment sound so insulting?

"But don't you mind Will," Mary Ann counselled. "He's always been a flirt—he probably just never thought to turn his charm on you before."

Paulie scowled. Mary Ann was trying to tell her Will didn't care a fig for her. But Maudie had said that he probably did. And there was the matter of those three kisses. "I've never known Will to be insincere."

A peal of laughter escaped Mary Ann's lips. "Then you can't know him like I do. You'd be better off guarding your heart against Will before it's too late," Mary Ann counseled her. "I know I am. I don't care how much he declares he still cares for me."

Paulie sat stunned. "He said that?"

Mary Ann stared at her as if she were a ninny. "Why did you think he came all this way looking for me?"

Why, indeed. Paulie felt her skin turn clammy. She'd known from the first that Will was carrying a powerful torch for Mary Ann. Why had she allowed herself to forget that? Probably because of the way she'd caught him looking at her sometimes—but Mary Ann said that was the way he looked at every woman.

And yet…the idea of trying to stop loving Will caused something in her to rise up and rebel against Mary Ann's advice. "But Will kissed me!"

Mary Ann smiled pityingly at her. "A kiss isn't enough to build a future on."

At the woman's patronizing tone, Paulie's fists balled at her sides, and she couldn't help herself from blurting out, "He kissed me *three* times!"

Despite her prior certainty that the number three was evidence of a serious interest on Will's part, she immediately felt foolish.

It didn't help when Mary Ann began to laugh at her again. "Three kisses or twenty—that just means a man's healthy, not that he cares about you. Kisses and even love-making can be vain promises, Paulie."

Paulie looked long and hard at Mary Ann. Will was right, she was beautiful. Men had loved her. And things still weren't working right for her. The idea depressed Paulie. Mary Ann was so experienced, she must know what she was talking about. She'd had three different men love her, and Paulie was having a hard time nailing down just one. And now she learned that she couldn't even trust the indications she'd taken as positive signs!

She stood on wobbly feet and careened toward the door, shaken by their conversation. "I think I'll go up to bed now. It's been a long day."

Mary Ann nodded. "'Night," she said casually, as if they had been chatting about something completely insignificant, like the weather.

Instead, Paulie felt as if the very earth beneath her feet was untrustworthy. Her hopes kept getting built up, only to be dashed again soon after. She wasn't sure who to believe—Mrs. Worthington or Mary Ann. Or whether she could be certain of either woman's version of Will's feelings toward her.

But she knew Mary Ann was correct in one respect. She would do well to be a lot more guarded around Will from now on, if for no other reason than to keep from making a damn fool of herself over the man. Again.

Where the heck was Paulie?

Will sat up in bed, his stomach grumbling, watching the door impatiently. Ever since sunrise, he'd been waiting to see Paulie again. Would she look as pretty in the morning sun streaming through the windows as she had in the candlelight last night?

Despite the insistent gnawing in his stomach, he was feeling much better today. His arm ached like the dickens, but that was an improvement. What troubled him more was his state of mind. He couldn't believe that he was developing such a yen for Paulie Johnson, of all people. All his life, he'd been sure of himself. His goals were always clear. He was going to save his money, buy a horse ranch, marry Mary Ann, and that would be that. Now the world seemed to be standing on its head. He was dreaming about a strange girl he'd never thought of apart from her being someone to tease, and buy liquor from, and talk to. And to top that, *she* wasn't even in love with him!

Oh, she'd kissed him all right, but she hadn't been happy about it. The second their embrace was over, she had fled the room as if a swarm of hornets were after her, Will remembered uncomfortably. Perhaps her hasty exit was an indication that she still harbored feelings for Trip Peabody, that she didn't want to be held by anyone besides Trip. She might have sent Trip back to Possum Trot, back into the welcoming arms of the widow Hale, but doing so was an act of self-sacrifice.

He drummed his fingers impatiently against the covers, then detected footsteps coming up the stairs. Finally! He sat up a little straighter, rubbing his hand over his stubbly jaw self-consciously. Paulie might be pretty as a picture, he thought ruefully, but there was no telling what *he* looked like!

"Why, Will! You're up!"

At the sound of Mary Ann's voice, Will sank down against the pillows in disappointment. She floated into the room carrying his breakfast tray, but he didn't feel nearly as hungry as he had when he'd expected Paulie to be the one doing the serving.

He looked her in the eye and remembered that he had failed to accomplish what she had hoped for. "I'm sorry I couldn't bring Oren around, Mary Ann. All my talking to him managed to do was get me shot, it seems."

Her face froze for a moment. Then she forced a smile. "That's all right, Will. I guess everything's worked out for the best."

He peered at her suspiciously. "Where's Paulie?"

"Downstairs, having breakfast," Mary Ann said. She chuckled. "My, my, I never knew a woman who could put food away so handily as Paulie Johnson. Last time I looked she was on her fourth biscuit."

Will smiled. "Really?"

Mary Ann shook her head. "I suppose I should take that as a compliment, since I made them myself." She eased the tray in front of him, and to his dismay, sat herself down in the chair next to him.

Will looked dubiously down at the plate with its fluffy browned biscuits. In all the years he'd been acquainted with Mary Ann, he'd never known her to be much of a cook. "Did Paulie say anything about coming up to see me this morning?"

"I don't believe so." She shrugged impatiently. "Really, I don't know what she's doing here at all, except getting underfoot."

Will tilted his head. "I would have thought, since you two were such good friends, that she might have told you a little of what was going on inside her head."

"Good friends?"

"Yes, Paulie said you and her are...well, that you'd become close over the past few months."

Mary Ann levelled a pitying look on him. "I'm afraid

she's been deceiving you, Will. Goodness, what in heaven would we ever have in common!''

That's what *he* had always wondered. But why would Paulie lie to him?

Mary Ann dimpled sweetly. ''I guess all women keep their little secrets. I doubt Paulie would appreciate it if I told hers.''

''If you mean her feelings for Trip Peabody, I guessed those a long time ago.''

She blinked. ''Mr. Peabody?''

''Yes, she told me all about it. And now Trip's gone, back to Tessie Hale, and I suppose she's pining for him.''

Mary Ann bit her lip. ''Oh, I see… Well, that's right. And you know, Will, women are apt to do the strangest things when they're disappointed in love. You have to be careful.''

''What do you mean?''

''Well, for one thing, I guess a woman's first instinct when disappointed by one man is to throw herself into the arms of another.''

Which, as Will suspected, would explain Paulie's mixed reaction to his kiss last night.

''Why, just look what happened to me!''

Will shot her a distrustful glance. He knew it was hard for Mary Ann to go long without talking about herself, but he couldn't imagine what parallels she would manage to find between her life and Paulie's.

''After I got your letter I was so heartbroken I didn't know where to turn,'' she explained, ''so I turned to Oat.''

''You turned to Oat because you were pregnant, remember?''

She frowned. ''That's right. I turned to Oren because I was heartbroken, and *then* I turned to Oat.''

Will laughed.

Mary Ann tossed her curls and pouted becomingly. "Oh, I know I've made bad fudge out of my life. But it was only because I was heartbroken." She leaned forward. "Heartbroken over you, Will Brockett."

Will couldn't believe his ears, which was a good thing, because his eyes were almost won over by Mary Ann's superlative job of acting out of contrition. "Next you'll be telling me that you've given up on Oren and want to marry me instead."

"But that's just what I *do* want!" she said, her blue eyes wide with surprise.

Will chortled. "You can't think I'm fool enough to believe you really love me?"

"But I do, Will," she said, "and I know you love me, deep down. Why else would you have come all this way?"

He rolled his eyes. "Because I made a promise to your father."

"You know you've always loved me."

Wrong. He'd loved the idea of her. Her seeming innocence. Her beauty. Her family. He'd felt responsible for her. But he knew now those things fell short of love. Love was something else. Love was…

Well, hell. He wasn't an expert on the subject. But at least he was beginning to understand what it wasn't.

To his dismay, Mary Ann rose out of her chair and sat gently on the edge of the bed, leaning toward him. "And I know you haven't forgotten how it used to be when we kissed, Will."

His lips instinctively pressed into a frown. "As a matter of fact, I haven't," he told her, "so I don't need a reminder."

She blinked, amazed that he would turn down the delectable offer she'd made him. "Are you saying you *don't* want to kiss me?"

"Let's just say I don't see the point."

"The point!" she exclaimed. "The point is this. You might think a match between us would be all to my benefit, but you're forgetting Oat had land. Oh, not much of it, I'll admit, but land and a house would be enough for you to start that ranch you've always dreamed of. And let's not forget Oat's bonds."

Will smirked. "I never expected you to."

"I'm just being practical. Oat's dead and the money's there. What difference does it make whether I take it now or I had waited six months to get around to finding it? I've got one more bank to visit, and Oat's bound to have put it there. Just think, Will. If you married me today, that money could be yours by this evening. You could buy horses with it…anything."

"What happened to Oren?" Will asked. "Last I heard, you were waiting for him to come to his senses."

She swept her eyelashes up and down like a dark velvet curtain. "You were right, Will. He was just using me. I agonized all last night, realizing what a fool I was pining for Oren when you were right here all the time."

"A convenient victim," he finished for her.

"No!" She tossed her hands up in frustration. "Oh, you're not taking me seriously."

"No, I'm not," Will admitted bluntly. "I'd be a fool to, at this juncture."

She slapped her hand down in dismay, nearly upsetting his breakfast tray. "You're just saying that because you think you've got someone else!"

Will froze. "Who are you talking about?"

"That little ruffian girl, Paulie Johnson!" Mary Ann clucked her tongue in disgust. "Honestly, Will. It tears me up inside to think that you've sunk so low that you would consider courting *her*."

"Paulie's good company. I've always liked her."

"But you never would have considered kissing her!"

He tilted his head, studying her. News certainly travelled fast. "Just how did you come by the knowledge that I have kissed Paulie?"

She rolled her eyes toward the ceiling in exasperation. "That poor girl practically blurted it out to God and everybody last night. The poor thing. She didn't realize how foolish she sounded."

"Why? Because she seemed to think that a kiss was significant?" Had she really thought that? Will wondered fervently, clinging eagerly to the scrap of information. "Some women don't give themselves to every man who comes along with a flirtatious word."

With a huff, Mary Ann jumped off the bed. "I won't stand for your insults! Here I am, offering you everything I have, and all you can think to do is throw my unfortunate past in my face." She wagged a slim finger at him in warning. "I'll give you a day to think over my offer, Will, and one day only."

She twirled and prepared to march back toward the door when Will stopped her.

"Mary Ann, wait."

She spun around, a hopeful expression on her face. "Yes, Will?"

"I just wanted to know… Is your generous offer of marriage being put forward because you discovered I'm interested in someone else, or because you realized that Oren Tyler wouldn't have you on a bet?"

Her blue eyes narrowed dangerously. "The offer still stands. You'd better think it over, Will!" Cheeks flushed, she turned and slammed out the door.

Paulie climbed the stairs one at a time, slowly, feeling that her dainty new shoes had cast-iron soles. She'd eaten way too much at breakfast, trying to pass the time and get her mind off her troubles by wolfing down one biscuit after another. Now she felt as if she'd swallowed a boulder. And there was scant room for a boulder inside her tight dress.

She stopped, looked up at the landing, then took another step, trying to keep her gaze focused on her bedroom door. She was *not* going to visit Will. Maudie had seen him early this morning before breakfast and reported he was alive, which was all she needed to know. Going into his room would just be leading herself into temptation. Mary Ann had taken him his meal, and would probably tell Paulie all about how he was doing and what he had said—if she really needed to know.

Not that she wanted to talk to Mary Ann about Will if she could help it. Their conversation of the night before had been enough for her.

A door slammed—so loudly Paulie jumped. As if summoned by Paulie's thoughts, Mary Ann appeared outside Will's door. She spun around in surprise when she sensed Paulie behind her. Her face was flushed, and her blue eyes almost glistened with some feverish emotion that made Paulie's heart stop. What kind of activity had been going on in that sickroom to put such a fiery bloom in Mary's Ann cheeks?

"Oh! Are you going in to see Will now?" Mary Ann asked, recovering her composure.

"No," Paulie said shortly. It took every ounce of restraint she had in her not to pounce upon the woman and demand to know what was making her blush. Had Will kissed her, too? Had they been discussing the possibility of a reconciliation?

A secretive smile touched Mary Ann's lips and Paulie

balled her fists at her sides. "I see you're taking my advice then."

"Don't worry. I'm not chasing after Will," Paulie said.

The smile broadened and became more sickeningly condescending. "'Course not. Will always wants to be the one to do the chasing." She darted out her pink tongue and licked her lips. Almost as if she could still taste his kiss on them. "And he always catches what he wants." She tossed her head, giggled, turned and scurried down the hall toward the little staircase that led up to her room.

For a moment Paulie worried that her heart was pounding so hard it would shake the very foundation of the house. She didn't have to feel her cheeks to know they were red hot, flaming with anger. Anger at Mary Ann, for setting her sights on Will the moment she saw that another woman might be interested. Angry at herself, for *being* interested in a man who was apparently as fickle as a saloon girl on payday. But most of all, she was angry at Will. How dare he kiss her one night and then kiss Mary Ann the very next morning? She would like to give that man a piece of her mind!

She knew what Maudie would say. Yelling at a man was no way to catch one. But that was the rub—she didn't *want* to catch Will. Right this moment she decided very emphatically that she *didn't* want him. No sirree. She didn't want Will Brockett any more than she wanted a case of yellow fever.

So what did she have to lose?

She surged toward the door Mary Ann had just come out of, not bothering to knock before barging right in. Will was sitting up in bed, happily eating one of the biscuits that she herself had made for him, looking as if he had not a care in the world. He saw her and smiled broadly, causing her stomach to flutter weakly.

At the unwelcome sensation, Paulie scowled. "Will Brockett, you're the biggest fool this world ever made!"

He dropped the biscuit down to the tray, but otherwise didn't seem the least bit fazed by her outraged entrance. Instead, he treated her almost as if she were an amusing diversion—just as he had during all the years of their acquaintance.

"To what do I owe the pleasure of your visit, not to mention your compliments?" he asked in that maddeningly calm voice of his. It was just as if they were back at the Dry Wallow, sparring over her freckles.

"I didn't come here for pleasure!"

"Really?" he asked, his eyebrows raised comically. "I thought perhaps you'd like to prove again how you don't like me."

She couldn't believe he could just sit there, cool as a cucumber, and joke about it! "No one could like you as much as you like yourself," she said through gritted teeth. "I was just coming here as a friend."

He laughed. "And what exactly did you want to say to me, as a friend?"

"Just that if you're in love with Mary Ann, then you're a fool and welcome to her!"

"In love with Mary Ann?" he repeated, pretending amazement. He *had* to be pretending.

"If you're not in love with her, you're just leading her on like that Oren Tyler, and in that case you're lower than a snake's belly and the two of you deserve each other!"

He blinked. "Say, you're really angry, aren't you?"

"I am not! It just burns me up to think I actually wanted to save you from Mary Ann's clutches. Now I hope you strangle in them!"

He frowned, then looked back up at her in understanding.

"I get it. You're feeling guilty for kissing me the moment Trip went away. Don't worry, I won't tell."

That was just the last straw. Wasn't he listening? "Land's sake, Will. Would you use your noggin for once? Why on earth would I be in love with Trip Peabody?"

He blinked. "You said you were."

"No," she said, sashaying forward until she was a mere foot away from him and could punctuate her words with a jab to his chest. "*You* just decided I was. But I'm not. And if I were, what would I run around kissing you for? I'm not like Mary Ann!"

He stuttered in confusion. "B-but Trip…"

She stomped her foot. "Trip's in love with Tessie Hale and always has been! He hasn't ever loved me, and even if he had it wouldn't have mattered because *I've* only loved one person my whole entire life, and it's not him. And if you can't figure everything out now, Will, then you're just as blind as a mule in a barn fire!"

Chapter Fourteen

Will stared in amazement at the door, which had just been slammed shut for the second time in ten minutes. He could hardly take in the strange conversation he'd just had. What could it mean? Could Paulie possibly be in love with *him?*

It seemed too incredible. He had known all along that she *liked* him. Lord knows, they had been friends forever. But beyond that, he had assumed she had saved all her deepest feelings for Trip.

If she hadn't, it changed a whole lot of things. Like who it was she was talking about that night she'd told him she was in love. Could it really be himself? The thought made him feel as thickheaded as she'd accused him of being. There was nothing standing between them and never had been—besides the fact that she seemed to think that he had some residual feelings for Mary Ann.

Paulie…in love with him. He felt a surge of contentment. He couldn't pinpoint exactly when he'd begun to think differently about his old friend. Maybe that night after Oat had died. Or maybe the first time he'd kissed her. Or maybe, somewhere in the back of his mind, he'd always known there was more to Paulie than met the eye.

A rap sounded on the door, and Will sat up again,

straighter, prepared to meet an apologetic Paulie. She always did regret these pets she got herself into.

"Come in," he said, putting aside the tray in case he decided to accept her apology by taking her into his arms again.

The door opened slowly and quietly—the first sign that his visitor wasn't Paulie. Will's brow puckered, and he looked up to see Oren Tyler standing in his doorway. He didn't flinch at the sight of the gambler, exactly, but he did wonder for a moment whether the man had heard he was still alive and had come to finish him off.

"Hello, Brockett," Tyler said. He closed the door behind him and took a few tentative steps into the room.

"Tyler." Will nodded tersely, watching the man closely for some clue as to why on earth he would have come calling. "To what do I owe this pleasure?"

The gambler stepped forward. "I won't mince words, Brockett. I've come about Mary Ann."

Thank goodness! Will thought.

His visitor chuckled. "Your speechifying yesterday began to weigh on my conscience. I'll admit I had a sleepless night last night, but I've finally come to see where my responsibility lies."

Will nodded, feeling more optimistic than he had in days. After all this trouble, it was beginning to look like things would work out. Mary Ann would have her gambler, he would have Paulie, and they would all begin to have some peace. "Mary Ann's in the house, you know," he informed the gentleman. "Sure you wouldn't rather say whatever you have to say to her directly?"

Tyler's eyes flickered in surprise, then he shuffled his feet uncomfortably. "I don't think so." His dark eyes looked into Will's imploringly. "It would probably be best if I didn't see her again, don't you think?"

"Not see her?" The words turned Will around.

"I've given some thought to what you said about Mary Ann," Oren said. "And especially about the child. And it's my feeling that I do owe it to the little fellow to see that he has a good start in life. Good as I can make it. So I brought Mary Ann this." He tossed an envelope on the bed in front of Will. "There's two hundred dollars in there."

Will stared at the money as though he could see through the white paper of the envelope to the individual bills concealed beneath it. "Two hundred dollars," he repeated numbly. The man hadn't come here to reconcile with Mary Ann. He'd come to buy her off.

So much for optimism.

The gambler rocked back on his heels as if he had just made an unspeakably grandiose gesture. "I worried a little about the sum at first. But I think this will be enough to get Mary Ann safely home, with a little left over." He continued to stare at Will, whose lack of response caused him a moment of doubt.

"Maybe it is best that you don't see Mary Ann," Will agreed finally.

Oren's brows drew together. "You do think that's enough, don't you?"

Two hundred, four hundred, even a thousand... Will doubted any of those sums would satisfy Mary Ann. Her wanting Oren seemed to have something more to do with what she wanted out of life than any monetary gain that union would achieve. After all, as Oat's widow and with the money he set aside, she would probably have enough money to keep her comfortable for a while. No, Will was willing to bet two hundred dollars of his own money that Mary Ann wouldn't be pleased by Oren Tyler's largesse.

"I'll make sure she gets your money," Will said, dodging his opinion on the matter.

Oren shifted his weight from one foot to the other. For some reason, he seemed uncomfortable leaving Will with an unfavorable impression of himself. "After all, I never said I'd marry her," he explained. "And then when she came here, she was another man's wife."

The strange thing was, the man seemed honestly to believe that fact absolved his own behavior...though he appeared nervous enough to know that others might not let him off the hook so easily. Will certainly wasn't about to give his approbation, but neither was he going to argue with the man.

"I'm sure this is more than what Mary Ann expects from you, Tyler."

A ray of hope lit his face. "Really?"

Will nodded. For Mary Ann's sake, he wasn't about to tell him that the woman had already moved on to a new plan—namely himself. Besides, he was hoping she had already given up on that false hope, despite her generous pledge to give him a day to think it over.

"Good," said Tyler. Then, standing before Will in awkward silence, he repeated, "Good."

Will cocked his head, wondering how long it would take for a man like Tyler to clear his conscience of any memory of Mary Ann. "I know you're a busy man, Tyler. Don't let me keep you."

"Actually, I *am* busy today. I'm leaving for Denver."

It was probably just as well that the man put as much distance between himself and Mary Ann as possible. "I wish you a pleasant journey."

The gambler grinned. "Oh, I usually do try to keep things pleasant."

And after a quick nod of his hat, the man was gone. Will looked down at the two hundred dollars, wondering how long he could put off giving Mary Ann the distinctly *un-*

pleasant news that she had just been paid two hundred dollars to forget Oren Tyler.

A brisk walk cooled Paulie down considerably. She felt like a darn fool now for having blown her composure with Will. What must he think of her?

She stopped at the gate in front of Mrs. Worthington's boardinghouse, idly studying the fine carriage parked in the street in front of the house, and considered whether she should go upstairs and apologize for telling him he was a fool. Just as she was debating the advantages and disadvantages of grovelling after having so embarrassingly revealed how much she cared for him, the front door opened and Oren Tyler emerged, looking handsome in a dark suit and hat and new boots so shiny she was almost blinded by them.

Her mouth popped open in astonishment. Tyler was the last man she'd expected to see coming out of Maudie's house this morning. Had he spoken to Mary Ann? Had the two of them reconciled? Oh, she hoped so! Then this whole ordeal would be over, and they could all go home. Of course, she would still have an awkward situation with Will to deal with, but in a few decades she might get over the humiliation of it all....

Paulie surged forward but skidded to a stop when the man stopped on the lowest porch step, pushed his hat back, stared straight at her and let out a low whistle. She whirled to stare behind her to see if the man had brought a dog with him, which would have explained the whistle. It wouldn't have accounted for the peculiar way he was staring at her, however.

Not seeing a canine of any description behind her, she turned back around to face the gambler. "Did you come to talk to Mary Ann?'' she asked, unable to corral her curiosity.

He smiled a big broad grin that about stopped her pulse completely. Lord, she'd never seen such white teeth! It looked like the man brushed them with laundry blueing. ''I came for some business, but if I'd known what a pretty little lady resided here, I might have made a pleasure call long ago.''

Again Paulie was tempted to turn to see what pretty little lady Oren Tyler was talking about, but incredibly, she could only deduce those fantastic words referred to *her!* She felt an odd fluttery feeling inside her, and couldn't help smiling. He apparently didn't recognize her from the Three Queens, or from the time she'd seen him in Possum Trot. ''You probably don't remember me...''

He didn't even let her finish, but let out a low, teasing laugh that seemed to rumble right down to the tips of Paulie's toes. ''Oh, I'd remember you, miss.'' He winked. ''I hope it's miss...?''

For some inexplicable reason, she was quick to assure the handsome stranger, ''It sure is!'' Something about the gambler's manner made her feel unsteady, almost giddy.

He feigned surprise. ''Now what are the men around here thinking, letting a sweet little sugar lump like you get past them?''

Sugar lump? She would have paid anything for Will to get an earful of the flattery the man was laying on so thick. She was sure Oren was simply pretending, and yet his words had a ring of authenticity—probably because he'd had so much practice being a slick piece of work.

Still, she couldn't stop the flush of pleasure that leapt to her cheeks, any more than she could help returning that infectious grin of his. She'd never flirted like this before. ''But I swear you *have* seen me before, Mr. Tyler.''

His eyes widened. "You know my name."

"Your reputation preceded you."

He threw back his head and laughed. "I hope you only believed the good things."

"I don't recall there being any good," Paulie said saucily. "From what I've heard and witnessed, you're a thoroughly unrepentant scoundrel."

"Maybe." He came a few steps closer, then took a long moment to drink her in appreciatively from head to toe, which caused the heat to stay aflame in her cheeks. "But you have to admit there's not much attraction in a repentant scoundrel, now is there?"

She bit back a laugh. "Or any scoundrel."

He looped a thumb rakishly in his belt and gave her another sizing up. "Now I know we've never met."

"How?"

"Because I would never forget a woman who was both beautiful and sharp-tongued."

"I don't even look familiar to you?" Paulie asked.

He shook his head. "No ma'am. For one thing, if I had seen you before, I wouldn't have failed to remark that your eyes were two pools of exotic jade," he cooed. "Do you remember a man telling you that recently?"

Paulie felt as if the wind had been knocked out of her. Exotic jade? She didn't even know what the heck it was, but it sure sounded good. She shook her head.

"Then we couldn't have met, could we?"

She gazed up at his dark eyes. There was some strange logic in his words that made her want to throw contrary things like cold facts to the wind. His eyes mesmerized her. She would have paid good money just for the chance to stare into those hypnotic orbs, which seemed to twinkle at her in some mysterious way that no other man's did. Will's eyes were handsome, and affected her in a deeper, more profound way. But sometime before she died she wished that Will would twinkle at her the way Oren Tyler did.

Tyler reached out and lightly touched her elbow, causing her to jump nervously. "Perhaps I was mistaken," she murmured, suddenly seeing no point whatsoever in telling him that she was actually the strange girl he had seen yesterday trying to help Will at Las Tres Reinas.

"We've both erred, then," he said in a husky voice. "My mistake was not discovering you sooner. Now it's too late."

She blinked. "Oh?"

"I'm leaving today for Denver."

This news startled her. "Denver?"

He nodded. "Would you care to join me? Who knows, if we enjoy each other's company, we could keep going until we reach San Francisco."

She flushed again at the bold suggestion. "N-no...I couldn't."

He cocked his head and smiled. "Pity." He pointed behind her, to a fine, sturdy black coach led by two beautiful chestnut horses. "I could convey you in style."

Paulie was surprised. "You would go all the way to Colorado in that thing?" Sure, it was a fine rig, but she wouldn't want to be cooped up for days in it.

He chuckled. "It's much more entertaining being able to stop at will, get to know the territory, and the people." He winked. "Especially the women." He leaned close to her again, so that she could feel his breath tickling her neck. "I also have three bottles of fine imported bourbon. Think of the romance of it, camping under the stars..."

Her stomach did a shocking flip, but Paulie tilted her head and leaned as far away from those cunning eyes as she could possibly get. "I've camped under stars before, mister. Believe me, there's nothing romantic about worrying about snakes in your bedroll and waking up with a backache. Though maybe a little bourbon *will* make it more bearable.''

He blinked in surprise, then chuckled. ''Ah, well. Like I said, it's a pity.''

Then, taking a step back, he tipped his hat and went on his way, climbing into his smart rig. Paulie watched the man go, knowing a million questions should be racing through her mind. Unfortunately, all she could really think about were those dark eyes, and the outrageously flirtatious things he'd said to her.

He hadn't made fun of her for wearing women's clothing, and she guessed Oren Tyler was as much an expert on that subject as practically anybody! She turned and went up the boardinghouse stairs two at a time, winding her way through the house directly to Will's room. Her step was so light that she floated. She rapped once loudly on the door and walked right on in. She barely noticed that Will was actually sitting up in the chair beside the bed in which she had kept vigil the night before.

Will waited for Paulie to speak. She looked distracted. It wasn't like her to be so silent.

''Paulie?''

Finally she appeared to focus on him, as if noticing that she wasn't alone in the room. ''Did you see him?'' she asked by way of greeting.

''See who?''

''Oren.''

Will flinched. She was calling him Oren now? ''I spoke with Tyler just a few minutes ago.'' In fact, he was glad to see Paulie here. He still wasn't certain how to broach the subject of the gambler's latest move with Mary Ann. Maybe Paulie could give her her opinion. He couldn't imagine her not giving it, in fact. "Look at this," he said, holding out the envelope. "He came here to give me two hundred dollars for Mary Ann."

"That was nice of him," Paulie said.

"Nice, my foot!" Will scoffed. "He wants me to give it to her as payment for…" His mouth snapped closed.

"For what?" Paulie asked, immediately curious.

Will swallowed. It was just as well Paulie knew the truth. "For Mary Ann's child."

She sucked in a surprised breath. "Mary Ann's going to have a little one?"

"Yes, and this two hundred dollars is to ease his guilt. The only thing I can hope is that it will show him for the cad he is and Mary Ann will forget about him."

Paulie shook her head. "She won't forget about him."

Will tilted his head and studied her. There *was* something queer about her. For one thing, the last time he'd seen her, she'd been hopping mad. Now she was almost eerily serene. "You seem awfully sure of Mary Ann's feelings on the matter."

"I am." She propped herself up on her elbows and looked into Will's eyes, and let out a long dramatic sigh. "Now that I've talked to him, I understand Mary Ann's attraction to the man."

"You do?"

"You know what he called me?"

Will balled his fists. "If he said something to insult or offend you—"

Paulie shook her head. "He called me a sweet little sugar lump."

Will stared at her in shock. For some reason, those words seemed even worse than he'd expected. "What!"

"He said my eyes were two exotic jade pools," she went

on dreamily, just managing to suppress another sigh. "Can you imagine?"

Will laughed, hoping to shake this odd mood of hers. "And I always thought they were more grasshopper green!"

She pursed her lips and sent him a scathing glance. "That's just the difference between you and Oren."

Will groaned in distress. "Don't tell me you're stuck on him, too. Especially not after what I've told you!"

"No, but I can definitely see that Oren Tyler is a man who knows how to turn a woman's head."

"I'm sure he's made an art of it," Will said bitterly. What was Tyler up to, flattering Paulie like that?

"He certainly has," she said with another languorous sigh.

Will cocked his head and studied her objectively. In a simple navy serge dress, she did look beautiful today. It could be that the gambler was just doing what came naturally. But fancy compliments were never Will's strong suit. Jade pools! Hadn't he himself noticed Paulie's fine green eyes before anyone else?

Her wholehearted defection to Tyler's camp rankled. "Lord, Paulie, I never thought I'd hear you singing that varmint's praises."

"Me, neither," Paulie said. "But I've never had a man look at me like that before."

Will's brows shot up suspiciously. "How was he looking at you?"

"Like he was a kid and I was birthday cake. It made me feel all jittery inside, unbalanced."

Will's mouth set in a grim line. "Sounds wonderful."

"Oh, it was very uncomfortable," Paulie agreed reasonably. "But just think, that's probably how poor Mary Ann's felt for months now."

"*Poor* Mary Ann?" Will repeated.

"Gracious, Will, it's like the man's cast a spell on her."

"Sounds more like he's cast one on you!" he said.

She let out a light chuckle, as if the very idea were plainly absurd. "I know that. Goodness, if that were true, I imagine I'd be on the road to Denver right now."

"He told you he was leaving town then?"

"Told me!" She laughed merrily. "He invited me to go along with him."

"What!"

"Don't worry, I told him I couldn't possibly."

Will felt his temper rising. "I should hope so."

Paulie looked at him, a half smile touching her lips. "Why?"

"Why?" he repeated hotly. "I would think it would be obvious why!"

She flicked at an imaginary piece of lint on her skirt. "Is it Tyler in particular you don't like, or do you simply despise the idea of any woman running off with a man besides yourself?"

"It's Tyler!"

"You didn't seem too happy when Mary Ann married Oat, either."

"Well of course I wasn't, but I didn't know…" It was his turn to let out a sigh this time. A ragged one.

She looked at him squarely. "Why should you worry about who I talk to, or where I go, Will?"

He hesitated. "I just feel responsible for you, is all."

"That's all?" she asked.

"Naturally," he said, barely reining in his temper. "What else should I feel?"

She sucked in a breath, and for a moment she simply looked at him sadly. "Nothing, I guess," she said, standing. Her good mood and teasing manner disappeared. "But don't think I'm sitting around hoping you'll take care of me, Will. I've done pretty well all these years without you. You shouldn't let responsibility for me weigh down your shoulders.''

She turned and stalked out of the room, and once again, Will felt bewildered. And this time, he felt a little angry. Didn't women ever stay on an even keel? It seemed they were always flying off the handle about something!

He tried thinking over his words to figure out what he could have said to make her so snippety with him. He'd told her he felt a certain responsibility for her. What was so wrong with that? Weren't women supposed to want to be watched over, and be taken care of? She'd looked at him as if even hinting at such a thing should have been a hanging offense. But when she was talking about running off with Tyler...

Maybe he should have owned up to how much he cared for her. But it was a new feeling for him. Besides, he wouldn't have been surprised if she'd laughed in his face if he'd told her the truth.

But clearly he had to say something to patch things up between them now. He got up slowly from the chair, glad that he didn't seem to feel any dizziness. The pain in his shoulder had subsided a good deal too, down to a dull throb. He could live with that for a while. What he couldn't live with was Paulie not understanding that he didn't think of her solely in big-brother terms.

He took a few more tentative steps across the room, pleased by his progress, when the door flew open and Mary Ann dashed in, breathless and flushed.

''Where is it!'' she cried, practically flattening him. She rushed into his chest, causing a riot of pain to rush through him.

He bit back a groan. ''What?''

"Paulie said Oren was here and left something for me," Mary Ann said impatiently. "Where is it?"

Biting his lip, he nodded toward the envelope on the table by the bed. "There."

She ran over, snatched it up, and tore it open. "I knew it! I knew he'd want to see me again. I bet he's sending for me, isn't he?"

As she said the words, she shook the envelope and the two hundred dollars came spilling out. She checked the emptied envelope for a message that wasn't there.

But almost immediately, the expression on her face said that the message had come through loud and clear.

She shook her head, in denial. "You sent him away, didn't you, Will?" she asked, her voice quick and breathy as she searched in vain for some positive slant on this slap in the face, this payoff. "You've thought over my offer and told him that you intend to marry me, didn't you?"

Sadly, Will shook his head. "I'm sorry, Mary Ann. I can't," he said. "And now Oren's left for Denver."

And almost immediately, the boardinghouse was rocked by the sound of a piercing wail the likes of which no resident there had ever heard.

Chapter Fifteen

That afternoon, a pall fell over the boardinghouse. The members of the household walked on eggshells and spoke to each other in hushed tones. Even Maudie appeared to feel the void created by the gambler's leaving town and the passing of Mary Ann's ill-fated romance. She lost five straight games of poker to Paulie.

After recovering from her first stroke of shock, Mary Ann began to dash in and out of the house, a black-draped flurry of purpose. What exactly she was doing, no one could tell, and no one was about to ask her point-blank, but the young woman seemed to be intent on something, even if it were simply taking short, frequent walks. At the same time, she had the distracted, feverish air of a person about to become permanently unhinged from reality.

When she left the house for the third time in an hour, Paulie could stand no more. She put her cards on the table and pushed her chair away. "I think I'll take a walk," she told Maudie.

"You mean you're going to leave me five games down just so you can go spying?"

Paulie gasped, shocked that she was so transparent.

"Don't worry," Maudie said, winking. "You have my blessing. I also want to know what the girl's up to."

"She sure looks distraught, with all her running in and out."

Maudie crossed her arms. "I'd be distraught, too, if I'd just been widowed by one man, abandoned by another, and had a little one on the way."

Paulie nodded, not bothering to add that it must seem twice as dismal to be abandoned by such a good-looking fellow. Then she snapped her head up. *With a little one on the way?* "How did you know?" she asked.

"I had a child myself, you know."

Paulie shook her head. Maudie had probably known before any of them. "You may not believe this, but I'm beginning to think Mary Ann really did love that gambler."

Mrs. Worthington considered that hypothesis with a doubtful squint. "Anyways, the girl's got a tough row to hoe ahead of her. I guess I can keep her on here."

Paulie jerked her head up in surprise. "Here?" She wouldn't have imagined Maudie would feel so generous towards Mary Ann.

She knew plenty of people, even men, who would have tossed her out on her ear once they learned of her unseemly conduct and its consequences.

Maudie waved a hand at her. "Sure, I've criticized her, and I do wish she could sit still long enough to play cards now and then. But where else is the poor thing going to go?" Before Paulie could voice the obvious, she pointed out, "If Mary Ann had wanted to live with her parents, I don't suppose she would have run off and married a man three times her age to begin with."

Maybe Mary Ann would be grateful to hear that she wouldn't be tossed out of Maudie's, Paulie thought as she made her way down the street towards town. It was another breezy, fine day, so she enjoyed the walk. Once in the center of town, she stood on a sidewalk and looked around at the people milling about, trying to find any sign of Mary Ann.

She finally spotted her coming out of a bank on the opposite street. She was carrying a large envelope in her hands, and staring intently at it as she walked, but when she stopped at an intersection to let a wagon pass by, she looked up—right in Paulie's direction.

Paulie panicked. Suddenly, it felt underhanded to be spying on her this way. How could she explain her curiosity? She darted back into the shadow of a building and ducked into the first doorway she saw.

It was the postal and telegraph office. Luckily, the building had a large glass window, so she watched Mary Ann as she headed back in the direction of Maudie's street, following her bobbing blond ringlets until they disappeared from view completely, and she knew it was safe to go home.

"Is somebody after you?"

Captured off guard by the strange voice, Paulie turned and found a short balding man behind the post office counter looking at her with interest. "No," she replied. "Just the opposite—I was watching someone else."

He chuckled. "I see. I thought maybe I had me a real female desperado on my hands—maybe a new name to add to my gallery." He nodded toward a wall where several Wanted posters had been pinned.

A face on one of the posters—one that appeared to be brand-new—caught Paulie's eye. "Night Bird," she said. On this particular poster there was a rudimentary drawing, but the cold eyes were unmistakable. She walked over to read the litany of his crimes listed beneath his likeness.

The man squinted at her, then stepped out behind his counter. "You ever seen him before?"

"We're old friends."

"First he was wanted for killin' the three men with the railroad payroll. Then just yesterday he killed another man."

"Who?"

"Some fellow who'd been chasin' him for a while. Used to be a Texas ranger once, but I think they kicked him out. Name was Cal Tucker. Wasn't too far from here, either."

Paulie felt a chill sink deep into her bones. "Cal?" she repeated. That man had to be the man they'd seen at Roy Bean's! But his being killed was almost incredible. He'd looked so able, so...mean. She couldn't believe that Night Bird had gotten him. More than that, she was amazed anew that she and the others had actually had the good fortune to escape the fate Cal had met. She felt clammy with relief—and renewed anxiety.

She turned, thanked the man for letting her use his post office to hide in, then rushed for the door. She couldn't wait to tell Will the news about Cal. Her pace was brisk as she began to walk down the street, but moments later she found herself transfixed in front of a store window.

It was a general store, the same one Will had gone into the other day. With the memory of Night Bird's latest attack fresh in her mind, she went inside it for the same reason that Will had gone in before his meeting with Tyler. A gun. She and Will would be heading back to Possum Trot soon, and she didn't want to be on the road without a weapon again.

She bought the best piece she could with what little money she had left over from paying Maudie. It was an old revolver, none too solid looking, but she imagined it would do in a pinch. She just hoped the pinch never came.

She stopped in an alley and tucked the revolver away under her skirt. Just having the gun in her possession made her feel a little safer as she walked back to the boarding-house. The cold that had crept into her bones when she heard about Cal dissipated a little.

"Mary Ann got back a while ago," Maudie said as she walked into the house. "Where you been? You must have missed her."

Paulie's mind was miles from her spying mission now. "I suppose so," she said, heading straight for the staircase. She wanted to talk to Will.

"You might tell the others that dinner's ready," Maudie said. "I don't suppose Mary Ann's going to be much help serving tonight."

Paulie hated to tell the woman her doubts about Mary Ann's helpfulness on *any* night, so she simply nodded and started up the staircase. She raced all the way to Mary Ann's attic room, deciding to save talking to Will for last so they could have a leisurely discussion about their rene-gade acquaintance.

She rapped lightly on Mary Ann's door and stepped back, waiting for either a shouted reply or for the door to be flung open. Neither happened. Paulie accompanied her next knock with a whispered, "Mary Ann?" When that also failed to garner a response, she carefully pushed the door open, just enough to peek inside and discover that no one was in the small chamber, there was a note on the bed.

Paulie edged toward it, feeling somehow guilty for being in Mary Ann's private space, which had such an eerily deserted feeling, and dreading, too, being the one to dis-cover whatever was contained in that note. She was certain it couldn't be good news. A quick perusal confirmed her fear.

I have gone to Denver. Please don't worry. I have Oat's bonds.

                                                    Mary Ann
P.S. I had to take one of the horses so I could catch up with Oren. I'm not sure whose it is—the pretty dark one.

I know you won't mind!

The short missive was addressed to no one in particular. Paulie rushed to the window and looked out, half expecting to see Mary Ann in the yard below. How had Mary Ann sneaked out of the house? She must have just left while Maudie was busy in the kitchen. But if she was on Will's horse, even a few minutes' lead would put her well ahead of anyone who wanted to catch up with her.

A shiver worked its way from the crown of Paulie's head to the tips of her toes. Denver! On horseback? Alone? Didn't she realize there were miles and miles of rough country between her and her destination? What if she never did catch up with Tyler?

Shaking her head in disbelief and yet unable to take her eyes off the note, Paulie hurried back down the flight of narrow stairs, knocked quickly on Will's door, and strode right on in.

The man turned and shot straight up about two feet into the air at the sight of her. When Paulie looked up from her note, she jumped, too. There stood Will, gloriously bare-chested in front of her. She'd seen him like this before, of course, but it was an even more impressive sight when the man was standing up. Vertical, he looked more imposing, more dangerous. Especially with that slash of white bandage covering his shoulder.

"Don't you ever knock?"

Paulie licked her lips, sure she didn't have enough spit in her to answer. "I did knock," she finally managed.

He rolled his eyes and quickly snatched a waiting shirt off the bed. "That's fine. Now all you have to do is learn the second part. There are two magical words called 'come in.'"

She shook her head, marvelling at the speed that Will's large but nimble fingers could work those buttons. He seemed so self-conscious about being shirtless in front of her, which wasn't like him. Of course, the fact that she was gawking at him probably didn't put him at ease.

"I just came in to tell you dinner was ready," she said slowly, knowing there were other things she had to talk to him about, too, and yet not being able to call them up at just this moment.

He nodded at the all-but-forgotten note she held in her hands. "Your racing in here didn't have anything to do with that?"

She glanced down, almost as startled by his perception as she had been by his nakedness.

"I heard you come clattering down from Mary Ann's room," he explained, taking the note from her hands. "What kind of a fix is she in now?"

Paulie didn't have the nerve to tell him. Instead, she let him read for himself, watching his face as he did so, waiting for the shock or anger to register. To her surprise, it was a long time coming—not until he'd read and reread the last line.

"Damn!" he cried, looking up sharply at Paulie. "Did you see this? She stole Ferdinand!"

Paulie blinked. This wasn't the reaction she had expected. "Don't you understand? She's gone after Oren Tyler!"

"'Course I understand," Will said. He ran a hand

through his hair. "I also understand she ran off with the best horse I ever had."

She couldn't believe her ears. "Just think how dangerous it is for her. How is she ever going to catch up with him? Do you know how many miles are between here and Denver?"

Will nodded, his lips twitching in disgust. "Good luck to her."

"But Will!" Paulie stamped her foot excitedly, but the gesture didn't result in a decisive *clump* in her new shoes like it always had in her old work boots. "Mary Ann's in danger, Will. Night Bird's out there somewhere."

Will looked at her oddly. "Of course he is, but hundreds of people still travel the roads every day."

She shook her head. "I was just at the post office. That man Cal who we met at Roy Bean's got killed by Night Bird."

Will's face paled a little. "What do you suggest?"

Paulie didn't have to think two seconds to come up with an answer. "I think we should go after her."

"We?"

She nodded fervently. "Right away."

"*We?*" Will repeated.

"Of course!" Paulie said. "I can't just stand by while Mary Ann goes riding off all alone," she declared. "I can't believe you would, either."

"Why not?" he asked. "We both could probably spend the next few decades of our lives trailing after Mary Ann to keep her from making mistakes, but that wouldn't keep her from making them. At some point, you have to put a stop to nonsense, or you'll just be encouraging it. You said yourself—it's time to let her make her own decisions."

Paulie couldn't believe this was Will talking. Will, who

a mere three days before had been intent on trailing after Mary Ann forever like a knight on a white horse!

Of course, thanks to Mary Ann, he now had no horse at all.

"The Breens could arrive here any time after tomorrow to fetch Mary Ann back home," she pointed out.

"That was your doing, not mine."

"All right, but what will we say to them—'Sorry, after making you come all this way we just stood by while your daughter ran off after a stranger'?"

"He's not exactly a stranger."

"What do any of us know about Oren Tyler?" Paulie asked. "The only thing we can be certain of is that he's callous and disreputable. That's not the kind of man Mary Ann needs in her condition."

Will's eyes narrowed on her. "You seem awful keen to rescue poor Mary Ann."

"I risked my neck finding her, and you almost got yourself killed. Why should we stop now?"

"My question is, why shouldn't we stop before we *do* get ourselves killed. Unless there's some reason why you think the risk would be worth it. Some reason aside from Mary Ann…"

Paulie snapped her head up to stare into his speculative eyes. His lips were set in a grim line. He definitely had something on his mind, she just couldn't figure out what it was.

"Is it just chance that your newfound concern for Mary Ann just happened to coincide with your being so taken with Oren Tyler?" he asked.

She sucked in a breath. "That's absurd!"

"If you'd told me three days ago that levelheaded Paulie Johnson would have been prancing around mooning over some fancy-talking gambler, I would have said that was absurd, too.''

Paulie set her jaw and glared up at him. ''I wasn't mooning.''

''I don't know what else you'd call it,'' Will said, an edge to his voice.

Paulie thought about the strange weightlessness she'd felt just having a man shower her with empty compliments. ''All right, maybe I was *mooning* just a little,'' she admitted. ''Is that so strange after being around a bunch of heathens all my life who don't know how to relate to a woman except to make love to her or slap her on the back?''

Will stepped forward and grabbed her by the shoulders. ''I didn't notice you minding lovemaking so much when we were doing it,'' he said. ''Or do women naturally prefer empty words to real kisses?''

She wriggled in his grasp, to no avail. Even with the bum shoulder, the man was strong as an ox. Now that she thought about it, she *would* have preferred Will's kisses over a lifetime of sweet words from a no-good gambler. But she didn't like his tone. And dress or no dress, she hated to lose an argument.

''I just prefer someone with a few manners!'' she said, giving him a mighty shove that, when he loosened his grasp, sent her reeling backwards. She caught herself from tripping and smoothed her skirts down in a calming gesture. Will Brockett was not going to best her this time. What in tarnation was wrong with him?

''Anyone would think you were jealous, Will,'' she said.

Every rugged wrinkle fell out of his face. ''Jealous? Of whom?''

Paulie shrugged. ''Of Mary Ann and Oren Tyler, I guess. He's stolen your old sweetheart, and now you can't stand to hear a good word said about him.''

He looked at her long and hard. "I don't care about Tyler one way or the other. I just don't see the point in chasing after a woman who doesn't want to be caught."

What a turnaround! Paulie marvelled that her arguments had finally sunk through Will's skull at precisely the wrong time. "What if something terrible happens to her? Won't you feel responsible?"

That hypothetical scenario gave Will pause, and Paulie watched as the possibilities played across his eyes. At last he shook his head. "We should concentrate on getting you back to Possum Trot."

"Me?" she asked. "What's the matter with me?"

"The city air seems to be giving you strange notions. Or maybe it's a lack of air from that corset you're wearing."

Though angered at the implication that she had gone addle-brained, Paulie felt some of the fight drain out of her. She gaped at him in amazement. "How would you know what I've got on under my dress?"

Will lifted his hand to his mouth and cleared his throat. "Uh…just a wild guess."

She shook her head uneasily. The notion of any man being conscious of her underwear was unsettling. Having that man be Will made things a thousand times worse. Could he also tell that she had a gun in her drawers?

Lord, right now she would have given anything to have things back as they were in the good old days back in Possum Trot, before everything started getting so complicated. What were they going to do now? They just couldn't give up and go back home. Or at least, Paulie wouldn't feel right doing that. Maybe Will had ceased to feel sorry for Mary Ann. But having suffered from unrequited love herself, and now understanding firsthand the appeal that the gambler might have for a susceptible woman, Paulie actually felt sympathy for Mary Ann. She didn't accept that they could just let her go.

Maybe some of Will's craziness had finally rubbed off on her.

Besides, Will had been absolutely right about one thing. It *was* her fault that the Breens were now probably on their way to San Antonio. If they showed up and discovered that she had simply allowed Mary Ann to run off, she would feel like a damn fool. She had to do something, even if she did it by herself.

"Are you going down to dinner?" Will asked her.

Paulie's head snapped up, making her realize how deeply she had already been immersed in plans. "Oh...I don't think so." She feigned a yawn. "Actually, I'm a little tired...and I have a headache. I might try to sleep it off."

Will looked at her curiously. "You want me to have Maudie bring something up?"

"No—no, I'll get something later."

At the store on her way out of town, she thought. She gazed at Will for a long moment, then forced herself to turn and go back across the hall to her room to pack.

In his room after dinner, Will felt a little guilty. He hadn't heard a peep from Paulie's room. Most likely she was angry for his seeming to dismiss her notion of running after Mary Ann. But he just couldn't see chasing Mary Ann anymore. Instead, he thought perhaps they could try to do things right for a change, and wire ahead to Oren Tyler that he was being followed. Let Mary Ann be the gambler's headache.

Will was amazed. In a few short days, Mary Ann had completely turned herself around in his esteem, only to have her place filled by the last woman on earth he thought he'd ever fall in love with.

He stopped in midstride as abruptly as if someone had hit him on the head with a log. *In love?*

He tried to think for a moment, to test himself. But what was the proof of love? It surely hadn't been what he'd felt for Mary Ann. The minute he'd met up with her in San Antonio, the protectiveness he'd mistaken for love had turned into impatience and mild disgust. What he felt for Paulie was completely different…deeper, as though it had always been a part of him. There was nothing forced about the tenderness he felt for Paulie. But even so, how could he be certain that wasn't just a passing emotion, too?

Shaking off the perplexing question, he crossed the hall to Paulie's room, eager to talk to her, and to ask her if she wanted to go with him to the telegraph office. Hell, he'd send Tyler a telegram in every city between here and Denver, if that would make Paulie feel better. Tyler was a rake, but he wasn't a demon. He would try to convince Mary Ann to go home. And if he couldn't, she would probably just stay in Austin or Dallas or Denver until her money ran out.

He smiled, knocked once on Paulie's door, and deciding to give her a dose of her own medicine, walked right on in. "Say Paulie, think you're up for a trip to—?"

He stopped, sensing immediately that something was very wrong. The room was dead silent. No room this quiet could have Paulie in it. He looked around. Paulie wasn't sitting in the rocking chair in the corner of the room, or standing by the wardrobe next to him, or lying on the bed. But something else was. A note.

At first Will thought the note was Mary Ann's; they were written on identical paper. Then he remembered that Mary Ann's short letter was still folded in his pocket, where he'd tucked it away while talking to Paulie before dinner.

He walked toward the white envelope, dreading the bad

news it was certain to contain for him. Already he was cursing Paulie, cursing himself for letting her out of his sight, cursing Mary Ann for getting them all into this mess. Practically no one he'd ever met escaped his mental castigation in the few seconds it took to reach that darn note, which he ripped open and read without delay.

Will,
Since you don't seem interested, I'm going to fetch your horse back myself. Please wait here for the Breens, and explain to them that Mary Ann will be back as soon as I can persuade her to return. If I can!
Yours,

Paulie

He stood in the middle of the silent empty room, reading the thing over and over, but the words never changed as he prayed they would. They never delivered more information, or better news, or delivered it in a tone that would have given him any sort of comfort. If anything, her little letter was shorter and more curt than Mary Ann's!

His vision snagged on the greeting. *Will.* Not "My Dear Will," or even a plain "Dear Will." Just *Will*. There was little more satisfaction to be gleaned from the closing, either. She would have sounded more affectionate, he thought, if she had been writing the note for Maudie.

But no matter how the letter sounded, it still translated to the same meaning: Paulie was gone.

And what choice did he have but to follow her?

Chapter Sixteen

Paulie rode far and fast, and as dark night fell, she realized she'd ridden long enough to land herself in a place she was unfamiliar with. There was a road, but she suddenly began to doubt its ability to take her in the right direction. Peering fruitlessly around the hilly countryside, she could see no recognizable landmark that would answer her question. But then, she'd never been at her keenest in the pitch black of night, which is why she'd decided to stop riding and get a few hours of shut-eye.

Now, staring sleeplessly up at the stars, her old revolver hugged tightly to her chest, she wondered whether that was the wisest decision. For one thing, she'd never been out by herself at night, and so had never noticed the innumerable, disturbing noises that could keep a body from getting forty winks. There seemed to be a whole slew of critters whose sole purpose in life was to come out at sunset and keep unfortunate souls like herself from nodding off.

Then there was the din sounding off inside her own head. Worries. What if she never found Mary Ann? It was a big state, and now that she was out in its vastness, she could see how easily she could miss spotting someone, even if they were travelling in the same direction. And there were also fears to contend with. Fear of running into unsavory characters. Night Bird.

That name sent a shiver through her, and she bolted up, just like Oat had done so many times. At the time she had laughed at the old man's antsiness, but she wasn't laughing now. Sometimes fears, like a child's cries in the dark, were caused by ignorance. But this, unfortunately, was the fear of experience. Oat had probably known that all along.

And now he was gone.

Cal was gone, too.

The world around her dimmed a shade. She repeated Will's words to herself—hundreds of people travelled the roads unmolested every day. Of course, from her vantage point now, those hundreds of people were just fools. How sure of herself she'd been when she'd galloped out of San Antonio—how full of herself, she realized now. It never occurred to her that maybe she should have listened a little harder to Will's argument for staying put, and that she could be galloping off toward her doom.

After they buried Oat, Trip had decided that life was too short to waste. How true that seemed to her now—now, when she might very well never see Will again. The possibility seemed horrible, unthinkable. And yet not a few hours before, she'd thrown a few things in her saddlebags and run off without stopping to tell him goodbye. Instead, she'd only written a note. And in writing it, she had been too self-conscious to say what she really felt. She'd given him only the barest of facts, and had taken pains not to make it sound like she was in love with him. Of course anyone could see that she was. Anyone, that is, except Will.

Now, it was too late to let him know.

Somewhere in the distance, an animal let out a long howl. A wolf, maybe. Or was it a coyote, or some animal she had never even encountered before? She began wondering about bears—an animal she'd previously never given much thought to. No one she knew had come up against one, but that wasn't saying much. Back in Possum Trot she was generally concerned with more mundane animal life like skunks and mice and snakes. From where she was sitting, an encounter with a snake would be far preferable to meeting up with a hungry wolf, or a bear. Bears were probably more ferocious than any other animal she could think of…and hadn't she heard somewhere that they travelled by night and liked especially to prey on small campsites?

In an instant, Paulie was on her feet, shaking the dirt off her blanket and herself. There was no sense in stopping if she was just going to huddle in wakeful anxiety. She began quickly packing up her horse again. Luckily, she hadn't really made much of a camp. It was a relatively warm night for November, and she hadn't wanted to bother with a fire. So all she had to do was gather up her things and…

At the sound of a twig breaking nearby, Paulie whirled away from her horse and squinted into the darkness. She couldn't see, but she didn't have to. She knew immediately that she wasn't alone. Her entire body froze, except for her heart, which was beating violently. The night sounds that had so occupied her thoughts suddenly evaporated, replaced by the rushing of blood in her ears and the faint but unmistakable rustlings of something trying to sneak up on her camp. She dismissed the possibility of its being a bear. An animal that big would have made more noise.

Indians. Night Bird's approach wouldn't have been quite so noticeable, of course, but he wasn't the only Indian in the state. Maybe some of them were clumsier than others; in any case, she wasn't going to stick around and find out.

Unfortunately, she had loosened the saddle on her horse, and so would have to waste precious moments tightening the girth before she could mount up. Or she could simply run for it. She was wearing a dress—Maudie had never returned her britches and shirt to her—but she had managed to retrieve her old boots from beneath Maudie's bed, and knew that she could run fleetly if she had to. And when she detected the sound of a footfall not twenty feet away, she decided then and there to run. Maybe leaving her horse behind would throw her pursuer off for a short while, allowing her a head start.

Not bothering to strategize beyond the need to run for her life, Paulie did just that. She ducked under her mount and took off at a sprint, amazed that she could keep her footing at all, her legs were shaking so. Then there was the problem of the darkness. She expected at any moment for her foot to land in a hole, or to come straight up against a bramble or even a tree. She was running blind, but she didn't care. If she hit a tree, that would simply give her something to hide behind. Until then, she wasn't going to waste precious seconds searching for cover, when she felt instinctively that her pursuer was gaining on her.

He was so close she could hear his breathing—heavy breathing. Whoever was chasing her was practically wheezing with the effort it was costing him, which gave her hope. If the rascal was tiring out already, maybe she could outlast him. Maybe she could circle back around even, and return to—

Her ankle caught on something and turned, sending her flying forward. For a split second in midair it felt almost as if she were going to soar away from her attacker. She couldn't have picked a better time to sprout wings. But inevitably what went up had to come down, and she fell to earth in a heavy, painful thud that knocked the wind clear out of her. Worse still, the man behind her lost his footing, too, and landed practically on top of her with a raspy *humph!*

Only sheer panic could make her lungs draw in air again. Gasping for breath, she turned on the ground and started pushing herself back with her elbows, freeing her legs and feet to kick the man if he so much as crawled toward her. Poised with her booted foot tensed inches away from her pursuer's skull, she discovered precisely who had been chasing her. Not an Indian, and certainly not a bear.

Will!

She nearly shouted for joy—until the sheer absurdity of their predicament hit her full force. "Land's sake, Will! Were you trying to scare me to death?"

"I didn't know you'd be so jumpy."

The comment smarted. She *had* been uncommonly frightened, and hated for Will to know it. "What are you doing here?" she asked, covering her embarrassment.

"Oh, just thought I'd do some fishing." He caught his breath and looked up at her with some amusement. "I'm following you, what did you think?"

"You could have saved us both a hard sprint and countless scrapes and bruises if you'd just announced yourself." Even as she said it, she began to feel the palms of her hands, which had attempted to break her fall, begin to sting like the dickens.

"I couldn't be sure it was you."

"Well I sure as heck didn't know it was you!" she retorted. "'Sides, who else would it be but me?"

Even in the darkness, she could see him lift his shoulders in his familiar shrug. "I didn't know until you started running."

"Then why didn't you tell me to *stop* running?"

"I did. I called your name several times."

Paulie thought back, and suddenly realization dawned.

"That was *my name?*" she asked in amazement. "Lord, I thought you were some wheezing devil about to get me!"

His lips formed a scowl, and he began to stand, wincing as he worked his shoulder. Paulie felt bad about that, but she had her own aches and pains to take stock of. Besides, if he hadn't snuck up on her like that…

"What were you doing running off half-cocked to begin with?" he asked, his impatience all too evident.

"I told you, I heard you coming and I—"

He waved a hand dismissively, almost disgustedly, at her. "No, I meant, what made you run off after Mary Ann this way? I would have come with you, you know."

Of all the exasperating people she'd met in her lifetime— and there were quite a few of those just in Possum Trot alone—she was beginning to think Will topped them all. "You told me point-blank that you *wouldn't* come!"

"I didn't know you'd go running off by yourself." His eyes pinned her in the darkness. "Maybe you didn't want me to come with you."

"Land's sake, why wouldn't I?" she exclaimed, thinking about the dull hours she'd spent riding, and the fearful time she'd passed attempting to go to sleep.

Her question was met with a snort, but the set of his lips held little humor. "I reckon Oren Tyler might have something to do with that."

"Of all the silly things!" In irritation, Paulie began to slap furiously at the dust on her skirts.

"Is it silly?" he asked. "I see you still dolled yourself up for this little trip."

She planted her hands on her hips. "Only because Maudie hid my pants!" she brayed in her own defense. Why did Will persist in saying she had a weakness for the gambler? Was it just to irritate her? "I couldn't very well ask her for my britches without rousing some kind of suspicion.''

He appeared to accept this answer, though he clearly wasn't through needling her. She supposed he'd accepted it as his life mission to point out how harebrained she was. ''I don't understand what all the secrecy was for,'' Will said. ''If you'd just tried talking to one of us, we might have told you how foolhardy it was to go chasing after a no-good gambler.''

Paulie thought she might shriek in frustration. ''Aren't you listening to a word I'm saying, Will? I'm *not* running after Oren Tyler. I have no interest in that man whatsoever. I just decided it was my place to try to fetch Mary Ann back.''

He harrumphed his disbelief.

''It's true!'' she cried. ''What you said about my being responsible for the Breens coming to San Antonio was right, so I decided to make myself responsible for seeing that Mary Ann was there to greet them when they arrived.''

He looked at her skeptically. ''I don't know if we'll make it back by then. I told Maudie to keep an eye out for the Breens and to tell them to sit tight till we got back.''

Paulie was comforted by his use of the word ''we.'' He was with her for the long haul, it seemed—an idea that warmed her more than she wanted to admit at the moment. Lord knows, she loved him. If only the man weren't so darned difficult!

Paulie turned and began to tramp back to her little camp. Now that Will was here, maybe they could build a toasty fire. To this end, she began picking up anything that looked combustible as they walked. But she hadn't given up on letting him know how idiotic some of his notions were.

''I can't believe you'd think I'd go chasing after Oren Tyler,'' she said scathingly. She tried to make it sound as if that would be the same thing as running after a skunk, which actually wasn't quite the truth. Oren Tyler was a good-looking fellow—but not nearly as handsome to her as Will was. She stopped a moment, just to drink him in. Lord, she was so glad to see him she wanted to yip for joy.

But for some reason, he wouldn't stop snapping at her. "What else was I to think, after the way you were sighing after the man this afternoon?"

"You must not have a very high estimation of my character!" Paulie said with a sniff.

He shook his head. "You have to admit, you've been acting mighty peculiar lately," Will said. "Running around when Night Bird's on the loose…"

"You didn't seem to care so much about that this afternoon."

"You didn't tell me Cal Tucker's murder took place near San Antonio," Will said bitterly. "I had to learn that myself from the man at the telegraph office."

Paulie frowned. "I'd have told you if you'd asked me."

"There are some details a person shouldn't omit." He shook his head. "I don't understand you."

"You couldn't have tried very hard then."

Will, too, began wandering and scooping up firewood, which became more plentiful as they neared the tree where she had snubbed her horse. "That's not true. It seems I've been thinking of nothing but you lately, Paulie."

She laughed. "Thinking of ways to annoy me, I reckon," she clarified. "You always were best at that."

For the first time that night, he smiled too. "You've got it exactly backwards. *You* were the expert on badgering me." He entered the clearing and dropped the wood he'd gathered. "I never did think you'd get under my skin this way, though."

The rough tone in his voice sent a little shiver through

Paulie, and she too dropped her wood, although not entirely voluntarily. Her limbs felt suddenly unsteady somehow, and her head seemed a little foggy. Sort of like in a dream when familiar people start doing unexpected things. She'd had a dream once in which Trip had turned into a bird. He hadn't grown feathers exactly, but perched on a bar stool at the Dry Wallow, he'd begun chirping just like a bluebird. That had been startling; yet not as startling as being full awake and sensing this strange shift in Will.

She looked up at him and swallowed hard. "What have I done to you lately?"

He shrugged wordlessly a few times before finding his voice again. "I don't know. This afternoon...all that business with Oren Tyler calling you silly things like sugar lump..."

Paulie cocked her head, studying him. As she stared into his anguished eyes, an idea struck her—struck her with such force she felt thrown off balance, like the world had just started lurching and tilting in weird and unexpected ways. Why, just that afternoon when Will had been grumbling about Oren Tyler, she had naturally thought that he felt sore because he was still jealous of Mary Ann's unflagging interest in the gambler. But now a very different possibility struck her.

It wasn't on account of Mary Ann that he was jealous of Tyler—it was on account of herself!

For the second time that evening, it felt as if the wind had been knocked clear out of her lungs. "Why, Will!" she exclaimed, rocking back on her heels from the force of her discovery.

He glanced at her warily. "What's the matter?"

She remained speechless for a few moments, savoring the delicious wonder of her position. For years she had pined after Will, for years she had been secretly envious of his attentions to Mary Ann. Why, just before they'd set out from Possum Trot, she had been bemoaning the fact that he was willing to go to the ends of the earth for Mary Ann, who had never deserved him. Now it appeared that he had been willing to go to the ends of the earth for her, Paulie Johnson. She could hardly believe it!

"Why, Will," she repeated. Her voice was hushed with awe, but the rest of her couldn't keep so calm. She almost hopped with excitement at her new discovery. "You're in love with me!"

Able to control her legs no longer, Paulie launched herself at Will, wrapping her arms tightly around his chest and squeezing with all her might.

He pried her away, but only for a few seconds, so he could look into her eyes. "Wait a cotton-pickin'—"

"You can't deny it," Paulie said, practically dancing with joy now as she took note of the red flush creeping into the man's cheeks. "You *are* in love with me, aren't you?"

"Have you gone loco, Paulette?"

"That's what this was all about—why you followed me."

He rolled his eyes as if searching the heavens for patience. "I came out here because I knew you'd get yourself in a fix if I didn't."

"You were worried because you're in love with me," she told him, still smiling. She didn't think anything could wipe the happy grin off her face now. "Just like you were worried about Mary Ann when you thought you were in love with her. Only you were all wrong about that."

He let out a bark of a laugh, but when he found his voice again it was lower, more serious. "What makes you think I'm not wrong this time?"

"Because Mary Ann didn't love you back." The unspoken admission that she *was* in love with him dangled heavily in the air between them.

"I never knew you were a love expert," Will said.

"I guess you taught me a few things."

He cocked an eyebrow upwards and sent her a questioning glance. "Like what?"

"Like this." Shyly, but nonetheless enthusiastically, Paulie stood on tiptoe and planted her lips against his. She counted this as their fourth kiss, but she wasn't tired of the activity yet—not by a long shot. Their tongues intermingled for a long pleasurable time before she pulled away, a little breathless.

To her surprise, his eyes narrowed and his arm around her waist reeled her in closer to him. "You're a quick study," he said in that gravelly voice that never failed to thrill her.

"I guess I like kissing about as much as anything," she said. Then, with more boldness than she would have ever thought herself capable of, she asked, "What else can you show me?"

She didn't have to wait a split second to find out. Will enveloped her in such a passionate kiss she thought her toes might not uncurl for decades. But this embrace was different from all the rest. This time she could feel a tenseness in Will, as if he were feeling the same coiled-up pressure building inside him that she was experiencing herself. Warmth pooled in her belly, and with it, a desire to be even closer to Will, though it was hard to imagine how that could even be possible. Unless...

She moved her hips, eliciting a groan from somewhere deep inside him. Her first thought was to pull back a little, but he hiked her firmly against him, letting her know that he didn't mind the movement one little bit. He seemed to welcome it, even, and responded in kind in such a way that she couldn't help but try again, this time less tentatively. Within moments, still standing in the little unmade camp, they seemed to be moving as one.

As one. Paulie let the phrase repeat through her mind, savoring the sound of it. The feel of it. It seemed to her that she had always wanted Will, without ever knowing exactly what it was that she wanted. She would have never believed that Will would crave her so fiercely, too—so fiercely that the hand roaming up and down her spine seemed to move more frantically, as if it wanted to claw right through her dress.

She was having similar thoughts. She didn't think that she would mind taking off her clothes. His, either. Days before, she had been too shy to want Will to see any part of her. Now her mind began searching for ways to move her hands between them surreptitiously so that she could undo the many little buttons that ran down the front of her bodice. To her amazement, he seemed able to read her mind. Only he didn't wait for her trembly hands to begin unbuttoning. He took on that task himself.

Paulie draped against him as he worked at the buttons and lightly nibbled the sensitive skin around her cheek and ear. She marvelled at how adept he was at making every caress feel as if it were the most earth-shattering thing that ever happened to her. Just to feel the inadvertent brush of his thumb against the sensitive skin beneath her bodice made her knees go weak with longing. She held on to his shoulders, enjoying every minute he held her. She feared he would suddenly stop—and at the same time she was aware that she should *want* him to stop.

She wasn't completely naive. She knew where all this could lead—to the same place that had left Mary Ann with child and without husband. There were sometimes dire consequences for women who let themselves get carried away with a man. A woman was supposed to wait for a man who would love her and take care of her.

Yet in the heat of the moment, those rules seemed ludicrous. In her world, in this darkness, there was only herself and Will, and the wonderful pleasures he was introducing her to. She loved him. She had never been surer of anything in her life. When they kissed, when they moved against each other, she felt as if they were touching soul to soul. There had never been and never would be a man she cared for so intensely.

Trouble was, he had never said he loved her—not in so many words—and maybe he never would. But he had followed her, when she knew he would rather have stayed in San Antonio. Besides, she realized with sudden clarity, it didn't matter whether he loved her or not. She loved him, and would go on loving him all her life. She had been willing to follow him blindly into Mexico after a renegade; now she would follow his lead into the mysteries that men and women shared. She wasn't certain which destination was the more dangerous.

She moaned in response to his rubbing the tops of her breasts with the back of his hand. His touch almost sent her off balance, so unsure were her legs beneath her; she was grateful for his strength, or else she might have toppled to the ground just as surely as she had when she had tripped earlier. Only now there was a strange energy building inside her, a melting warmth, making her bold and almost delirious.

"Oh, Will," she whispered, throwing her head back to allow him to trail kisses down her neck.

To her shock and dismay, he answered her hoarse voice of passion by stepping away from her, nearly sending her reeling from his absence. Didn't he know that her legs had turned to water?

He turned away only long enough to snap the blanket off her saddle and spread it on the ground. Then, lying down himself, he pulled her down on top of him. She'd thought she might collapse; instead, she felt almost as if she were being poured onto the ground, and ended up straddled on top of him. He reached up and pushed her dress off her shoulders so that the whole thing bunched at her waist.

Paulie felt fire in her cheeks. Before leaving Maudie's she had dispensed with her corset. Now she wasn't wearing anything more than a thin shimmy beneath her dress, and Will had untied that, too, so that her breasts were exposed to him, pale in the moonlight. "You're beautiful, Paulie," he whispered, teasing one peaked bud with the tip of his thumb.

Paulie drew in a sharp breath, both at the shockingly pleasurable sensation and at his words. Beautiful? *Her?* She could hardly believe he'd said such a thing, and yet when she looked into his eyes, glittering at her through the moonlight, she *felt* beautiful for the first time in her life.

Paulie thrilled at his glance and quickly wriggled out of the rest of her clothing, so that she was completely bare on top of him. Then she started working on his buttons, slowly, kissing the skin beneath each as she uncovered it, as he had done for her. She took special care around the bandaged shoulder where the bullet had hit.

His whole body tensed beneath her lips, and she felt a strange power she'd never dreamed of before. And a growing impatience. She looked up into Will's eyes and he shifted slightly, so that she would feel the swollen length of him against her thigh.

He was apparently impatient, too. "Do you have any idea what you're doing?" he said, his voice a hoarse rasp.

She smiled, and rubbed against him instinctively. "Not a clue."

He shut his eyes as if in prayer. "I didn't think so."

"You told me I was a quick study, though," Paulie said.

Will opened his eyes again and ran his hands up and down her arms. "Quick isn't what we're aiming for, Sprout."

At his use of his old endearment for her, she felt her last shred of control slipping away. Not that she cared. There was such a fire building inside her that she felt as if she might happily turn into some wild beast, if Will would just stop being so darned cautious.

"This is your first time," he whispered. "I want you to have something to remember."

She could have laughed at the irony. "I don't think I'll be forgetting this anytime soon, Will."

He smiled, and pulled her down to him again, kissing her hard. At the same time, he rolled onto his good shoulder so that his body was pressing her to the earth. Paulie sensed that she should have been nervous, but all she felt was more heat coiling urgently within her. Then, with his free hand, he untied his belt and began to shuck off his pants, a task she was eager to help him with. She tugged off his boots, then sidled back up against him, shamelessly eyeing his impressive masculine body.

After allowing her to look her fill, Will pulled her toward him again. This time when their bodies touched, skin to tender skin, it was chain lightning going off inside her. The soft friction of their bodies made her senses fog, and yet she felt she would remember his every touch and movement to the end of her days.

When he poised against the most vulnerable part of her, hesitating slightly, she enfolded him in her arms, eager to quench the throbbing desire inside her. She pushed herself against him so that their joining was complete, and an unexpected sharp pain shot through her, causing her to gasp. Will froze, looking into her eyes with concern, but the pain slowly subsided, replaced by stronger, more urgent sensations.

When Will sensed she was ready, he moved more deeply inside her, and from that moment, Paulie really did feel as if some wild thing had taken over her being. She couldn't stop the primal heat that built inside her with each thrust, any more than she could hold back the moans and heartfelt whispers that escaped her lips.

Will whispered to her, too—sweet words whose meaning she could only believe because they were so entwined in the frenzy of lovemaking. When that frenzy built to a fever pitch and the heat between them spiralled out of control, their bodies shuddered in release as one, which was sweeter still.

Minutes later, still wrapped tightly against Will, Paulie felt rather than heard the night enveloping her. This time as she shut her eyes, no thoughts of bears or Night Bird haunted her. All she was aware of was the sound of Will's steady breathing, and her own as she drifted off to sleep.

Will awoke in the dark with a start, amazed to find Paulie snuggled close to him, asleep. He smiled. His shoulder ached like fire, but the pain had been worth it. He reached over and combed his fingers through a strand of Paulie's hair straggling across her cheek.

Silky. He hadn't expected her hair to feel so soft. But Paulie never failed to surprise him. Her wiry body was covered in skin so soft that if he hadn't known better he would have sworn she spent her days doing nothing but soaking in a tub full of rosewater. There were other things that had shocked him that perhaps shouldn't have. Like her complete abandon during lovemaking. He'd been bowled over—and delighted—by her boldness. But when did Paulie Johnson ever do anything half-heartedly?

He sighed contentedly, wishing only that they were in a fancy hotel somewhere, in a feathery bed, with nothing but leisure ahead of them. He wanted to do nothing but spend a few years making love to her—but he doubted there would be time for that now.

They still had work to do, people to track down. His heart wasn't really in the chase, though. How could it be? His heart was already full to bursting with love for Paulie; there was no room left. He wondered how it would be when she woke up, and they had to speak to each other. What would he say? Gabbing was never his strongest suit, like it was with Paulie. But he didn't want her just to start nervously chattering on like nothing had happened, which, being Paulie, he feared she would. Something *had* happened, something that changed their lives forever.

For so long, he had wondered why love, which came to so many so easily, seemed so elusive in his own life. He'd tried to manufacture the emotion with Mary Ann, a project that had taken him a long time to give up. But when he looked at Paulie now, he understood why it was he'd been so confused about love. Because he'd never been without it. Ever since he was a young buck and had first run into Paulie Johnson in her pigtail days, he'd never lacked for a female to lavish his affection on—or one to lavish it on him. He wondered now if there had ever been a day since that he hadn't loved Paulie. They just had a more roundabout way of expressing it than most people.

Maybe he wouldn't give either of them a chance to talk anymore, he mused. The minute she opened her eyes, he might just take her in his arms and kiss her again like there was no tomorrow. Maybe he'd never give her a chance to talk again.

After a few moment's consideration, he decided he wouldn't want that either, though. Chatter was an essential part of Paulie, and he didn't want to change a thing about her. Besides, he would miss talking to her, sparring with her. Somehow, they would just have to find a balance between kissing and talking.

Chuckling silently at his foolish frame of mind, he bent and placed a whisper-light kiss on Paulie's cheek. She felt warm, and he moved closer to her to ward off the night chill. Their fire had never got itself built, and now they only had their two blankets for heat.

The strange thing was, he could *smell* fire. Very faintly. He glanced around, wondering if maybe Paulie had built a little cook fire somewhere, and he was smelling the ashes. But the coals were nowhere in evidence, and besides, he could swear the smell reaching his nose was smoke. Fresh smoke.

Frowning, he got up, pulled on his pants and boots, then ambled slowly to a rise in the land. His eyes squinted west, from where the wind was hailing, and could just make out a dot of light in the black horizon far, far away. A campfire.

"What's going on?" Paulie said.

He nearly jumped in surprise. He hadn't heard her sneak up on him, but there she was, covered only by a blanket slung over her shoulders, peering off into the distance. She looked beautiful, and his body responded instantly.

"You see something out there, Will?"

She seemed unmoved by the fact that she was standing naked next to him. He wasn't, though. He shifted, trying to keep his eyes from straying up and down her gloriously naked figure. "Fire," he replied. The word came out more gruffly than he'd expected.

Paulie's breath caught. "Maybe it's Mary Ann!"

"Maybe." Will glanced back mournfully at Paulie, who he could tell was already caught up in the prospect of trailing Mary Ann again. Then he looked at their private little campsite. So much for kissing instead of talking. Or making love for weeks on end.

"Who else could it be?" Paulie said excitedly, oblivious to his regretful mood.

Will turned back to the pinpoint of light and drew a steadying breath. "Maybe somebody we're not so eager to see."

Chapter Seventeen

"Looks like we were both right," Paulie said. But as she peered over the hillside, looking at the little camp below, there was no joy in her tone. Nor was there any in Will's expression.

They had found Mary Ann, and her gambler. Unfortunately, at some point, either together or separately, those two had come across Night Bird and his three cohorts. Now they were his prisoners.

"Damn," Will muttered. It was all he had said for five minutes now.

"What the Sam Hill are we going to do?" Paulie asked, looking up at him. Will studied the lay of the land with a tense, anxious expression on his face. She couldn't believe that just an hour before they had been entwined in each other's arms, making love on a blanket on the ground. She had never felt such happiness followed by such despair.

"We've got to get them out of there."

The words made Paulie's heart sink. How on earth were they going to do that? "We got away from Night Bird once. Do you think we'll be that lucky again?"

Will looked at her and crooked the corner of his lip up into a wry smile. "If Mr. Bird's in a generous mood."

Paulie glanced back down the hillside, squinting. She had fairly good eyesight, but from the position of the prisoners, she could tell frustratingly little about what was going on. Oren's rig had been overturned. Mary Ann was tied sitting down as Night Bird had positioned Paulie and the others during their captivity on the border. The most disturbing thing about the picture was that Oren Tyler was lying on the ground next to Mary Ann, and appeared to be hurt.

Were murdering, thieving Indians ever in a generous mood? Is that really how they had escaped before—because Night Bird hadn't cared if they survived or not? She'd thought it was because of Oat's ingenuity. Now she wondered. "He doesn't seem in particularly high spirits."

On the contrary, Night Bird was stalking around the circle impatiently. A shiver ran down Paulie's spine. "Remember what he said, Will? That he only cared about the white man's money?"

Will nodded, and she knew instantly that the thought had occurred to him long before she had remembered it. "He only kills for money. Large sums of it."

Oren Tyler had made enough money to pick up and move to Colorado. To run after him, Mary Ann had cashed in Oat's bonds, and she had Tyler's two hundred dollars. Between them, they probably were carrying nearly as much as the men guarding the payroll had been when Night Bird decided to cut their lives short. With a price on his head already, he would have nothing to lose by killing these people. If he did kill them, they wouldn't be able to run to authorities.

Paulie shivered. "We've got to attack them."

When Will turned his head, his face bore an expression of pure incredulity. "*Attack* them?" he repeated, his voice a whispered croak. "Have you lost your mind? We've got two pistols, and they have our old rifles and then some. We're outnumbered and outgunned."

Paulie shook her head. "We can't just watch them be butchered."

"We won't," he said with determination. "Or at least, you won't. You're going to ride for help."

"Me?" She blinked. Immediately, she hated the plan. "By myself? That doesn't make any sense."

"It makes more sense than you and I charging down there and both getting ourselves captured."

"What if we got in position and tried shooting them?"

Will frowned. "That doesn't change the fact that there are four of them and two of us. The odds aren't good, and besides, you're a lousy shot."

Paulie bit her lip to keep back a tart reply. Now was no time for unnecessary boasting. She could hit a target most of the time...as long as it wasn't moving. She doubted once the shooting began the group of outlaws would kindly sit still long enough for her to take aim. Besides, Will was right about their weapons not being up to snuff. When she had bought her puny gun, she had only been thinking in terms of self defense, not leading a charge against an armed camp.

"You'd better leave now." Will grabbed her arm and started pulling her back down the other side of the hill, toward their horses, which they had tethered well out of distance from the camp. They were just lucky to have been downwind from the Indian, or else they surely would have been caught, too. "It's a long ride to San Antonio, and we don't have any time to lose."

She wasn't about to leave Will again without a fight. "What do you intend to do here while I'm trotting around the countryside?"

"I'm going to keep watch, and try to make certain those two don't get hurt."

She looked at him skeptically. "What will you do if something happens?"

Will glanced back for a moment, scoping out the terrain. "There has to be a place where I can get close enough…"

"Close enough to what?"

"To shoot."

He was going to try to kill Night Bird? Paulie shook her head. "If you think I'm leaving you here, you're crazy! If you're going to try to shoot Night Bird, why wouldn't you want me here for backup?"

"I won't fire unless it looks like something's about to happen—or if they find me."

She shot him a distrustful look.

He tightened his grip on her arm and hauled her close to him. "If you stay here, you might be signing all our death warrants. We need men with real guns. You need to locate the federal marshall in San Antonio."

"What if I can't convince them you're in danger?"

Will obviously didn't think there was much chance of that happening. "If you so much as whisper the name Night Bird we'll probably have a stampede of rangers and angry citizens coming our way."

"But I can't just leave you here, Will. You're hurt!" She knew that wasn't much of an argument. Will had made it out this far, and he'd certainly engaged in some pretty strenuous physical activity without any adverse affects.

"I'm all right," Will said.

"Why can't I stay?" she asked. "You go to San Antonio."

"Because you've probably got more stamina right now. I've just been laid up in bed with a fever. Besides, if one of us has to run the risk of being captured by Night Bird, I want it to be me."

"We don't agree on that subject."

He smiled encouragingly. "Just think of this as your opportunity to rescue your friend Mary Ann."

Paulie didn't mind admitting her fib now. "That was a lie, Will. I just followed along because I wanted to be with you. *You* were the friend I was worried about. Still am."

He smiled warmly at her. "I know, Sprout. And I'm glad you came along—more than I can say."

Paulie felt light-headed. If only they were somewhere else—somewhere private, and out of harm's way. More than anything, she just wanted to crawl under their blanket and make love again. But she knew she was living in a dream if she actually thought that was going to happen. And Will was right. Given the fact that he was still recovering from a bullet wound, she would be the faster of the two.

She always did hate to lose an argument with Will, and in this case, capitulation was doubly hard to accept. What if she never saw him again? What if the first time he had taken her in his arms and showed her the joys of being a woman was also to be her last? She looked into his eyes, hoping to see some of the same desperate longing in them that she felt inside herself. But all she saw was worry—and his trying to calculate whether their plan would actually work.

He was right, of course. Their future didn't bear thinking about, right at this moment, not when the future might be cut tragically short. She had no choice but to ride for help, and the sooner she left the sooner she would get back to Will.

"I'm leaving, but I'm not happy about it," she said.

"You better promise not to do anything stupid and get yourself killed."

To her surprise, he crossed his arms and smiled at her, just like in the old days. "I wouldn't worry about me. Seems my life only comes into danger when you're around."

Her lips twitched into a smile, but the situation was too dire for laughing. Besides, she feared if she started laughing she would start crying, too, and she didn't want that. Not when this might be the last time she ever saw Will. "You *would* give me your lip at a time like this, Will Brockett," she groused as she reluctantly mounted her horse. She would have to be very quiet riding out, until she was absolutely certain that she was far enough away that Night Bird wouldn't be able to hear her. Jeopardizing Will's safety was the last thing she wanted to do.

Once she was on her horse, he reached out a hand and held her lower leg, then looked up into her eyes. "The only lip I'm interested in is that pouty one of yours."

His words were like liniment to a sore muscle. She was beginning to think that he had forgotten all about the intimacy they had just shared. But if he could stand there talking about her lips, things couldn't be as hopeless as she had feared. "Maybe it wouldn't pout so much if you'd kiss it more often," she said.

He grinned his irresistible grin, and still holding her leg with one hand, he brought her down toward him with the other. "I wouldn't worry about your lips getting neglected," he whispered. "From now on out they won't be."

And then he gave her a little demonstration of how well he planned to take care of them in future. At the mere touch of his mouth against hers, Paulie felt her insides melt like a wax candle in a bonfire. How could a man affect her so? She felt almost dizzy again, and her body, which had seemed a little sore on the way over to find out whose campsite they had seen, had apparently recovered and was aching for more.

"Oh, Will…" In spite of her determination not to cry, Paulie felt tears burning her eyes. What if they never had the opportunity to be together again? What if she came back and discovered that Will had been captured, or killed? Anything could happen…

Will stepped back, his mouth set in a tense line. He gave her leg a final pat. "Ride fast, but be careful."

She swallowed back her sob and managed a shaky smile instead. She could cry all the way to San Antonio if she wanted, but right now she was just wasting time. "I will. You be careful, too, Will."

He nodded. "I'll try to stay in one piece."

They weren't the most encouraging words she could imagine, but they would have to do until she got back from San Antonio. She turned her mount and tried to tamp down the acute feeling of disappointment as she trotted away. What had she expected, a declaration of love?

She shook her head, sending her tears, which were flowing freely now, flying away from her face. After all these years, she *hadn't* expected Will Brockett to tell her he loved her.

She'd just hoped he would.

Waiting for Paulie was even harder than Will would have expected. After she left, he made the long walk to the crest of the hill where they had been before, to keep an eye on Night Bird and his captives. The Indian looked more agitated than Will could remember seeing him, and yet he did nothing to his prisoners. One other Mexican stood guard, and the other two seemed to be dozing, not far from Oren Tyler.

Will wondered what kind of wounds the gambler had suffered. He should have told Paulie to bring back a doctor, in case there was something seriously wrong with him, but he supposed Tyler would be lucky just to make it out of his current predicament, doctor or no doctor.

And yet, so far, Will hadn't noticed Night Bird making a move toward his two prisoners; he didn't seem to be paying them much attention at all, in fact. He could only imagine why the Indian was stopping in one place for so long. Maybe he wanted to keep his captives around for as long as possible, just to see their nerves become increasingly frayed as the night wore on.

Will dreaded dawn. Surely something would happen then. Night Bird would want to move before daylight, which meant that his prisoners would have to be dealt with. But what exactly would he do with them? When he had left Trip, Paulie, Oat and himself by the Rio Grande to die or escape, they had been in the middle of nowhere, a good day's ride from being able to report what happened to them.

But now they were in central Texas, and not too far from a road. The outlaw couldn't trust that his prisoners wouldn't be found. Which gave him another reason to kill them.

Where was Paulie? He would have given anything for her to come riding up, for her to be by his side. Unfortunately, his side wasn't the safest place for anyone right now.

Yet when he thought about Paulie he smiled for the first time since she'd left. Her first instinct had been to attack. He could just see what a sight she would make, charging down the hill with her rusty revolver like a crazed woman. Maybe that would have scared Night Bird after all.

He wished he had had more time to talk to her, to tell her how much their lovemaking had meant to him. He wasn't certain he could come up with the words to really express what was in his heart, but he could at least have tried. When Paulie rode away, she'd looked sad, as if she'd been expecting him to say more. What woman wouldn't?

But then, what woman would land herself in the middle of a situation like this one? Just Paulie, he thought ruefully.

As the minutes went by, he felt his eyelids grow heavier. His shoulder ached, but he could ignore that. The desire to sleep, however, was a dangerous feeling right now, and he fought against it fiercely. Unfortunately, the fire around which the captives were sitting was dying, and it became harder and harder to see them in the dark. Without something to focus his vision on, his mind kept returning to the appealing idea of slumber.

Then he saw something that put any idea of sleep out of his head. Movement below. He sat up ramrod-straight and tried to make out exactly who was moving. It was one of the Mexican bandits and Night Bird, arguing over Oren Tyler. Was Tyler still alive?

A few moments later the gambler moved slightly, relieving Will no end. He didn't want any deaths on his watch tonight. Things were bound to get much worse later, when the bullets started flying. Until then, he wanted to keep Mary Ann and Tyler in the land of the living.

That wish seemed more unrealistic when Night Bird took a rifle and pointed it at Oren Tyler's head. Will shot to his feet and then froze in concentration, never taking his eyes off the scene below him. They were talking, but the Indian wasn't putting his weapon down. He could see Mary Ann trying to plead with Night Bird, whose gun was still aimed at Tyler.

Will crept closer. There was little to use for cover on the barren hillside—just a few scrubby-looking bushes that wouldn't hide a squirrel, much less a man. Every step he took made him feel more exposed. Yet if he didn't get closer he would never be able to get a bead on Night Bird. If he crept too close, however, any one of the Mexicans could turn and shoot him down. Then they might take revenge on their two prisoners.

He eased himself down beside a bush, wondering whether the darkness would camouflage him. He would have given all he owned at that moment to hear the sounds of approaching hoofbeats, but he knew the timing would be too providential. He lifted his gun and sighted down the renegade, but he could tell immediately that the distance was too far. If only he had his own rifle—the one Night Bird had stolen... Just a little bit closer.

As he crawled out from behind the bush, he heard Night Bird yell something below, and then to his horror, he saw the Indian cock the hammer on the rifle. The next moments were a blur. Mary Ann screamed and looked away, and Will lifted his gun, knowing any shot he got off would probably be wasted. Night Bird drew the gun close to Oren Tyler's temple.

Time had just run out.

"Don't shoot!"

Will hadn't expected the words to come out, and once they echoed down the hillside, he began to wonder whether they had really issued from his own mouth. And yet, all eyes suddenly turned to him. Three Mexicans sprang to their feet immediately; one ran toward him. Will knew after a few yards he could have killed the man, but was fairly certain he would be captured or killed in the process. He wasn't in the mood to die just yet.

Taking a gamble, he lowered his gun to his side and began to amble down the hill, trying to look casual even though his heart was beating like a jackrabbit's. It was best to appear as though he were interrupting a picnic, not a killing.

One of the Mexicans approached him, his rifle pointing directly at Will's chest. Will slapped the barrel away. He might be walking into a nest of thieves, but that didn't mean he was going to pretend to respect them. The other bandits looked back at their leader—for permission to kill him, no doubt—but Night Bird merely smirked. Will nodded coolly at his would-be assassins and strolled into the circle assembled around the fire.

Mary Ann gasped. "Will!" she cried, looking up at him with mournful eyes. "Oh, Will, you shouldn't have come after me!"

Something in her voice startled him and made him feel an unexpected tug of fear for her. Maybe it was the sincerity in her tone, and the regret. He looked down at Tyler lying on the ground and immediately understood. The man had been caught in some gunplay, but he hadn't been as lucky as Will had been in his wound.

"He's pretty bad off."

Will could see that. One whole side of the gambler's face looked bloodied, especially around the eye. "How are you, Tyler?"

The man let out a groan, holding a hand over his wounded eye. "Not so good. Mary Ann was right, you shouldn't have come here, Brockett."

At the sight of the once cocky gambler brought so low, Will felt a rage building inside him, one he feared might get the best of all of them if he vented so much as a tiny portion of it. He forced a casual shrug. "Just thought I'd pay a social call."

The renegade wasn't amused. "Where are your friends?"

Will wasn't about to answer that.

"Where is the old man, and the boy-girl?"

"The old man is dead," Will told him. "The young lady is in San Antonio."

Night Bird shook his head. "I could have used such a one as she." He pointed to an empty bottle of bourbon on the ground. The gold label looked unfamiliar, and expensive, so Will guessed it was probably from Oren Tyler's private stock. "My men capture men, money and whiskey. Now they are useless."

Will inspected the Mexicans' appearances more closely, and felt anguish shoot through him. Two of them were bleary-eyed with drink. Paulie had been right; he and she probably could have attacked the encampment. This was also why Night Bird had been sitting out the night with his captives, and had been pacing anxiously. He was waiting for his men to sober up.

The Indian's lips curled up into a lopsided smile. "Yes, you could have, señor," he said, as if reading Will's mind. "But now you are my prisoner."

Before Will could gather his wits, the Mexican standing behind him kicked the rifle out of his hand, and Night Bird tied his hands. The two drunker bandits held their guns on him. Not another word was spoken as they trussed Will up just like Mary Ann, but after they were done, Night Bird inspected his handiwork approvingly.

"You will not get away this time."

Will tensed; every length of rope that bit into his arms seemed to sap away a little of his hope. The next time Paulie suggested a harebrained plan like charging a campful of bandits, he would take her more seriously.

Night Bird put his rifle aside. "Before you came here I was going to put the rich man out of his misery." He nodded toward Tyler. "Also repay him for getting my men drunk."

"Is it his fault they stole his whiskey and drank it all?" Will asked.

Night Bird shook his head. "Not all. There is still this." He held up an unopened bottle for Will's inspection. "Now I have decided a better way to kill the man would be with his own medicine."

He threw the bottle to one of his men, barking out orders in guttural Comanche. Will was startled. He hadn't heard the renegade use his own tongue before—just Spanish or English. He didn't know why, but the strange language sounded ominous.

The Mexican understood the command, took the bottle, and walked away from the camp and the overturned wagon.

Mary Ann let out a whimper and focused her luminous blue eyes on Will. "Oh, Will... This is all my fault." She gestured with her head to the wagon, Will, and Tyler. "If it weren't for me, none of this would have happened."

Before he could respond, Oren Tyler lifted his head. "Don't blame yourself, Mary Ann. I guess it's my fault a little, too."

"Oh, Oren..." Tears streamed down her face. "I'm so sorry. If there was only something I could do for you. I love you so much!"

The gambler sent her a lopsided smile. "I guess I can see that now, sweetheart." He swallowed, then continued in a humbled, emotion-choked voice. "I want you to know, Mary Ann, that I love you, too. And if we ever get out of this, and if you would still want a blind man, I'd be honored if you'd be my wife."

For a moment, it looked like Mary Ann might faint. "Oh, Oren! I'd be proud to be your wife."

Will stared at the couple, dumbfounded. This was a fine time to be making fancy promises! Most likely they would all be dead before long. Why the hell couldn't the man have declared his undying love this morning and saved them all the inconvenience of being captured by bandits?

Then he remembered. *He* hadn't told Paulie he loved her when he'd had the golden opportunity, either, and now he might not see her again. That thought sent a cold chill through him.

Night Bird, standing at the edge of their little circle, laughed. At the unexpected sound, Will looked up and discovered that the man's mirth was all aimed at him. "You are a fool, señor. Twice you have chased *la bonita,* and the woman does not love you." He laughed again. "I am glad you will die knowing you are a fool."

Will would have agreed that he was a fool, but not for the reason Night Bird believed.

"What's that man doing?" Mary Ann asked fearfully, gesturing to the man who had taken the bourbon bottle from Night Bird. He was now walking in a semicircle around the camp, pouring out the contents of the large bottle on the dry grassy ground.

A cold shard of dread knifed through Will, who understood immediately. Night Bird was going to burn them all. The whiskey would ignite the grass in back of them, and the light breeze would slowly fan the flames toward them. They would be unable to get away in time. The fire would creep up on them, and they would be able to move no faster than caterpillars to escape it.

He didn't want to say anything that would alarm the others, though they would soon find out the renegade's plan. As if in answer to Mary Ann's question, Night Bird picked up a length of wood and held it over the fire, making a torch that would ignite the fire that would kill them.

Will tried to breathe steadily, to think clearly. He looked away from Mary Ann, away from the campfire. And then he saw it—a figure not too far away, darting behind a bush.

His heartbeat began to speed up. Was it Paulie? He didn't hear the hoofbeats of a posse approaching, and he didn't see any other movements, either. Paulie alone probably couldn't rescue them. He had to pray that she had brought reinforcements—and be thankful that, if it was her out there in the darkness, he might at least have been given an opportunity to say goodbye to her the right way.

He looked at Night Bird and smiled. "You're wrong about one thing, Night Bird."

As he pulled his torch away from the fire, the Indian raised a brow.

"I'm not in love with Mary Ann, and never have been. It's the other woman I love. Paulie Johnson."

The renegade looked incredulous. "The boy-girl?"

Will nodded. "I guess I always have, since I met her." Night Bird looked less impressed with this news than Mary Ann, whose blue eyes rounded in surprise at this tidbit of gossip. "And if I ever get out of this, I intend to marry Paulie straight away."

"But you will not get away," Night Bird said.

"We'll see," Will replied as the Indian touched his torch to the ground. Within seconds, the ground circling the back of them was ablaze. Mary Ann screamed in surprise.

At the same time, a cry went up not far from their camp. Paulie stood and waved her arms, sending fear shooting through Will. Was she crazy? But her gesture was followed by the distant squeak of saddle leather and men spurring their horses. Hoofbeats thundered closer and closer. The world around became a frenzy of movement and firelight. Gunfire sounded, and nearby, one of the Mexicans dropped to the ground. Will looked quickly around, and saw Night Bird disappearing into the night just as a small army of men crested the hill and swooped down upon the campsite.

* * *

Paulie ran with all her might, tears streaming down her face. *He'd said he loved her—right there in front of everybody!* Drawing a knife, she ran right into the middle of the group, the first person to reach them. Thirty men were behind her, she knew, half of them firing guns, and others on horseback flying past her at a gallop after Night Bird and the other two men.

She skidded to a stop next to Will and fell to her knees. He smiled up at her. "What took you so long?"

She could have whacked him over the head, but she was just too damn happy to see him all in one piece. Besides, she had a knife in her hands.

"Quick, untie me," he said, and she cut frantically at his bonds, slicing through them faster than she would have ever thought possible without taking a foot or hand off, too. Nerves and the growing heat around them brought beads of sweat to her brow, which poured down her face, mingling with her tears.

When she cut through the last cord, Will jumped to his feet, grabbed up his rifle from near the wagon and dashed toward the horse of the man who had been killed. Paulie ran after him. "Where are you going?"

"After Night Bird," he said, swinging up on the saddle.

Paulie grabbed his leg before he could spur the animal. "Wait, Will—let the others go."

"The others aren't as mad as I am," he answered. "Help Mary Ann and Tyler—he's hurt bad."

And then he was gone, riding like lightning into the darkness, disappearing from her once again. She dashed back to the two by the fire, who were being helped out by a few of the men she had brought from town. She knelt by Mary Ann, and cut through the ropes binding her hands as another man worked on her feet. All the while, Mary Ann told them about their capture, and how the Indian planned to burn them alive. Two men were beating the fire with blankets, trying to put it out. Their efforts kicked up hot sand that Paulie and the others turned away from.

"How did Will get caught?" Paulie asked Mary Ann.

She nodded toward Oren Tyler, who was lying nearby. "Night Bird was about to kill Oren, when Will came out of hiding—I guess to distract him. Will saved Oren's life." Tears streamed down her cheeks.

Paulie looked at the gambler's bloodied face and shivered. He had to be in quite a bit of pain, but he didn't look like he would die.

She cut the last strand of rope from her hands. "I've got to go after him."

Mary Ann looked alarmed. "After Will?"

She nodded, scoping out the area. She eyed one of the horses of the men taking care of Tyler. "I'll be right back— I hope," she said.

She made a dash for a little sorrel gelding and jumped on before its rightful owner could discover her commandeering his mount. She spurred the animal and galloped like thunder into the night. Where could Will have gone?

Somewhere in the darkness lurked Night Bird. Like the winged creatures he was named after, Paulie knew the man had the power to swoop down on her out of nowhere. She only hoped that he wouldn't want to bother with killing or hostage taking when he had a herd of bloodthirsty Texans on his trail.

She heard a gunshot and without stopping veered her horse in that direction. Her heart was pumping like mad. Night Bird had had a gun, she knew. Had *he* fired the shot? One of the other men? Or was it Will…

Please, God, don't let Will be hurt!

Knifelike dread pierced through her, and she galloped so fast that she nearly passed them by. She sawed on the sorrel's reins and screeched to a halt, throwing up clumps of dirt as she stopped next to Will.

He was standing over Night Bird, whose painted pony lay dead on the ground nearby. Will had shot it out from underneath him, and now Night Bird was immobilized by a broken leg.

Paulie got off her horse, and fired another shot in the air so the others would know where they were. Will didn't take his eyes or his gunsights off their captive.

Captive. It seemed odd to use that word in reference to a man who had held most of South Texas captive to fear for months and months. Now, on the ground, bent over his twisted leg, beaten, he looked smaller and much less formidable. She almost couldn't believe she'd been so afraid of him before. Then she remembered the evil he had done, and that he had almost killed Will. She felt more sympathy for his horse.

She walked over to Will. "Thank God you got him." Now that she was standing next to him, and sure that he was, as promised, all in one piece, her knees felt rubbery with relief. "Thank God you're safe!"

Will looked at her only long enough to give her an intimate smile that told her all she needed to know about how glad he was to see her. "I'll feel a lot better when the law takes this fellow off my hands."

She nodded and heard hoofbeats coming in their direction. It wouldn't be long now. And once Night Bird and the others were gone, she intended to give Will the longest kiss the world had ever known. "Did you really mean what you said earlier?" she asked.

Will's brow wrinkled in thought. "Let's see... Do you mean that part about loving you since the first time I met you and intending to haul you to a preacher at the first opportunity?"

Paulie nodded enthusiastically.

He shot her a sideways glance. "I guess I must have." He looked away and shrugged, a wicked grin tugging at his lips. "Or maybe it was just nerves."

Paulie was just about to tell Will what she thought of his jokes, when Night Bird looked up at her, his face registering confusion for a moment. Then he smirked. "The boy-girl," he remarked.

Paulie felt herself tense at his description of her. Here she was about to become an engaged young lady, and she was *still* being undermined. "I told you before, Mr. Bird, I'm not a boy!"

The Indian nodded. Then he gave her dress another up and down glance. "No, you are not a boy," he conceded. "In a dress, you are also a *bonita*."

"You see, Night Bird," Will said. "I'm not such a fool after all."

Paulie wasn't sure she understood Will's remark, but to Night Bird's comment, she could only roll her eyes. A *bonita*, indeed! "What did you think I'd look like with a dress on?" she asked the Indian tartly. "A June bug?"

Captor and captive both barked out a laugh as Paulie folded her arms crossly over her chest. Honestly, men had so little imagination!

Epilogue

It was easier to go to a preacher than get a preacher to come to Possum Trot, but Paulie persuaded Maudie to bring one down with her from San Antonio. It wasn't often that five people from one town got married on one day—especially when the town was no more than a little dusty burg with a store and a saloon. It would have seemed a shame to have the ceremony anywhere else but the Dry Wallow.

Paulie had festooned the old place with as much ribbon as could be had at Dwight's store, and decked the tables and doors and bar with cedar boughs. "Looks festive, doesn't it?" she asked Maudie as all the participants were assembled for the big day.

Hands on hips, the other woman gave the room a long considering glance. Of course, she'd never seen the Dry Wallow before, so she couldn't know how many sand dunes Paulie had swept out just the previous day.

"It looks…" Maudie paused to think, then smiled. "Well, it looks just right for a Christmas wedding." She sidled nearer to Paulie, nodded toward the preacher standing forlornly by the long bar ogling the half-empty bottles of spirits, and lowered her voice. "I didn't tell him he would be performing a ceremony in a barroom, Paulette."

Paulie laughed. "The Dry Wallow's my home. *Used* to be my home," she said, correcting herself. "Trip's taking over the saloon, but he's going to live at Tessie's house." She glanced over at Trip, stiff in his new suit, and pulled her own husband-to-be closer to her.

Will looked unbearably handsome in his wedding duds, and she could tell Maudie thought so too by the way she blushed when she looked into his eyes. Paulie knew that feeling well.

She and Will were going to start that horse ranch he'd always wanted, and would live above the saloon until they built their new house on Oat's land, which they had bought from Mary Ann. It seemed right, somehow, taking over that property. After all, in a strange way, Oat and Mary Ann's ill-fated union had been what finally brought her and Will together. If they hadn't hunted down Mary Ann together, they might still be what they had been for so long—frustrated friends.

Trip, hearing his name, hurried over and nearly knocked down four chairs in the process. "Ain't we gonna start this thing anytime soon?" he said, his weathered face contorted anxiously. "I don't want to give Tessie any time to change her mind."

Paulie hooted at that idea. "I guess if she hasn't changed her mind about you in twenty years, she won't in the time it takes Mary Ann to primp in front of a mirror on her wedding day." In fact the woman who was soon to be Tessie Peabody looked perfectly serene standing by a table with refreshments as she talked to the third groom, Oren Tyler. Tessie, a widow, had on her old wedding dress, which had stood the test of time a little better than Paulie's mother's had.

But in the week prior to the wedding, Tessie had helped Paulie fix her dress up so that it looked a mite less odd than the last time she had tried it on. Gone was the hoop skirt, and Tessie had gathered up the excess material into a swag in the back, creating a kind of bustle. The change made Paulie feel just as ridiculous, but a little more stylish. Her hair was pulled up simply this time, styled by Maudie, so she didn't have to worry about her groom making jokes about her head being caught in a cactus. On this day when Will looked at her, she saw only sincere admiration and love in his eyes—emotions she returned tenfold.

"I must say," Maudie whispered fervently, "Mr. Tyler certainly is handsome, even after his little accident."

Paulie found her gaze drawn, as so many of her guests' were, to the stranger in their midst. Tyler's more superficial cuts had mostly healed in the weeks since their run-in with Night Bird, but he had lost the use of his left eye, which now was covered with a black patch.

"He looks dashing—almost like a pirate," Maudie observed with a sigh. "It'll be nice to have a man around the house again, especially one so good-looking."

Paulie chuckled. She had been surprised when Maudie had offered to let Mary Ann and her one-eyed gambler stay on at the boardinghouse, but now that she thought about it, she shouldn't have been. Now Maudie would always have someone to play cards with.

"Say…" Will said, taking Paulie's arm and drawing her aside. "The way you're ogling that gambler fellow is making me mighty jealous."

Paulie smiled. "You? You don't have anything to be jealous of."

He shrugged immodestly. "I guess not, when I've got the prettiest girl in the room about to marry me."

She shook her head, brimming with love for her soon-to-be husband. Standing across the room from Mary Ann, who had just swept into the room in a burst of bridal glory, beautiful in a new white dress dripping with lace, her curls looking neater and blonder than ever, and her blue eyes shining with excitement, Paulie knew Will's compliment was grossly exaggerated. "*Not* the prettiest," she corrected.

He wasn't giving up. "The prettiest and the best."

She looked across the room at Tessie, and smiled. "No woman's better than Tessie. She's never said a bad thing about anybody."

But Will still wouldn't cede Paulie's superiority. "You're prettiest and best, *and* you've got the most freckles."

As if from instinct, Paulie whirled on her groom and practically hopped up and down in agitation. "Will Brockett, you better just drop *that* subject for the next fifty years."

The stubborn man shook his head and pulled her a little closer. "You might have been able to argue the point once," he allowed. "But that was before I had seen *all* your freckles."

Paulie gasped and felt a blush creeping up her face. During the past few weeks, they had made love enough times for Will to have counted every mark on her body. "Hush, Will!" she whispered frantically. "There's a preacher here!"

He shamelessly used her embarrassment to win his argument. "Then you'll admit that you're the most superlative bride in the room?"

Happily, she relented. As arguments went, it was not

such a bad one to lose. "All right," she said, standing on tiptoe to plant a kiss on his cheek. "How can I bicker, when I certainly have the best groom?"

* * * * *

COMING NEXT MONTH FROM

HARLEQUIN HISTORICALS